W9-ATQ-895

3 4028 08770 1655

HARRIS COUNTY PUBLIC LIBRARY

YA MacKis
McKissack, Jennifer
Sanctuary DISCARD

$17.99
ocn899880444
First edition.

SANCTUARY

SANCTUARY

JENNIFER McKISSACK

SCHOLASTIC PRESS

New York

Copyright © 2015 by Jennifer McKissack

All rights reserved. Published by Scholastic Press,
an imprint of Scholastic Inc., *Publishers since 1920.*
SCHOLASTIC, SCHOLASTIC PRESS, and associated logos are trademarks
and/or registered trademarks of Scholastic Inc.

The publisher does not have any control over and does not assume any
responsibility for author or third-party websites or their content.

No part of this publication may be reproduced, stored in a retrieval system,
or transmitted in any form or by any means, electronic, mechanical,
photocopying, recording, or otherwise, without written permission of the publisher.
For information regarding permission, write to Scholastic Inc., Attention: Permissions
Department, 557 Broadway, New York, NY 10012.

This book is a work of fiction. Names, characters, places, and incidents are either the product
of the author's imagination or are used fictitiously, and any resemblance to actual persons,
living or dead, business establishments, events, or locales is entirely coincidental.

Library of Congress Cataloging-in-Publication Data

McKissack, Jennifer, author.
Sanctuary / Jennifer McKissack. — First edition.
pages cm
Summary: After the sudden death of her aunt, Cecilia Cross is forced to return to the old
mansion on a remote island off the coast of Maine, ironically named Sanctuary, the place
where her father and sister died, and from which her mother was committed to an insane
asylum soon after—and it is also a place of dark secrets, haunted by the ghosts of its original
owners, and inhabited by her vicious uncle.
ISBN 978-0-545-58758-7 (jacketed hardcover) 1. Haunted houses—Juvenile fiction.
2. Ghost stories. 3. Murder—Juvenile fiction. 4. Uncles—Juvenile fiction.
5. Families—Maine—Juvenile fiction. 6. Secrecy—Juvenile fiction. 7. Maine—Juvenile
fiction. [1. Haunted houses—Fiction. 2. Ghosts—Fiction. 3. Murder—Fiction.
4. Uncles—Fiction. 5. Family life—Maine—Fiction. 6. Secrets—Fiction. 7. Maine—
Fiction.] I. Title.
PZ7.1.M4355San 2015
[Fic]—dc23
2014046789

10 9 8 7 6 5 4 3 2 1   15 16 17 18 19

Printed in the U.S.A.   23
First edition, October 2015

Book design by Mary Claire Cruz

For my brothers and sisters, and our father

I fitted to the latch
My hand, with trembling care,
Lest back the awful door should spring,
And leave me standing there.

I moved my fingers off
As cautiously as glass,
And held my ears, and like a thief
Fled gasping from the house.

—EMILY DICKINSON

CHAPTER 1

THE LAST TIME I SAW SANCTUARY I WAS TWELVE. NOT LONG AFTER THE FIRE and my sister Tess's death, my aunt took me away from the old mansion and the island and settled me into a boarding school in a remote area of Maine.

"I can't see beyond the trees," I told her as she tried to get into the cab. "I can't see the ocean."

I clung to her like a small child would, despite being the taller of the two of us, burying my face in her hair, thinking it smelled of the sea. She'd untangled from my grasp, her delicate face set and grieving, and waved out the back window as the cab pulled away. At her yearly visits after that, her hair smelled of lilies and sadness, but never the sea. I longed to see the sea again, but longing was intertwined with tragedy like thorny vines. So I'd made myself forget.

On my aunt's last visit before her death, as I walked her to the door, at seventeen and no longer the child, she'd been the one to reach for me, with an almost desperate clasp on my hand, whispering fervently: *Don't come back to Sanctuary, Cecilia. Ever.* Her nails dug into my skin, and her eyes were frantic. My aunt had seen the wildness in me, the part of me like my mother and my sister, and it frightened her.

Now I was in a boat in the middle of the open bay, the green-gray of the sea in chaos around us. I'd missed it so much. I wanted to reach for the water, feel its coldness stun my fingertips and its seaweed twist about my wrist. The salt thick in the air made me think of my aunt's hair, full and flowing and smelling of the sea. So one thing I loved had been given back to me, but only after another had been taken away.

The island was growing larger, a dark blob in the gray dusk. I tried to remember it now, to bring back the joy of early childhood, running our forested and rocky island with my cousin Ben and my older sister, Tess. We were wild children. No one cautioned us against the perilous high cliffs above the sea or the devilish rip currents while swimming. We were an afterthought, but free to do as we wished, gone from the manor all day, returning only when hunger brought us scrambling to the kitchen.

Tess had always been the leader, taking us on adventures to find pirates' lost treasure or the ghosts of Sanctuary's dead, with me following her, and Ben following me. Ben was the oldest, but slower in mind and body. Tess and I watched over him.

Tess's death abandoned me to roaming the island alone, the pain so raw and lonely I didn't know how to feel it. I'd pretend she was still with me, so I could cope. Walking along the windy cliffs alone, I'd talk to her as if she were still beside me, my child's imagination holding her fast to me. But after my aunt forced me to the boarding school, I could no longer catch Tess in my mind. She twisted away gleefully, eluding my grasp. Now I was returning to find her again—or at least I thought it was Tess who yanked at the rope wrapped around my heart, pulling me back to Sanctuary. I could already hear her saying, *Our home, is it?*

Uncle was at the helm of the boat, Ben beside me. My stomach rolled with the waves. I wasn't used to the motion anymore. But the sea lapping against the boat seemed to be welcoming me home, even if my uncle wasn't.

Uncle looked back at me, but I couldn't see his face in the low light. I knew he was glaring. At the bus stop, I'd been startled by the vicious look he gave me. My memories only had him hovering off to the side in a vague, tense way. He was at the forefront now. The lines in his face had deepened in the five years I'd been gone, especially the ones around his tight mouth. I wondered if my aunt's recent death had sliced them deeper.

Lights were sprinkled along the mainland we'd left behind. The small village of Lady Cliffs was much as I remembered, but I'd noticed a new filling station on the corner. In its window was a poster with a yellow crown above the words KEEP CALM AND CARRY ON. When Uncle saw me looking at it, he barked, "English fellow trying to bring the war to us." But the war in Europe was far away. Only the dangerous pull I felt toward Sanctuary was real. I didn't know what I would find there, and I was fearful of who I would discover myself to be.

We pulled into the harbor. I spoke silently to my aunt, almost like a prayer: *Watch over me, Aunt Laura.* I could feel only her displeasure.

Ben jumped out of the boat and secured the line while Uncle barked needless orders. I was paralyzed by a sudden bout of fear, sitting in the boat as it rocked on the waves. I thought of the men who took my mother away and feared I would end up like her. My cousin looked at me with a question in his eyes, but didn't speak. We were quiet people anyway. Uncle made a disgusted smack of his lips as he looked at me and, without a word, turned away.

Ben grabbed my suitcase with one of his large hands, giving me a final look of concern before he followed Uncle down the pier and up the white gravel footpath that I knew led to Sanctuary.

Still unable to get out of the boat, I looked again at the Maine shore. My hands trembled to start the motor to return to the mainland and my boarding school in the trees and my dear friend Elizabeth who'd replaced my lost sister.

It wasn't Elizabeth's calming voice I heard; instead Tess's taunted me as only an older sister could: *But, Cecilia, this is what you wanted, isn't it?*

A terrible feeling stirred deep and true inside of me, that if I stepped out of the boat, I would never get away. Sanctuary wasn't visible from the harbor, but I knew the house waited for me. I stood, wavering just a little as the boat shifted on the water, and stepped out onto the pier. I was home.

CHAPTER 2

My city heels were clumsy on the planks of the piers and the gravel of the path. I caught a glimpse of Uncle and Ben as they rounded a turn toward the back of the house, and followed, remembering more of my way with each step.

I looked up at our French Gothic home, which stood aloof and forbidding on a grassy hill in the middle of the island, at its most narrow strip. Its power clutched at my heart. Its magnificent white façade, now lit up by the almost full moon, was worn a little by the sea air, but was still stirring and stark against the black slate roof. Narrow white brick chimneys rose up, breaking the roofline, along with many gables across the front, and the two large towers on either side.

It was an old manor house of forty rooms, which didn't include the labyrinth of service activities in the basement. The original owner, the mysterious and wealthy Captain Winship, had spent precious years and money to build it. He'd been set on recreating the Old World in the New, calling his home Sanctuary to be his sanctuary from the England that didn't appreciate him. The house was finished in 1754.

The old captain's spacious, lovely room—the manor's best—was on the southwest corner, and had been my aunt and uncle's. My aunt would take her morning coffee on that balcony, hiding from life as the days slipped away. So many had lived in this house, lingered on that balcony, and now they were gone. Sanctuary still stood.

It's just a house, I told myself. It doesn't hold the dead, only the memory of them. It doesn't turn sane people insane. It doesn't kill people. It's just a house—a very large, very old house.

Something caught my attention in the trees to my right. I remembered the graveyard was there, a place my sister haunted. Suddenly, I was ten again: frightened and looking for her, hearing her laughter, not able to see her behind the branches. I closed my eyes, tasting the memory in the scent of the trees the wind brought to me.

I was lingering too long. If you did that, the memories caught you by the throat. Turning from my mind's tricks, I made my way to the back of the house.

The worn knob seemed smaller and darker. At the bottom of the door were scratches my dog, Jasper, had made. I knew he would remember me, his constant companion. Taking a settling breath, I steeled myself against the sad so I'd be open to the good.

Strong feelings rushed toward me as I opened the door. They pressed on my heart, so powerful I stepped back, feeling both a pull and a push—like a ripping inside. I clutched my chest and closed my eyes against the onslaught of emotions, so many, so piercing.

I forced my eyes open, unsteady on my feet. I wanted to run back to the boat. I'm not supposed to be here, I thought. The house doesn't want me.

Dizziness overcame me as I took in the familiar things—the same black kettle on the stove, the same gray raincoat hanging on a nail by the door. I felt like a child again, expecting to see Tess come around the corner and grin mischievously.

I shut the door and backed away. Stumbling to the old stone bench in the herb garden, I breathed in the fragrance of the herbs, trying to slow the beating of my heart. Not yet an hour in Sanctuary's shadow, and I was imagining things and shaking with fear.

But something was wrong. Something was wrong in that house.

No, I thought. *No.* It's Sanctuary. It's my home.

I had to calm myself. I wouldn't be accused of being like my mother.

A wave of homesickness came over me, but not for Sanctuary. I needed to see my friend Elizabeth and the others too. All those years there wanting to be here, and now I *was* here, and wanted just as strongly to be there.

What was I *doing* here? Why had I felt compelled to return?

One of the girls at school had told me, matter-of-factly, that I didn't quite belong with them, that there was something different about me. I'd pressed her to tell me what it was. Her eyes narrowed as she thought. "Maybe the sea, something to do with being from an island." She shook her head, clearly frustrated. "I can't say exactly. You seem like you're from someplace else."

In her soft British accent, Elizabeth had gently explained it to me.

"Cecilia," she'd said, grasping my hand and groping for words, "not only do you look a little exotic with your loose hair and dark eyes and positively luminous skin, you have a habit of staring at people a bit too long and of making remarks that are sometimes disconnected from the conversation."

After that, I tried to fit in more. I listened carefully to the others, like when they were trying on the latest college fads their older sisters had sent them: folding their hair into crocheted snoods, dancing around in saddle shoes or shag socks, or modeling a Tyrolean hat covered in pins. I laughed with them, liking them very much, but feeling apart, separate. At Christmas, after waving good-bye to them as they departed with holiday excitement for their real homes, I'd roam the school's empty halls, feeling like I was disappearing—already a ghost.

Coming here hadn't been to escape there. I hoped to find something here that would make me feel whole. I wanted to find the place I belonged.

Sanctuary loomed, observing, waiting to see if I'd flee.

But I wasn't going back on the sea tonight. And I'd yet to see Jasper, and my old bedroom, and my library. I stood up, ready to face the house again.

CHAPTER 3

THE LARGE HEARTH OF THE IMMENSE KITCHEN WAS EMPTY AND COLD, BUT it was early September and the weather still mild. Ben was at the table, Uncle by the hearth, and a stout woman at the sink: our cook, Anna.

She glanced at me, smiling, saying, "Hi, Cecilia," as if I'd just returned from a day-trip to Lady Cliffs and hadn't been gone for five years. I hadn't expected a warm embrace—she'd never been demonstrative—but disappointment washed over me. I knew the reason. I'd seen her look back at Uncle as she'd spoken.

Better than the pinch on the cheek and the "How you've grown" comments that Elizabeth complains about with her relatives over the pond, I told myself. And the only blood relation I had here was Ben.

I sat next to my cousin at the long table. Anna gave me a bowl of hot stew without asking if I was hungry, and then left the kitchen, her small hands moving nervously as she did. The smell of wet dog hair mingled with that of her cooking.

And then little Jasper came skidding into the kitchen, barking once, twice, then cowering at the sight of Uncle and slinking around to me, his tail wagging. I fluffed his black ears and whispered to him, "You remember me, darling puppy," although he was no longer a puppy. I played with him for a moment, his happiness at seeing me taking the sting from Anna's distant welcome.

Out of the corner of my eye, I saw Uncle watching me, the brim of his cap pushed low, his chin up a little to get a better view of me. He stepped forward, saying harshly, "Out, dog!" Jasper's little paws scuttled him backward, and he shot from the room.

I stared after my sweet little dog, stunned, then at my uncle. "But why would you do that?"

Uncle seemed surprised I'd spoken. "This is my house. I do what I want."

I looked at Ben, but he wouldn't meet my eyes. I thought of going after Jasper, but hesitated, thinking he might be difficult to find in this large house I no longer knew. And I didn't want to see any more of it just yet. It was hard being here.

Slowly, I pulled off my gloves and unpinned my hat, placing them on the stout oak table. With my bare fingers, I caressed the soft felt and realized my hand was shaking.

"Are you pregnant?" Uncle asked in his gruff voice.

"What?" I asked, blushing and confused. I could see Ben beginning to blush as well, the red creeping up his face.

Something twisted was in Uncle's eyes. This was the man who had pulled the money to my school—immediately—upon my aunt's death. Summoning me to her office, the headmistress had gently told me I had to leave, just moments after she'd given me the news my aunt had died.

"Better for the fellows if they stay away," he said. "There's something wrong with the females in your family."

I looked away at his cruelty, unable to answer, a voice inside me telling me he was right.

Then he leaned toward me, his eyes snapping. "'Greedily she engorged without restraint, And knew not eating death.'" He threw his hand at me. "Women are dunces, man's downfall!"

Ben sat silent, staring at a red apple. That apple was too bright for this gray place. It stood out, like it had toppled off a branch in Paradise and dropped straight into this hell.

I looked down at my hands and then back up at him. "Are they dunces, Uncle," I said as evenly as I could, "or cunning temptresses? They can't be both." These words were familiar to me, as if I'd heard them spoken before.

His lips twisted in anger, and he spat the words: "Your blood runs mad."

I didn't know what came over me. Maybe it was the built-up grief over my aunt's death and Uncle's refusal to let me attend the funeral, or even his caustic allusion to my mother's insanity. But I said in a quiet voice, "It isn't blood, Uncle. We're made of the sea, don't you know? Stab me and watch the water flow."

He was stunned, stepping back. I was shaken too. I felt confused, slightly off-balance, like I was on a pitching ship. I didn't know why I said those words to him, but I felt an intoxicating rush of power. A small smile flickered across Ben's face, gone in a flash.

Uncle pressed his lips tightly together and leaned against the hearth. The color was returning to his face, but his cheek twitched. "If it wasn't for your aunt, I wouldn't have let you come back. This is my home. I don't want you here."

"You shouldn't have stopped paying my tuition, then," I said, trying to keep my voice from shaking.

"Why should *I* pay for you to go to that school?" he asked, not looking for an answer. "I know why you came back. It was because of your mother and your sister."

"They were my *mother* and my *sister*. And my father also is buried here." I looked down, playing with my hat, not able to look at the manic glint in his eyes any longer. "Sanctuary is my home too."

"You don't fool me, acting like you don't know," he said. "I know what you seek here. You won't find her, do you understand? You won't."

"You're the mad one," I said quietly.

"Me? You're the one who thinks her mother is dead." At my perplexed look, he exclaimed, "You said *were*—that your mother was, not is! Well, your mother is alive, and mad. She's mad!"

I stayed silent. He was right. She was insane and put away.

He narrowed his eyes, and I could almost see him thinking, calculating. "There's a visitor in the house," he said finally.

He paused, but he had more to say. He tipped his chin at me. "I've put him in your old room."

Disappointment pierced me. I'd wanted to be back in my childhood bedroom, with my canopied bed and high wide windows, my chest full of a young girl's toys.

"Mr. Bauer's from the university," Ben said softly. "He's here to look at the books you used to like."

My library too! Sanctuary had an impressive collection. I'd been telling Elizabeth about it for years and felt ownership of it, like it was all mine. Many of those books had helped me through scary, lonely patches.

"He's young for a professor," Uncle said.

I said nothing, wanting him to stop talking, to leave the room, to leave Sanctuary, to leave me alone with my cousin.

"He'd heard about the library," Uncle continued, "and asked to take a look." He shrugged. "I said he could, for a fee. So I put him in your old room."

"Where am I to sleep, Uncle?"

"You'll be in Anna's room," he said.

All of these rooms in this house, and he was putting me in with our cook? For all my childhood, Anna had slept in a small room off the kitchen. I had been in there rarely, but I knew it only held a twin bed. "Where will Anna sleep?"

"Anna and I are married now," Uncle said with a sly grin.

"But . . . but," I protested in shock, "Aunt Laura hasn't been dead much more than a month." Ben shifted in his chair.

Uncle's face grew dark. He left the room, finally.

Shaking from this astonishing news, I looked at Ben. He bit his lip and gave me a sad smile.

"They are married?" I asked him.

He nodded.

"But . . . when?"

"Last week."

"But . . . no, it can't be. Who would marry them?"

"Reverend Miller," Ben said, quite sensibly answering the question. But then he looked at my face and must have seen something there that gave him pause. For he suddenly seemed sad and serious.

My cousin was simple-minded, yet fretted in a way too deep for his nature. I'd not seen him much these last few years, but he'd come with Aunt Laura on most of her visits.

I squeezed his hand quickly, not knowing if it was for his reassurance or mine. There was something about knowing someone you grew up with— even if you only saw them occasionally as time went on—as if a tight bond was set in young years that couldn't be easily broken.

Jasper came back in and settled down on the rough stone floor, laying his head on my foot, comforting me. The old faucet dripped.

My cousin handed me his apple. I pushed the stew away and took a cautious bite.

CHAPTER 4

"DO YOU WANT ME TO TAKE YOUR SUITCASE TO AN—TO YOUR ROOM?" BEN asked, pointing to the door to the service hall.

"Thank you, Ben," I said, "but I remember where the room is." I didn't want him to see how shaken I was.

Tossing the apple core away, I grabbed my hat and gloves in one hand and my suitcase in the other and nodded a good-night to Ben, who headed upstairs, looking back at me worriedly as he left.

Anna's room was off the dark service stair hall outside the kitchen. It was a gloomy area, dimly lit, with a servants' staircase on the right and several closed mahogany doors. I tried one, only to find the pantry. The next opened to the lone downstairs bedroom, a small windowless cove.

Anna had lived in this small place, waking before dawn, scurrying to the service bathroom before hustling to the kitchen to direct her large staff. But the old servants were gone, and most of my family dead. And here I was, sleeping in the cook's old room.

I set down my suitcase. I turned on the lamp, which sent out weak light, and sat on the narrow bed. The spare room had no pictures on the wall and only a wardrobe, the bed, and a bedside table.

No girls laughed around me and ran across the floor above my head. Instead, Sanctuary creaked and groaned into an eerie, unwelcoming silence. Sadness enveloped me.

Then I heard whimpering and opened the door to Jasper, his little tail wagging. Sitting on the floor, I kissed him on his sweet nose. "Did you miss me, boy? Did you miss me?"

I played with him for a while. Dogs were so forgiving. It hadn't been my fault I'd been sent away, but he didn't know that. Jasper had always been my dog more than anyone else's.

With one last lick on my cheek, he scampered out of the room. "Don't leave," I called out, going after him immediately. I'd wanted him to sleep in my bed as he used to, burying his head under my feet.

"Jasper," I said softly, going into the kitchen and through an open door into the formal dining room.

I hesitated, then turned on the electric chandelier, casting light into the magnificent room with its fine rosewood table. High windows graced the back wall, dark and mirrored from the night now. Into my mind came a wavy image of my family gathered around for dinner, with my father at the head, Mother to his right, and Mamie to his left. The memory was so vivid I felt I was there, back in the past, seated between Tess and Aunt Laura. I opened my eyes to find my family gone and cobwebs floating above my head, like waves on an invisible sea.

My aunt had shut up this room after they'd come for my mother. For those few months before the fire and before I was sent away, Aunt Laura had hardly left her bedroom, even taking her meals there with Uncle. The rest of us shared bleak evenings in the kitchen. The dining room had been abandoned.

I ran my fingers along the doorframe, wondering if a house could absorb conversations and feelings, releasing them when it wanted. Memories of moments, of whisperings, nudged at me. Was my family captured in Sanctuary's walls? I put my ear to the wood, listening. But instead of my father's calm voice, I heard another, harsh and unrecognizable. My eyes flew open. I stepped back, my heart speeding.

It's just rats or mice, I thought. At school, they'd climb in between the walls, sometimes hissing at one another.

Shutting out the light, I hurried past the long, lonely table and my imaginings into the high-ceilinged foyer. Jasper's paws made scampering noises up the wide oak staircase.

I treaded silently across the mosaic floor of the shadowy foyer. I didn't want to glance up to see if Jasper was there because I couldn't shake the feeling something was here with me, watching me. My stomach in knots, I made my way to the library, a place of refuge just beyond the stairs.

The door was solid mahogany and heavy, creaking as I opened it. I shut it and turned on my old desk lamp.

I smiled at the familiar sight of the wide, very tall shelves of books on the back wall, instantly feeling better. Opposite the shelves were windows that I knew gave a lovely view of the lawn during the day. I scented a sweet fragrance in the air that I couldn't place. It made me think of happy things I was impatient for, feel an acute sense of longing.

I stared at the books, drinking in the sight of each familiar leather binding. I'd read only a fraction of them as a child, finding comfort in rereading the ones I liked best. I had always been a slow reader, but that didn't stop me from doing it.

Many of the books were written in languages I didn't know, but the leather bindings, the black curves of the letters and marks, the radiant illustrations, the textured paper were all things I did understand. These books had been lovingly created; the tales they told must have value.

A long glass-topped case ran alongside the length of wall between the fireplace and the shelves. Inside it were special books. I never touched the fragments of clay tablets, which were fragile and inscribed with symbols that looked ancient and powerful, and I rarely rolled out the thick-skinned paper scrolls. But my eyes and hands always greedily went to the bound manuscripts, some with heavy leather covers and ornate metal clasps and corners.

I glanced around the shadows of the large room, past the quiet upholstered chairs in front of the fireplace, the small empty cart that had held bottles of liquor for our guests, the bare places on the wall where paintings once hung.

I went to the love seat by the window, glancing at yesterday's *New York Times* casually left on the side table with its disturbing headline GERMAN ARMY ATTACKS POLAND in bold print across the top. I picked up the fedora lying beside the paper.

A stranger was in this house, sleeping in my room, with his hands on my books. I played with the hat, resisting my urge to flatten it, and wondered about Sanctuary's guest, the young professor—wondering how young was young and what he taught and what he looked like. The boarding school only hired woman teachers.

Putting the hat on my head, tilting it over my eyes, I climbed up on the love seat as I used to do and looked out the window into the dark. Tomorrow, I had all day to swim in my wild, cold ocean, read a tantalizing novel in my library, and then explore the island. It would be a good day.

This thought lightened my mood, triggering a surge of courage. I found I wanted to be closer to her, to see her grave, even if it was night. Seeing her name, *Therese Cross*, might be a comfort. I had wandered the boarding school cemetery many times, not bothered by it. I wasn't a child anymore, and no longer the younger sister.

I left the library and the hat and went out the front door.

CHAPTER 5

As I stepped out from under the portico to the stone path, the breeze of the night air cooled my skin. I couldn't find where the path branched off to the graveyard. It was either because it was dark and I couldn't see, or because Uncle had long ago removed the old stones. Ankle-high grass brushed wet against my stockings as I left the path.

A short wrought iron fence surrounded the stones. The gate squeaked as I opened it, the high-pitched noise grating on my ears.

The cemetery was not a well-designed one. A large dry fountain stood in the center, but graves had been haphazardly dug around it, like someone had scattered seeds into the air for the planting of the dead. The graveyard's disorder didn't bother me—it seemed more in keeping with the wildness of nature—but the dead did.

The cemetery had been Tess's place, not mine. She'd known my fear of the *not seen* and liked to tease me about it—prick, prick, prick. I'd challenged her to cliff diving and exploring caves. And she'd return the favor by leading me into the graveyard at night, then breaking away to hide.

Her grave was next to my father's and grandmother's, abandoned in a deeply shaded corner, branches scraping their stones. Uncle must have laid Aunt Laura there too. The thought stopped me in my tracks. Her fresh grave would be there beside the others, my dear sweet aunt with her soft eyes and heart. It was too soon to stand before my family while they slept in the earth.

But I told my sister, as if she could still hear me: *See, Tess, I am in the graveyard at night alone without you.*

Sometimes I'd find her lying on a grave. Such an odd thing to do. She was very fond of one in particular. I felt pulled toward that one now, as if that was where I was supposed to go all along. I glanced around me as I walked, just to make sure I was alone.

I stopped and hugged myself with my arms, trying to warm up in the chilly air. It was too dark to read the headstone, but I knew what it said. "Amoret Winship," I whispered to no one. "Lost in 1756."

Amoret's grave. Tess's place.

The dark-haired beauty Amoret had been the first mistress of Sanctuary. Tess and Mother had been obsessed with her, talking endlessly about her while sitting right here by her grave or huddled with their heads together in a corner with one of Tess's books.

Tess told stories at the dinner table about Amoret, with Mother listening intently, a wineglass in her elegant hand, her dark eyes riveted on my sister.

Amoret had been young, the captain old. Living two hundred years ago. Some tragic mystery swirled around her death. Her life had been sad as well. Tess claimed Amoret longed to return to her home. I hadn't asked where her home was. Instead, I'd been watching Mother watch Tess and wondering what I might say that would get her to listen to me in that way.

I went to the headstone, dragging my fingers along the top of the rough stone. "Amoret," I whispered, and felt something tingle in my chest. Suddenly, I realized I was angry with this dead sea captain's wife. It made no sense, of course, but I blamed her for bonding my sister and mother so closely there was no space for me.

You were never interested in me, the wind seemed to whisper.

"You were dead and gone," I told the wind. There had been so many other things to explore on our rocky, wild island—caves, trees, sea animals. Especially the sea. I'd always loved the sea.

Yes, you did, came the whisper. *You were less interested in the dead.*

I nodded.

But everyone in your family is dead or near dead, Cecilia. Perhaps you should pay attention now.

About to nod again, I froze and squeezed my eyes tight, not wondering why I was talking to the wind, but *knowing* something was here, in the cemetery.

I caught a sharp scent beyond the wild fragrance of the bushes and the trees. It reminded me of what I'd sensed in the library—that longing—but there was nothing sweet about the longing floating about these dead stones. It was sharp and sad—and angry. I was transfixed, trying to listen to it as if it could speak or sing. It wanted me to do something. It was desperate for me to do something. I had no idea what, but the feeling was building. It was unbearable.

CHAPTER 6

I RAN, WINDING THROUGH THE GRAVES, NOT KNOWING WHAT I WAS running from. My foot caught the edge of a flat stone by the fountain, and I fell, ripping my stockings and scraping my knees.

Frozen with fear, I didn't want to look behind me. But I turned my head slowly, peering back into the deep shadows. I wanted to call out, to ask who was there, but my voice died in my throat. Not even the wind stirred now.

"No one is here, Cecilia," I whispered. "No one." No one is in the walls of Sanctuary. No one is in the graveyard.

I stared off into the past, remembering my aunt ushering me into the hallway as my mother's incoherent screams came from her bedroom. "Go find your sister, Cecilia," Aunt Laura had told me.

"Why is Momma yelling?" I'd asked. "She sounds scared."

"It will be all right. Go find Tess."

But it hadn't been all right.

My knees were stinging and the stone was cold beneath me. I pulled myself up, brushing off my hands and my dress. I threw open the squeaky gate and hurried to the house. As I got closer to Sanctuary, I began to run again. By the time I was through the front door, I was breathless. I shut it, not caring how loud I was. I leaned back against the heavy wood, shaken to my core.

"Hello," someone said. I gave a surprised shout.

I took a breath only when I realized it was a real person talking to me.

He stood on the stairs. Dull light from the second-floor landing cast shadows across his face. "I'm sorry," he said, coming down a few steps. "I didn't mean to startle you."

"You did," I accused, my heart still pounding.

"Did what?" he asked quickly, now at the bottom of the staircase, his face slightly more visible in the moonlight coming in the windows above the door. Even though Uncle had said that he was young for a professor, I'd still been expecting a man with gray hair and spectacles. He wasn't that.

"Startle me," I said slowly.

"You did too," he said, his voice amused.

I was quiet.

"Startle *me*, I mean."

"You came down for your hat," I said, gesturing toward his hands.

"Yes," he said, holding it up, then playfully twirling it around his fingers.

I stared at the spinning hat, blushing when I thought of wearing it, an act that seemed intimate now. "I saw it in the library," I said, not sure of what to say.

"Yes." I could tell he was smiling.

"Well . . . good night," I said, going past him.

"Wait."

"Yes?"

"Are you Cecilia? Cecilia Cross?"

"Yes. And you're the professor who's come to look at our books." I might have sounded resentful. I hadn't meant to reveal that.

"Eli Bauer," he said, stepping toward me with his hand out. I'd never shaken anyone's hand before. His touch felt nice and warm. We paused for just a second, looking at each other, our hands clasped together in the moonlit foyer.

He let go. I wondered if I'd lingered too long.

"Well, good night," I said again.

"But—"

"Yes?" I asked, turning back to him, wanting to hear what he had to say.

"What were you doing outside?"

I hesitated, and he waited. "I was just looking at the front lawn," I said, hoping I didn't sound as defensive as I felt. "I hadn't seen it in a long time."

"Since you were a child, I hear."

"I was twelve when I left."

"You went to a boarding school?" When I didn't reply, he added, "Your uncle told me."

I stiffened at the thought of Uncle talking to someone about me. I didn't even want my name on his lips. Aunt Laura should have told me what kind of man Uncle had become, instead of giving me vague warnings about not coming back to Sanctuary.

Mr. Bauer was still waiting for an answer from me, but I couldn't remember what he'd asked.

"What was it like, your school?" he asked, in a fumbling way, as if he were trying to think of things to say too. It made me like him better.

"All girls," I said.

"I know what that's like."

"What?" I asked, confused.

He laughed. "I have sisters."

"Sisters," I repeated. "How many?"

"Three, and two brothers," he said, a smile in his voice.

"I can't even imagine," I said softly, liking the smile in his voice.

"Did you find what you were looking for?" he asked. "Out in the front yard?"

I didn't think of Sanctuary's lawn as a yard. It sounded so quaint, and I wondered what kind of house he'd grown up in. "I wasn't looking for anything."

"You seemed . . . in a hurry when you came through the door."

We were quiet for a moment.

"I'm sorry about your aunt's death," he said.

"Thank you," I said, turning to go again, finding myself a little disappointed he didn't call me back a third time.

"Good night, Cecilia," he called out.

CHAPTER 7

I woke to a dark room. I'd dreamed of black things, of murder, although I didn't know whose, lost in a sea of nightmares. I blinked my eyes, trying to orient myself, remember where I was.

My knees stung, reminding me of my fall. I flicked on the lamp, hoping the light would chase away my demons or the ghost, whichever it was. Despite the cold, I threw off the covers, suffocating from their weight.

My knees didn't look too awful, and my hands were hardly scratched.

My suitcase was open on the floor, clothes spilling out where I had left them when searching for my night things. I pulled out a frayed bathing suit, another gift from Elizabeth. Money hadn't been flowing from Sanctuary to school—just enough to pay the necessary bills. Over my suit, I put on slacks and a blouse, grabbing a musty jersey sweater and an old towel from the wardrobe.

Digging in my purse, I pulled out a fragile gold wristwatch—my mother's originally, once Tess's, now mine. Five o'clock, I noted as I wound it. I usually liked to try to guess the time by the light in the room, but it was impossible in this dark cell. I wondered if Mr. Bauer was enjoying my beautiful bedroom with its view of the moon hovering over the sea and the sun rising in the morning.

I hadn't been able to see his face very well, but he did have a nice voice. I liked the way he spoke—not just the tone of his voice, but something in his manner that was endearing, an amused kindness or curiosity or . . .

To my surprise, Jasper was lying outside my door. I put my hands on my hips. "So now you return?"

He was on his feet, his tail wagging furiously. Not able to be anything but charmed by him, I knelt down and bade him good morning.

With him at my heels, I went out the kitchen door into the fading dark of the morning, not wanting Uncle spying on me. His room faced the front lawn. I crossed the east lawn. The sea lawn, I thought, Tess's words coming to me.

I glanced back at the house, not able to help myself, my eyes searching for my old bedroom window, half expecting to see someone looking out at me—not Tess, but Mr. Bauer perhaps. He was probably still asleep—*in my old bed*. An image of him tangled in the covers of my four-poster bed—his head on my white pillowcase—flashed through my mind.

I spotted my room on the second floor with its unnaturally high and wide windows. From those windows, I'd had a view of the upper and lower terraces, a murky fountain, the sea lawn, the vine-covered gazebo, the unused stables, the overgrown garden, a corner of the burned-out cottage where tragedy had struck, and, of course, the sea. I remembered how they looked in the mornings like this, the scent of the sea wafting through my open windows, the call of the sea driving me out of doors, into the water.

How I had loved standing at my childhood window with Tess on party nights, watching our guests on the lawn, listening to the jazzy music float up from the upper terrace, wanting to be one of the girls in dresses shimmering in the moonlight, dancing with boys who scooped up joy right out of the night and threw it back out for others to catch.

I remembered the feel of the glass against my nose and Tess's hand covering my own, the soft light of the Japanese lanterns, and the aloof gaiety just out of my childish reach.

Ten years ago, the crash of '29 had changed our lives drastically, stealing our money and our father. It was a few years after our father's death that Mother had been dragged out of Sanctuary screaming, leaving her own mother and two daughters behind.

And then the awful fire had taken my grandmother and sister. The horrible rush and crackle of the flames that night never left me. They came to me in my sleep, more often than my mother's screams.

I jerked my head from the house, away from its shadows, toward the wood. The sea was out there, just past the thick stand of trees, waiting for me. How I'd missed the frenzied joy of its waves, the salty taste of it, its *power.*

In the dark of the woods, I took a different path than the one to the boats, instead going to the other side of the island, the pines sharp and fresh in my nose. Jasper mostly led the way, but I liked to think I would've been able to find it on my own.

A wisp of light flew in front of my face. I stopped to watch it, turning round and round, as it circled me. I reached for it, in wonder, and it came to rest on my finger before flying off again. Others appeared, lightly brushing my cheeks. They were beautiful and mesmerizing.

Jasper barked, and more lights popped out of the early morning air, circling us both.

They were about my head, flying into my eyes, against my cheeks, now hurtful and sharp. I felt something *desperate* about them.

Frantically, I waved them out of my eyes.

"Run, Jasper!" I yelled, and we did, the lights trailing us.

I pulled them out of my hair, then stopped to get them off me as my heart beat wildly. Jasper jumped up, barking. But they only continued circling us. Running again, trying to avoid roots and rocks, we finally made it to the shoreline.

I continued to swat and swat until I realized they were gone, all of them. My heart pounded while Jasper barked. I stood at the edge of the woods, looking into the shadows, not seeing even one light left. *What were those things?* I felt tears on my cheeks. Surprised, I wiped them away. Jasper was jumping on my legs, still frantic.

I leaned down to pet Jasper, speaking soothing words to him, trying to calm us both down. "Come on, Jasper," I said, kissing his trembling head. "We're all right." He crawled closer, trying to climb into my lap, so I sat on the pebbly sand. "What were those things?" I asked him as he snuggled to me. Looking at me, he barked.

"I know, I know," I whispered to him. "Strange things."

I bit my lip, thinking, rubbing Jasper's chin. Some vision pushed and shoved along the edges of my memory, but it slipped and spun and I couldn't catch it. I buried my head in his fur, seeking comfort myself.

I hadn't been back a full day and all I'd been doing was running away. At school, they thought of me as the brave explorer, *the strange wild girl from the island*, but this wasn't the Sanctuary I knew. When I was a child, before all of the tragedy, it had been a place of natural wonder.

I continued to pet Jasper and breathe in the sea air. I looked around us at my favorite cove, mostly rocks and pebbles, but some sand. "Aw, Jasper, there is nothing else like this, not anything so beautiful." He barked again, but it seemed a happier bark. "I'm still scared too," I told him. "A swim will help." I gave one last glance back toward the woods, trying to laugh at myself for turning insects into things of terror. I kissed Jasper's sweet head again.

I shed my sweater, my slacks, my blouse, and, shivering in the early morning air, I quickly made my way to the small cliff. Jasper settled down very loyally on the beach to watch over me, thinking to guard me from the seals or the faded stars or any of the strange things living here at Sanctuary.

I was excited now that I was close. Birds were all about me, enjoying a dawn flight, as I climbed up on the jutting rock that enclosed the south end of the cove, ignoring the stabs of the jagged rocky edges bearing into my soft feet as I went higher.

At the top, I looked down on the crashing waves, the white crests catching the day's first light. For just an instant, doubt shot through me as I peered down at the water so far below. What if in my absence a boulder on the sea's floor had rolled just there, beneath me?

But then all I felt was a desire for the sea and a need to be courageous—and I raised my hands above my head and dove, taking the plunge down into a dark slate of a sea.

The cold was shocking. I swam, pushing one arm out, fingers stretched to the tips, then the next arm, my feet kicking, my body moving with the current, showing me the way. I tasted salt on my lips and felt its sting on my knees.

A deep, sweet peace began flowing without and within me, through me, into my heart, becoming part of my soul, until I was alone with the sea. There was no feeling like this, anywhere but here. It was exhilarating. How I'd missed this.

My body hummed with a serene calm, but the water was too cold. I pulled myself away from the sea and splashed up to the beach, shivering terribly. Jasper stood waiting patiently for me to do something exciting as I dried off and threw on my clothes. I sat down in my old spot, on a gray boulder with a flat top, gathering my legs under me. Jasper crawled into my lap, and we snuggled together, listening to the unceasing rush and hiss of the sea as it rolled in and out. The sun was slicing the sky with soft color.

Suddenly feeling unsettled, I turned to find my cousin watching me.

"You scared me," I told him, sharper than I'd intended. "I didn't see you."

He came toward me, stopping a few feet away. "I knew you would come here."

"How did you?"

"It was your favorite place." He gestured to the cliff. "Tess said you'd break your neck jumping off that one day."

"I can still dive off," I said, quite proud of myself.

He came to stand by me then, putting his hand upon my wet head for a moment. I could feel the wideness of his palm and the strength of him in his heavy grip. Then he reached into his pocket, bringing out a cap.

I took it from him. "I missed you, Cousin." I put the hat on my head.

"You're back now," he said. "Did you miss the island, and the swimming? I know Jasper missed you."

I kept looking at him. "I did. I missed Jasper very much."

"Jasper missed you," he repeated, saying it so low I almost didn't understand him. He looked so lost in that moment, I wanted to reach out for him, but I thought he might pull away.

"Thank you for the cap," I said tenderly, putting my love for him in the words, hoping he would sense it.

"You shouldn't come out so early in the morning. Wait until it's completely light."

"Whyever not?" I smiled. "Don't you remember how we used to slip out?"

"Things are different now," he said. "Momma said not to." He looked off at the sea, his eyes sad.

Now he was left to just his father. "Why?" I asked gently.

He shrugged. "Maybe because she's out after dark," he said directly, without drama or whispers. But I felt the sea's salty whisper in my ear as it slashed the shore.

"She?" I asked slowly. I shivered in the cool morning air and wrapped my arms about me.

"The ghost."

A sick feeling soured my stomach as I remembered standing over Amoret's grave last night, thinking the wind could speak.

"Amoret Winship's been dead for almost two centuries, Cousin," I said, trying to be calm, to not let him know how much this talk was disturbing me.

He looked at me. "I didn't say it was her."

I pressed my lips together, afraid for us both. "Who do you think it is?"

"I haven't seen her, so I don't know."

My heart pounded. "Aunt Laura saw a ghost?"

"I don't know. She just said that she was there."

"Are you trying to frighten me away?" I asked, trying to make light of it, but feeling my hands shaking. "I just got here."

"I don't want you to go."

"There is no ghost."

He didn't look convinced.

"Tess and I spent enough time out in that graveyard. Amoret or any other soul wouldn't have been happy with being bothered by children roaming about all the time. Remember how Tess would lie on Amoret's grave?" I asked, trying to joke, but even as I said it, I shuddered.

"I remember a lot," he said. In that moment, I saw things as he must see them: How all of us had been taken from him—his uncle, his aunt, his grandmother, his two cousins—and now his mother was gone too. Unlike Ben, I didn't remember a lot. My memories were hazy and fractured, sliced up by tragedy, then exile. It's worse for him, I thought, the loneliness of being the only one left in a place that triggered sharp memories, reminding you again and again of your loss.

I put my hand on his arm. "I won't go out at night." I wanted to say, *I'll take care of you again.*

"Do you promise?" he asked, as a child would.

"I do. I promise," I said.

"And you have to stay away from Papa." Ben's tongue went to the corner of his mouth, a nervous habit he'd always had. "Don't rile him up. He'll hurt you."

"Don't worry about me, Ben," I said, trying to reassure him. "I'm not afraid of your father." I wasn't being honest.

I felt his sudden tight grip on my arm. "You should be."

I put my hand over his. "Let go, Ben," I said quietly.

He released me, but said urgently, "You have to understand, Cecilia."

"Don't worry, Cousin."

"He's done it before."

"Done what?" I asked quickly.

But he shook his head.

"What did he do?" I asked him again.

But he wouldn't answer me.

My calm from my swim was gone.

CHAPTER 8

It was an eerie thing how we grew older, but the dead didn't. I was the younger sister, but only I had aged. Tess stayed the same, year after year, forever thirteen. And still, though I was seventeen and she was dead, I could feel her life force—very strongly now that I'd come home—and that life force was chastising me and pushing at me.

It was a strange, terrible comfort, being so familiar, a feeling like finding the place one was meant to be. But I fought the feeling, not wanting to feel second to Tess again, but at the same time, craving it.

I took out the one new dress I'd bought in Bangor and pulled it over my head, talking to Tess now. "You're not here anymore. Leave me alone."

My whispered words seemed to lie upon the air, shifting things around me.

And then as if something nudged the memory into my head, I recalled the wisps of light from my past. Or rather, Tess's past. When she and I had run the island at dusk or dawn, the lights had frolicked about her, round and round her head, almost as if they were a halo. Anna had said they were fireflies, but Tess had laughed at that, her nose twitching in that particular way she had, calling them ghost candles, saying they lit the way for her. She started calling them "our cousins."

In the kitchen, while I sipped hot coffee, Anna showed me how to roll out the dough for the biscuits, gently chiding me when I kneaded it too long, telling me the biscuits would be hard and tough if I didn't leave the dough alone. I couldn't help it. I liked the feel of it in my hands, liked sifting the flour on it, and stretching the dough out. We weren't supposed to be in the kitchen at my boarding school, but I'd befriended the head cook, Sheila. She'd taught me to bake.

Anna was stout and solid, but had never been remotely motherly to me while I was growing up. She was not only Sanctuary's cook; she managed the entire household, long before it shrank down to its current small size.

"How long has Mr. Bauer been here?" I asked, sliding a glance at her. Jasper, who was settled by the cold hearth, gave me an expectant look when I spoke, his little ears perked up.

"Came in yesterday afternoon, just before you."

The quiet of the kitchen cast a somber mood. At the school, Sheila always had the radio blaring out swing music while she danced around the table with a frying spoon. Our island had no telephones or radios. Electric lights and indoor plumbing had arrived only with my mother's marriage and my father's money (for Uncle was stingy with his), cushioning my life in relative comfort.

"Did he spend much time in the library?" I asked Anna.

"He was there for an hour or so."

We were quiet for a moment as we worked. My thoughts returned to my encounter—or imaginings?—in the graveyard last night.

"Anna," I began cautiously. "Do you know anything about the Winships?"

She tensed up and abruptly turned away from me, going to the icebox.

"Ben and I were talking about Amoret Winship this morning," I said, glancing at her while I worked the dough. "And I realized I don't know very much at all about—"

"It's about time, Patricia!" snapped Anna, looking around at a young woman coming in. "Where's Mary?"

"She's on her way, Aunt Anna."

Aunt Laura had written to me that Anna's nieces had begun working at Sanctuary when the last of the maids quit. I turned to look at Patricia, my hands still in the dough. Her brown eyes regarded me. "Hello," she said, a smile quirked on her lips.

I nodded at her. "Hello."

"You're Cecilia," she said. "Do you remember me?"

"Of course," I said. "You stayed with us occasionally." I was too shy to say, but I remembered a lot about Patricia. She was odd-looking, with blond fuzz for hair and dark brown eyes. Pools of mud hiding the reason for the lopsided smile she seemed to always have.

"What do you remember?" she asked in a teasing voice. Patricia had always seemed perpetually amused.

I blushed because I'd been thinking of how wild she'd been, sneaking out to see boys, who motored over on boats from Lady Cliffs. Tess and I spied on her once, creeping out into the dark after her. The memory of what we'd seen was still vivid. It'd been more educational than our governess's lessons. Tess was angry and testy afterward, which I'd never understood.

Patricia was watching me and laughed her great boom of a laugh I'd always liked. "Maybe I don't want to know what you're remembering," she said.

"There's a guest in the house," Anna snapped at her. "You and Mary need to be up earlier."

Patricia wiggled her eyebrows at me. "He's quite handsome."

"He looks smart," Anna said.

"He works at a university," Patricia told me.

"Isn't he a knockout?" swooned another girl as she rushed into the room.

"About time, Mary," Patricia said, repeating Anna's words, giving a teasing smile to her aunt. "Aunt Anna says we need to be down early, spit-spot ready to go, now that there's a guest in the house."

The top of Mary's brown hair was neatly pulled back and clasped with a bright blue bow. Mary was nothing like her sister—in looks or in personality.

"Go wipe that red lipstick off your face," Anna told her.

Mary ignored her, glancing up and down at me. "Is this Cecilia Cross, then?"

"Hello, Mary."

"You've come back. Why on earth would you?"

Where else am I to go? "Sanctuary is my home," I said.

"But things are different now, aren't they?" she said, laughter in her eyes. "With you in my aunt's old room and her upstairs in your aunt's room?"

"Mary!" Anna exclaimed. Patricia whacked her sister on the shoulder.

"I'm only saying the truth," Mary said, giving Patricia a little push. "It's just strange." She looked back over at me. "You've still got that long hair. Like your aunt, and your mother too. Very Victorian of you. I would have thought you'd cut it while at that fancy boarding school."

"The school valued learning, not fashion."

She burst into laughter. "You're just as serious as you always were, I see. Always so formal, with a dash of odd."

"Shush!" exclaimed Anna.

Mary shrugged. Her eyes darted in the direction of the hallway. "Ooh, I think I hear him," she said.

Patricia's eyes lit up. "I want another look at him. Particularly from the back."

"Patricia Marie!" Anna exclaimed.

"You're so uncouth, Patricia," Mary chastised.

"Well, have you seen his bum, as our British cousins would say?" She gave me a wink.

"Go ask him in for coffee and breakfast, Patricia," Anna said.

Patricia gave Anna a pleased nod, and she and Mary left us alone in the kitchen.

"Don't you want to see the young man as well?" asked Anna gruffly.

I didn't answer, just kept kneading the dough, but flipping and pounding more harshly than I should. Anna gave me disapproving glances because the biscuits would suffer. Finally, she couldn't take it anymore and gently slapped my hands, gesturing for me to move aside. With brisk efficiency, she rolled the dough out and began to cut the biscuits. I pinched a piece of dough and popped it in my mouth, thinking.

The biscuits came out of the oven hot and smelling like memories. I slathered one with butter, then another, and ate them quickly, burning my mouth. Jasper and I waited, but no one appeared—not Patricia, not Mary, not the visitor.

As Anna washed the pan, I stood beside her, fidgety, and played with the tin measuring cups. "I found the fireflies this morning." Anna's head was down, and I couldn't see her face. "They wouldn't stay out of my eyes," I said, still unsettled by the incident.

"I don't know what you're talking about," she said, vigorously drying now.

"The fireflies," I said. "Remember Tess calling them ghost candles? The lights, Anna. The tiny wisps of light."

"I've never seen them," she said. "But I believe your mother used to talk about lights. Of course your mother saw a lot of things."

"What do you mean?" I asked slowly.

She looked at me in a distracted way. "Your mother was trouble, Cecilia. For your uncle, but your father too." She put away the pan and hung up the rag. "Now where are those girls? I have work for them to do."

CHAPTER 9

ELI BAUER WAS IN MY LIBRARY SITTING ON THE LOVE SEAT IN FRONT OF
the window. He stood and smiled when I came in. Jasper gave a low growl
before losing interest and settling down at my feet. The feeling of longing I
had sensed in the library still lingered in the air.

Last night, the darkness had hidden Mr. Bauer's face. Now I guessed
him to be in his early twenties. He had sandy blond hair and inquisitive
eyes and a presence about him that made me feel suddenly shy, especially as
I thought of our talk in the darkened foyer, as if we'd shared something
illicit.

Why *had* we stayed in the dark last night and dallied in the hallway,
making awkward conversation?

"What book do you have?" I asked, trying to see around him. The
library was mine, not his.

He didn't even look at the book, just kept his quiet eyes on me with the
same look I'd caught on the faces of men on the train. But his gaze was
different than theirs, more one of surprise than anything. It made me hesitate for a moment, my eyes unable to leave his. He kept on looking, giving
me a smile so thoughtful and catching it made me want to smile back, but
I didn't.

"That book there," I said, gesturing to the open one on the love seat.
Then I noticed which one it was. My eyes darted to the case, the glass cover
propped open.

"Oh, no," I said, picking up the book, placing it back on the worn red
velvet, shutting the top. "You mustn't touch these books in here." I paused
and then grudgingly said, "You may look at the ones on the shelves."

I noticed he was wearing gloves. "What are those?" I asked, realizing he
hadn't said anything.

"What?" he asked, still looking at me. Then he glanced down, rubbed his hands together lightly. "The gloves? To protect the books from the oils in my fingers."

I rubbed my own fingers together, dismissing the thought of wearing gloves myself. I looked up into his intent eyes and his slight smile and, not able to help myself, smiled tentatively before glancing away. Something else was nagging at me, distracting me, but my thoughts were on Mr. Bauer.

"Your uncle invited me to stay for a few days," he said.

"Oh, all right, then."

"It's a long trip back and forth in one day. And I wanted some time to look over the volumes he has for sale."

"For sale?" I'd thought this was what Uncle had been planning.

"The university has some private donation funds to expand our collection. When I saw the books your uncle sent, I knew I had to come."

"He sent you books?" I asked quickly.

"He did," Mr. Bauer said with a nod. "Outstanding volumes. He has a 1594 quarto of Shakespeare's 'The Rape of Lucrece.'"

Oh, no, no, I thought. People might leave, but the books needed to remain. And these weren't Uncle's books. Uncle didn't use the library, except apparently to steal books to sell.

I went to the shelves, as if I could see which ones were missing. I ran my fingers over the spines, not liking that even one of them had left Sanctuary.

My fingertips slid through the dust covering a gold-embossed leather volume, the touch of it both bumpy and silky. I heard a soft murmuring in my ear, with insistence. I brushed the air with my hand.

When I turned, Mr. Bauer was at the desk—my desk—with his pile of books in front of him. He looked up. "These are remarkable. Many of them are first editions." He patted the stack with his gloves. "And some are original documents."

"Yes, they are remarkable," I agreed reluctantly.

"This is Greek," he said, tapping the book. "Modern Greek."

"Is it?" I asked, going over to him, looking at the script. "I never knew what language it was. It has so much depth—forceful and elegant at the same time."

He carefully pulled out a fragile manuscript. I appreciated his delicate handling of the material. I sensed that he felt, as I did, that the value of these wonderful volumes was beyond money.

"This one," he said, "this one is Egyptian."

I paused. "Do you read Egyptian and Greek?"

He gave me a quiet smile. "I recognize them."

"I'd like to study languages," I confessed haltingly. "I think my sister knew another language." I shook my head and smiled. "Well, it was probably gibberish she made up to fool me."

"But you could learn," he said. "Have you thought of going to a university?"

"No."

"Did you attend school on the mainland before you went to boarding school?"

I shook my head. "We had a governess for a year or two. She left."

He leaned back in his chair, looking interested. "Your education stopped for a time?"

Again, I heard whispering. I closed my eyes for a moment, remembering . . . something, but I couldn't quite catch it.

"Miss Cross?" he asked.

"What? Oh, yes. There was another woman, a Miss Owens, who was here when I was seven or eight, but just for a few months before my mother let her go." I smiled. "She was a strange governess. She had this way of talking, like a flapper girl stuck in the past."

I had tried to mimic her, using her words, like "hooey" and "gams" and "killjoy," even trying to do that little laugh in her throat that she had.

Sometimes she would laugh so hard that she'd double over, holding her sides, tears coming from her eyes. She'd told me I was quaint and must've been yanked out of the nineteenth century: "We gotta get ya off this rock, doll!"

"Why was she dismissed?"

"I don't know," I admitted. "But it was not long after the crash. Things changed at Sanctuary then."

He nodded. "The world changed."

"We lost our money. Anyway, by then, I was educating myself." I glanced about again, drawing back the heavy drapes to look behind them. But then the whispering came from over my shoulder, and I turned only to find Mr. Bauer looking at me.

"Do you hear that?" I asked cautiously. It was like two voices talking quietly to each other, like the ardent whispering of . . . lovers.

"No," he said, listening. "Hear what?"

Then the voices were gone as quickly as a snap of fingers. I listened, but there was only silence. They had felt . . . familiar, as if I knew them.

Mr. Bauer was looking at me, his brow furrowed.

"This is my desk," I said quietly, "that you're sitting at."

"All right," he said, still watching me, a thoughtful expression on his face.

"You can sit over there," I said, pointing to the love seat.

He picked up the books, being careful with them, and settled by the window. I could tell he wasn't going anywhere. I pulled a novel out of the shelves and returned to my desk, still shaken. But as the moments went by, I convinced myself I'd only heard Patricia and Mary talking outside the door, eavesdropping, or playing a trick.

I tried to pretend I was alone, but I couldn't shake his presence. I kept stealing looks at him, which wasn't easy to do because my back was to him. But he was engrossed in the manuscripts and didn't seem to be aware of my attention.

He was nice to look at. I could see what Mary and Patricia meant. But I didn't think it was only his features that made him so attractive. He was reading intently, with one hand up on his forehead, absentmindedly pushing back his hair. His body was relaxed as he focused on the manuscript. He was slumped in the seat a little, his long legs straight out in front of him. He seemed comfortable with himself.

Then he looked up, right into my eyes. I turned quickly around and didn't look back.

After a time, Mr. Bauer pulled off his gloves and placed them on the side table, saying he was off for breakfast in the kitchen.

"Anna is a good cook," I said and turned back to my novel.

"What are you reading?" he asked. I showed him the cover and he read the title out loud: "*The Castle of Otranto*. Are you enjoying it?"

"A helmet falls from the sky and crushes someone."

He raised his eyebrows. "So yes?"

"And portraits walk."

"Now I've got to read it," he said.

I smiled. "You're mocking me."

"Not you, the book."

"But if I'm reading the book . . ."

His eyes lit with amusement. "Why don't you come to breakfast?"

"I've already eaten."

"You could have a cup of coffee." He gestured to the book. "We can talk about the other strange things happening at the Castle of Otranto."

"I'd rather read."

"Oh-ho!" he said, his hands going to his heart.

"I mean rather than have coffee," I assured him.

"All right," he said, giving me a nod as he left. "Then I'm not so offended."

CHAPTER 10

I LAY DOWN ON THE LOVE SEAT, KNEES BENT, FEET TUCKED, SO I'D FIT, AND read my novel. The morning passed quickly, so immersed was I in the story.

But voices from outside pulled me away from my imaginary castle. Glancing at my watch, I was surprised two hours had passed. Laughter drew my eyes to the window.

Mr. Bauer was on the path in front of the house. It was Mary's laughter I'd heard. She stood beside him, touching his arm, lightly, briefly, as he spoke to her. They matched—her looks and his. She had none of my exotic wildness; instead, her American-girl naturalness blended with Eli's blond good looks to make them quite a pair.

My eyes went to the graves in the trees. Although I could hear no sound from the cemetery, I felt called and compelled to go there. I was still looking out the window, transfixed, when the library door opened behind me. Uncle was in the doorway.

He was a large man—almost as tall and broad-shouldered as Ben—with ugly hands that twitched by his side as if they longed to squeeze the life out of something. The library seemed to retreat inside of itself at his presence. I resisted the urge to flatten myself against the wall.

His eyes darted to the window and back to me. "Spying, aren't you?"

"What do you want?" I asked, trying to keep my voice steady, trying to sound confident and sure. I wondered where Ben was.

"Don't take that tone with me, girl." His whole body seemed about to pounce, as if he couldn't control it.

Tightness pressed against my chest. I kept my eyes on him, remembering a silver letter opener in the drawer of my desk.

"I should never have let you come here. I can see your mother in you, that crazy witch, with her nose in the air like she was some sort of queen.

She ordered me around in my own house, thinking she was the mistress here. But when your father died, she knew, she knew . . ." His voice trailed off.

I was determined not to be afraid. "What did she know?"

"I'm your guardian, did you know that? I can throw you out into the sea if I want," he said, thrusting his chin toward the window. Ben's words came to me. *He's done it before.*

"No one would care," Uncle said. "You have no one."

Don't listen to him, my books whispered. "No one," he repeated, as if arguing with the whispering. But then he bit his lip, as if he was surprised he'd spoken those words.

"I wonder . . . I wonder why you even brought me here."

"Brought you here! I let you come back. You are here because I let you stay. Do you understand, you . . ." I saw it in his face, a deep loathing or fear that twisted his mouth. But then something passed over his eyes, as if he was confused. His eyes grew fixed, like he was trying very hard to remember something. "I made a promise," he said finally. "But a man can only do what he can."

He slammed the door when he left.

I collapsed onto the love seat, shaking. I held my book against my forehead and took deep breaths. I had no idea why my uncle hated me so much. I thought it might be hatred and fear of my mother he was taking out on me.

Mary's laughter drifted in through the window. As I wrestled with fright and uncertainty, I resented her carefree happiness. I wanted to flirt with a handsome young man. I wanted a family living in a normal home in Lady Cliffs, and to not grieve or fret or fear. I sat very still until I was calm again.

The front door creaked, and steps echoed in the foyer. From the window, I could see Mary going around to the rear of the house with a basket. My head whipped back as the library door opened, revealing Mr. Bauer.

"How was breakfast?" I asked, glad my voice was steady.

He paused for a moment, then closed the door, saying, "Quite good. Those biscuits."

"I told you Anna can cook," I said, going back to my desk. "I used to think of her biscuits when I was at the boarding school, wishing for them."

"Even better than my mother's," he said, sitting on the love seat. His eyes lit up playfully. "But don't tell my mother."

I smiled at him briefly. I pictured him with a mother, the two of them together in their kitchen, him helping with dinner. I had always wondered what it would be like to have a mother who cooked, instead of one who danced and threw parties and then went insane. Was he kind to her? I thought he probably was very kind.

I realized I was staring at him while I was thinking all these things. Coming back to myself, I started. I felt the heat rise into my cheeks.

He smiled, looking not at all discomfited by my staring. He might've even looked a little pleased. "What are you thinking about?"

"Are you trying to trespass on my thoughts?" I asked, still feeling vulnerable because of Uncle's visit.

His brow furrowed. "Are you so private?"

I shifted in my chair. I didn't look his way, and he didn't say anything else, but I heard pages turning.

All was quiet. I continued to look toward the door, afraid Uncle would barge in. But I didn't think he would with Mr. Bauer here. And also I'd noticed Uncle had only hovered in the doorway, as if he didn't want to step into the room. That thought comforted me: that the library might be a place he didn't like to enter. I was safe here. Finally I fell back into my castle again, immersed in another world far from Sanctuary—interrupted only by occasional glances at Mr. Bauer.

CHAPTER 11

LATER IN THE MORNING, THE SMELL OF BAKING COOKIES REACHED THE library, making it hard to concentrate on my reading. I left quickly, before Mr. Bauer could say anything to me. I didn't know what to do about him yet.

I froze in the doorway. Uncle was sitting in his chair at the head of the table. Ben was there, in front of the hearth, with Anna hovering over him. When she moved, I saw that he was holding a wrapped wedge of ice over his right eye.

"What happened?!" I exclaimed, taking in Ben's look of shame and Anna's fearful one. I shot a glance at Uncle.

A pleased grin split Uncle's face, which made my stomach feel sick. Ben kept the wrapped ice on his face, not looking at me. Anna went to the sink. Uncle's smile faded, and he took one of the cookies off a plate set before him, eating it quietly.

"Ben?" I pressed.

"A father can punish his own son," Uncle said, turning to look at Ben, "especially when he's an idiot. Taking a perfectly good window frame apart!"

"I thought you said the wood joint was rotted," Ben explained.

"Not on that window! And then you spent all morning on it, a simple task, and now I have to put it back together." He mumbled something I couldn't hear. Then: "Not from my side of the family."

"I'm sorry, Papa," Ben said, pulling at his collar, letting the rag of ice slip a little, showing his swollen red eye. His tongue went to the corner of his mouth.

"Don't apologize to him," I said.

"I can discipline my own son!" Uncle shouted at me with such hatred I trembled inside at what he might do. He stared at Ben now. "Put your tongue back in your mouth, boy! No one wants to see your ugly tongue!"

Anna started to slip out the back door, a hatchet in one hand, the other on the knob. The door cracked open, when Uncle barked at her, "Where are you going?"

She looked back over her shoulder as she explained, "I have to get one of the chickens for our supper." She stood there, waiting for Uncle's reply.

Uncle reached down, scooping up Jasper, who yelped as he was captured. Startled, I shot toward him, but Uncle held him away from me. The poor thing immediately went limp in Uncle's arms, knowing not to fight the beast. Uncle held the dog firmly, his hand resting on Jasper's back. "Cecilia will kill a chicken for our dinner."

"What?" I asked in disbelief.

I watched his hands on Jasper and reached for the dog again, but Uncle held him tightly. "You're too soft. You care too much about them all," he said. "That's your weakness. Ha!"

I was frozen in place, thinking about what to do. Jasper looked at me with his soft, timid eyes. Uncle didn't pet him, just held him firmly so he couldn't move.

"I'll kill the chicken," Ben said.

"You won't either," Uncle growled. "And if I find you have, I'll be taking out that other eye," he added dramatically, as if he were a king and this his castle.

I grabbed the hatchet from Anna and went past her through the door, leaving the scene behind me, heading for the henhouse. Tess and I had spent a lot of time around the chickens.

When I came into the yard, hidden from the house by trees, the chickens looked at me, or so it seemed. I hid the ax behind a large island oak outside the wire fence and then went in, watching them strut around on their big claws, scratching in the dirt.

It was a heartless task, picking out one for slaughter.

Walking quickly, sending the flock squawking and flapping, I swooped one up by her leg. After she tussled for a minute, she calmed down, hanging there limp and sad. I pulled her up and tucked her under my arm, trying to be gentle and talking to her as if I wasn't going to hurt her.

Ben was waiting for me. He led me toward a bloodstained stump.

"I'll do it for you if you want," he said bravely, the area around his eye an angry red. He'd have a black eye by morning.

I studied him, petting the chicken to keep her calm. "Why don't you fight back?" There was a harsh judgment in my voice, which I hadn't meant to reveal. I was angry only at myself for what I was about to do and shouldn't have been taking that out on my cousin.

But Ben didn't look ashamed, and I wondered if whatever had touched his brain had touched his spirit too, making him the perfect son for my uncle. "I shouldn't have taken apart the window," he said finally.

"No," I said, shaking my head at him. "It wasn't your fault."

"You're scared of Papa too," he accused. "You don't fight back either." He pointed to the chicken.

"I'd fight back if he ever tried to hit me."

"You don't know what you'd do."

I sighed. "Let's not argue, Cousin." I gestured to the hen. "I'll do this. Just tell me how."

"The feathers around the neck are thick," he said, "thicker than you think. Where's Anna's hatchet?"

"Oh," I said, looking over my shoulder. "I left it by the tree outside the gate."

Ben left to retrieve it as I petted the hen's feathers. "It's a nice day today, little darling," I told her. "A few clouds are hovering over the coast there."

"Don't let her see it," I told Ben as he came back, so he put the ax behind him and stood waiting for me.

I approached the dead tree stump again and saw the two nails hammered into the top. "That's where the neck goes?"

Ben nodded, still hiding the ax.

"Will she die quickly?" I asked.

"If you do it right," he said bluntly.

I swallowed. "Put the hatchet by the stump."

Ben—in an almost comical way—kept facing me and the chicken, keeping the ax behind his leg. Then he placed it behind the stump, on the other side. "I'll hold the hen while you do it," he said, gesturing for me to lay her down.

I carefully placed her on the stump, positioning the neck between the nails, as Ben put his large hands on her body, keeping her in place. He looked at me as the chicken squirmed. "One strong cut."

I nodded at him, quietly grabbing the ax. I closed my eyes tightly, trying to take the sting away. I couldn't cry. I had to be able to see what I was doing.

The hen was facing the other way, toward the sea. I positioned the ax against her neck and put everything out of my mind except her neck and the weight of the blade in my hand, not wanting to slip up.

Still, I hesitated. But then a sense of resolve soared through me, and as if someone else more experienced was guiding me, I brought the ax down, forcefully, and as Ben advised, made one strong cut, a perfect slice really. The hen jerked about, and warm blood gushed out, onto Ben's hands, my clothes and feet.

Ben held the body firmly as it continued to move. I hadn't expected her to live with her head gone. I put the ax down and stroked her soft bloody feathers, saying, "Little darling, little darling," as I watched her life leave her.

Once she quieted, Ben released her, and he and I stared at each other. "You are good at this, Cecilia. It usually takes me a few tries."

I nodded silently.

He gestured to my face. "You have blood on your face, where you wiped away your tears."

I sniffed. "You'll clean her?" I asked, rubbing my fingers on my dress.

He nodded.

I stood, looking down at the two pieces of her. My eyes came up when I sensed someone else was there. It was Mr. Bauer, his hands in his pockets, staring quietly at us, and the hen, and the blood.

"I'll clean the hatchet when I get back," I said to Ben.

Without waiting for his reply, I took off running.

"I'll clean it!" I heard him yell after me.

My feet hit hard on the path, pound, pound, pound. When I got to the beach, while still hastening to the water, I threw off my shoes, my new dress now bloodied, my slip, my underthings, trying to push away all thoughts of that life going out of its body and me being the one to take it. The waves rushed up to meet me, luring me in, wanting to clean the blood and death off me.

I immersed myself under the cold water, thinking of the beauty of the books in the library and the soft feathers on the hen's neck and feeling the horribleness of her violent death gently float away until only peace remained.

CHAPTER 12

⁓

AFTER SWIMMING VIGOROUSLY THROUGH THE COLD WATER, I WASHED THE blood out of my dress and shoes as best I could and dressed in wet clothes. The sun was out, and I shivered in the heat. I walked back to the edge of the woods, stopping as I heard a twig snap loudly. I scanned the trees around me, but nothing stirred.

Hungry, thinking of blueberries, I took another path, meandering through the trees, marveling at the many shades of green. I headed toward the gardens of the destroyed cottage, a place we'd often retreated to on cold wintery days, a cozy house for Tess, Ben, and me to be with our grandmother, Mamie.

I hadn't been there since the fire and wondered if I could take seeing the place again. It was important to at least try because I didn't like being afraid of something on my island. Fear would only give my fear more power. Maybe all these years away had only made the memories worse than they'd have been if I'd never left.

Continuing on the path, I approached the remains of the cottage from the sea side. It was perched on a cliff overlooking the sea. A stunning drop, with waves crashing against the rock.

Wild blueberries flourished at the edge of an overgrown garden on the other side of the cottage from where I stood. Mamie had given us baskets, and we'd fill them with berries. She'd make pie with flaky crusts and serve slices with cream. The remembered sweetness filled my mouth. But the memory didn't make me happy; instead I felt a shock of pain.

To get to the garden, I had to walk through the ruins, or traipse through a thick tangle of brush grown wild after the fire, or go around the area altogether.

I raised my foot to step onto the plot of land that used to be the little house. Panic shot through me, tightening my chest.

I backed up, smoothing down my bloodstained dress. Stone slabs—once the foundation of the cottage, now cracked and overgrown with ivy—were buried in the ground between the garden and me. My eyes stung as if the fire were still blazing in front of me. My face felt hot.

I couldn't do it.

Frustrated, I plowed as rapidly as I could through the overgrown brush behind the house, scratching my arms and legs, talking to myself or to Tess all the while about how I just needed time to work up to it and to *please leave me alone* about it.

When I got to the gardens, I looked at the ruins, the crumbling stone staircase and hearth that hadn't burned, and the ivy and brush grown up around them. I sensed the presence of the dead there, particularly Tess. I looked up as if an upstairs window were still there and Tess was leaning over the sill, telling me to come in. I saw the confidence in her eyes. She was always so sure. I wondered how she could be so sure.

But that night, the horrible night that I didn't like to think about, I hadn't seen her, hadn't heard her at all. I'd stood there while the flames licked at the roof, feeling the heat on my cheeks, in denial, looking up at the window, not thinking about my grandmother, only Tess, crying out her name, telling Ben as we clutched hands, "She's not in there. I know it. She's not."

My appetite now gone, I sat down on the brick wall around the garden's perimeter, out of the view of the eyes of Sanctuary. I wondered if it had been my grandmother's intention to build a private place the main house couldn't see. There wasn't much left of her rustic cottage.

"What happened here?"

Startled, I turned around, almost falling off the wall. It was Mr. Bauer.

He walked past me to the ruins. My heart was beating rapidly as he approached the ground where the cottage stood.

"How did you know I was here?"

He hesitated. "I saw you from the house. What happened to this place?"

I studied him for a moment before answering. "A fire," I said softly.

He was quiet.

"My grandmother," I continued, "patterned her little retreat after Marie Antoinette's hamlet, with gardens of roses, that little pond, and the Queen's House."

"I think this would be the Moulin, not the Queen's House."

"Moulin?" I asked.

"It was the mill. Some say it's the most charming of the queen's structures."

I nodded.

I shuddered as he took a step onto the slab. He wasn't facing me and didn't see my reaction. He continued to walk around while I watched from the garden wall. "Look," he said, pulling something out of the overgrown brush. He gestured for me to join him.

I hesitated for just a moment, then jumped off the wall.

I stood at the edge of the cottage's imprint, watching Eli examine something I couldn't see. I didn't want him to see me frightened of a place, so I forced myself to take a step. Sickness hit my stomach, and pain shot through my head. I couldn't do it. I climbed back up on the brick wall and wrapped my arms around me.

Mr. Bauer came over to me. "I'm sorry." He hesitated, like he was trying to find words. "Did someone—?"

"What do you have there?" I asked.

He smiled at me, a sad quiet smile. He held up his prize.

"A horseshoe," I said, reaching over and running my finger along it, and feeling the nearness of Eli, our arms almost touching.

"Good luck, my father would say," he told me, handing it to me, as if he were giving me luck. My family needed the luck, I thought. Weren't we all cursed?

A rare memory of Ben, Tess, and me playing horseshoes with my father flashed in my mind. I remembered the weight of the iron in my young hands, but not much more than that. The look on my father's face, any words he might have said to me . . . it was all gone.

"What are you thinking of?" he asked.

I shook my head, studying the horseshoe. "Nothing."

He grabbed some berries off a bush, popping them into his mouth. "Would you like some?" he asked, offering them to me.

I shook my head.

He finished the berries in his hand and sat beside me on the wall. "I'm sorry to ask so many questions," he said softly.

"My sister died in the fire. My grandmother too."

He looked up, shock on his face. He touched my hand quickly and then pulled back, as if he'd suddenly realized he'd touched me. "I'm so sorry, Cecilia."

We sat quietly for a few moments.

I slid off the wall and ate some of the berries after all.

"Tess was obsessed with sticks," I said, glancing up at him and finding his eyes on mine. I sat back beside him, picking up the horseshoe and turning it over and over. "We had a large collection of twigs, and each of them was a person. Her stick family was huge, her children spilling out of their house of shells. She wanted to have lots of boys, she said."

"And your stick family?" he asked. "Who did it consist of?"

I paused. "You can't see the cottage from the house," I told him quietly, watching him.

He looked back at me silently.

"You couldn't have seen me from the house. Were you following me?"

His face grew red.

I jumped off the wall, leaving the horseshoe. "Did you see me swimming?" I asked, suddenly flustered.

"What? No, no," he said, shaking his head, turning an even deeper red.

"You did, didn't you?" I asked, horrified.

"I was worried about you when you didn't come back after . . . the chicken. I went to look for you and found you." He looked uncomfortable. "When I realized you were taking off . . . your . . ." His voice drifted off as he grasped for words.

I crossed my arms, feeling very exposed.

He looked over at me. "Cecilia," he said, "when I realized that you were going for a swim, I left immediately."

I pulled my arms in tighter. "Immediately," I repeated.

"Yes," he said. "Truthfully. At once."

"Then how did you find me here?"

He looked guilty. "I waited for you. I stayed in the woods—" He stopped when he saw my face. "But not near the beach. I know it sounds suspicious, but that's the truth."

"You were spying on me?"

"I wanted to make sure you were all right. I'm sorry."

I looked down at my blue-stained hands. "I'm going back to the house. Don't follow me."

He called out as I strode off. "What if I want to go back to the house too?"

Walking backward, I yelled at him, "Perhaps you should go for a swim!" I left him standing there.

CHAPTER 13

I READ IN MY ROOM ALL AFTERNOON, AVOIDING THE LIBRARY BECAUSE ELI was probably there. Every time I thought of him following me to the beach, I was angry all over again. It was true I'd spied on him too, but I hadn't followed him across the island to do it.

Ben came to the door. "Papa said to come to dinner." He gave me a broad, simple smile. "We're eating in the dining room tonight."

"The dining room?"

"Yes, Patricia and Mary have been cleaning for hours, and Anna has been cooking. It smells so good."

"I don't think I'll come, Ben. Thank you."

He still stood there, waiting.

"What is it?" I asked him.

"Uncle said you have to. He has a special dinner planned and you're to be there."

I shook my head.

"He . . . he said to remind you of what he said in the library." Ben didn't ask what that was, but he knew his father. He could guess.

Uncle was at the head of the carved rosewood table, dressed in dark trousers and a sweater vest, nice clothes I wouldn't have thought he owned. Ben was to the left of him, Mr. Bauer was to the right, and a place had been set for me beside my cousin.

"Good evening," Mr. Bauer said to me as if he hadn't done anything wrong. I gave him a reserved nod.

I played with my silverware, glancing around me nervously, remembering the odd sensation I'd felt in this room last night.

Anna was abandoned at the other end of the formal table for twelve. I realized this was Uncle's solution to the awkwardness of his quick marriage to the cook and that Anna's seat was also practical since it was closest to the kitchen. Our servers were Patricia and Mary, who looked slightly confused and relied on Anna's whispered directions. Jasper had been banished from the dining room and kept trying to get in whenever the door flew open.

It was soon clear this arrangement wasn't running smoothly when Patricia and Mary tried to bring out the entrée before the soup. Anna's little hands went flying, and she got up to tend to the matter. Ben giggled quietly into his hand, turning his dark hazel eyes to me. Uncle glared, sliding from his lord-of-the-manor ridiculousness to embarrassment, which only made him bark at Anna to hurry up.

She returned to the table, way at the other end, with three empty chairs between her and me. I took up my spoon to eat my soup.

Mr. Bauer was taking all this in with a very thoughtful look. He really shouldn't be here, I thought, eavesdropping on me, on our family, and reading our books. He has no right to be so interested in all of it.

I had been giving him the silent treatment all during dinner, but I didn't think he was noticing.

Uncle finished his rum, the bottle now empty, and Anna jumped up to fetch him some more, her soup getting cold. She pulled the liquor out of the mahogany sideboard against the wall. It had grown dark and overcast, so we weren't able to see the lawn before us and the sea beyond that. I had watched guests play croquet on that lawn.

"Eli," said Uncle suddenly, giving his empty glass to Anna, "I didn't get a chance to go to a university like you. I had adventures when I was young, but then settled down for a quiet life with my Laura.

"Of course I had to put up with Cecilia's mother, who disturbed my quiet, bringing her husband," Uncle continued, "her kids, then her mother came, everybody, for God's sake, until they"—he paused, taking a sip of his rum—"died."

He shrugged. "So." He let the word lie.

I held my tongue, despite feeling Tess in my head: *You let him talk of us this way, Cecilia!* I glanced at Eli, who was studying Uncle carefully.

Mr. Bauer wiped his mouth with one of the fine linen napkins Anna had brought out for the occasion. "You have a wonderful collection in your library, Mr. Wallace. What is your favorite volume?"

"I don't have much reason to read."

Eli looked at all of us, his face filled with incredulity. "So none of you have read them? Except for Cecilia?"

Uncle guffawed. "Cecilia can't read. She always had trouble with it."

I bristled at that.

"She can," Ben said very bravely. "Cecilia was reading in her room all day."

"Tess was always carrying around books," interjected Mary, while refilling Mr. Bauer's glass as he thanked her.

"That's right," Uncle agreed. "It was Tess who could read. Always—" He stopped, then paled, as if some unwanted thought came to him. He swigged down his rum and raised his empty glass again to Anna, who hurried over with the bottle once more. I couldn't help but feel irritated with her, wanting her to stand up to him.

"Cecilia's slow with words," Ben said, not meaning to be unkind, but still it stung. "But she would read me some of the stories sometimes."

Mary's lips turned into a smile as she left the room. I felt Mr. Bauer's eyes on me. Steeled with defiance, I looked up at him, only to find him giving me an encouraging nod.

"They are fascinating books," he said, just to me, it seemed. "Brilliant."

Uncle glanced at me, his eyes bright. "Valuable, then?"

My stomach felt sick. I drank some water. It tasted bitter.

"Oh, yes," Mr. Bauer said. I didn't think he was a very good negotiator if that was what the college had sent him to do. "The stories are compelling. Do you know—many of the texts are about women being persecuted."

"What?" Uncle rasped out.

I smiled into my glass. The library had some such texts, but not the "many" Eli claimed it did.

"Women being attacked, mistreated, murdered," Eli listed, "plundered, all sorts of evil deeds. One text addresses the witch-hunting that took place in the American colonies in most of the seventeenth century and into the eighteenth."

I nodded, remembering the books.

"Satan's minions!" Uncle sputtered, his fingers twitching as he picked up and put down his glass. He pulled on his nose in agitation, again and again.

But Eli was paying no attention to Uncle, which confounded Uncle so much I thought steam might erupt from his ears. Eli pressed on: "Many times financially independent women were the ones executed as witches."

"They only brought it on themselves!" spat Uncle.

"Some did see it that way, as ludicrous as it sounds," Mr. Bauer said. "Take the widow Ann Hibbens, living in the colonies in 1656. She was of fairly high social standing, but outspoken."

"I remember reading about her," I said. "She was excommunicated, wasn't she? She refused to apologize to some carpenters she'd accused of being dishonest."

"That's right," Eli said. "That was as far as it went because she was under her wealthy husband's protection. But not long after her husband's death, she was accused of being a witch and hanged."

Uncle's eyes blazed, and I knew when his lips started moving, it'd be another one of his wild speeches: "'So saying, her rash hand in evil hour, Forth-reaching to the Fruit, she plucked, she eat'"—I took a huge bite of my bread, trying to chomp through his words—"'Earth felt the wound; and Nature from her seat, Sighing through all her works, gave signs of woe'"—was I any better than Anna? Just sitting here, not defending my sex, my cousin from this man—"'That all was lost.'"

"Would you stop with that insane chatter," I snapped, surprising myself.

"Don't be blasphemous, you soulless creature!" he shouted at me. I steadied my chin, not wanting him to see me tremble. "Those are God's words, you wicked girl. You're one of the devil's imps, just like all your kind." His eyes were alight with the passion of a zealot. I thought him insane in that moment, as if he were possessed by a demon.

"Actually," interjected Eli, in a calm voice, but his eyes were hard, "those are Milton's words."

Uncle's head jerked. "What?" His eyes lost some of their crazed look. "My father taught me those passages. They're from the Bible."

"No, they're not. They're from the epic poem *Paradise Lost*, written by John Milton."

Uncle gave his guest a long stare, but Eli didn't seem agitated at all.

Disquiet settled over us. Even the room itself seemed to be disturbed by the conversation, the lights dimming, probably because Uncle had neglected to repair something. His beady eyes were fixed on the amber liquor in his tumbler. His shoulders were stiff and tense, as if he were a predator ready to pounce on prey, but without hunger as an excuse for killing.

He caught me staring. He settled back in his chair and said to Eli, while still looking at me, a challenge in his eyes, "Will that part of the collection be worth less because it's about a bunch of women?"

I sipped my water. *He's not getting my books.*

Eli studied Uncle for a moment. "They're valuable texts." He turned to me and asked quietly, "Did your aunt or mother add much to the collection?"

"Some," I said.

"Before I came to your island," Eli said to me, his eyes lit up by his subject, "I did some research, looking for something about the people who had originally settled here." (His voice *was* really lovely, with a slight gravelly undertone to it.) "I discovered that your ancestor," he said, nodding at

Uncle, "Captain Winship, was a witch-hunter before he settled on this island. Did you know that?"

I felt an unease come over all of us at this more personal turn in the conversation. The mood almost visibly shifted. Ben looked at Uncle, then quickly glanced away to study the wallpaper on the opposite wall. Uncle scowled at Mr. Bauer.

"The captain," Eli continued, "was also involved in the deportation of the Acadians from their home. He transported a shipload of them from their French province in Nova Scotia, abandoning them to the wilds of Virginia."

I felt Uncle's eyes on me then. He wasn't paying any more attention to Eli. He was focused on me, as if I had something to do with this story Eli told. Still watching me, he gestured in Anna's direction, down the long length of table. "Anna, where's the chicken?"

My head whipped over to Anna's tense face and back to him.

He glared at me, a smile on his face.

I left the table before the chicken arrived.

CHAPTER 14

I sat up, thrashing, waking to a gunshot. My heart pounded as I tried to remember where I was. This wasn't school; it was Sanctuary, Anna's room. A nightmare, only a nightmare: the same one that had haunted me many times before. In it, I was a child running across the sea lawn, desperate to find my father.

Taking deep breaths, I stayed still, listening to the night breathing of the house, its normal whispers and creaks, feeling something had woken me other than my dark dreams.

My feet were quiet, sliding over the small rug on the floor, as I crept toward my door. There, I stayed very still, waiting for some noise or movement. Someone was on the other side, waiting too, I just felt it.

I watched the knob to see if it would turn. If it was Uncle, I'd be in trouble; he was much larger and stronger than I was. Quietly I picked up the letter opener I'd left on my bedside table. I needed a real weapon, a knife from the kitchen, but this would have to do.

Gathering courage, with my blade at the ready, I flung open the door. But the service hall was dark and empty.

Determined now, I grabbed the flashlight off my bedside table. Turning on all the lights in the house might wake people upstairs, and I didn't want that. On my own, I needed to figure out who was here, because if it wasn't Uncle . . . The thought died in my head.

I looked around the hall and up the service stairs, and even in the pantry briefly, the smell of fresh yellow onions caught in my nose.

Next I searched the breakfast room, elegant in its day, abandoned now.

My light flickered across the white sheets draped over the small table and chairs at the room's center. It had been a morning ritual of my mother and my aunt to take coffee and cold bread in here, even while their guests were served a more formal breakfast in the dining room with the rest of the family.

I passed through the room into the foyer. Thinking I heard whispering, I shone the light up the wide stairs, but saw nothing but darkness. I investigated the shadows and corners of the lower portion of the stairs and of the large hall, but found only dust balls and scurrying spiders.

The vast ballroom pulled me to it. Opening one of the double doors just beyond the staircase, cringing at the loud creaking of its hinges, I stepped barefoot onto the cold marble floor of this grand wasted room. Two great cut-glass chandeliers hung from the high gilded ceiling.

On the other side of the wall stood three pairs of French doors leading to a stone upper terrace, stepping down to a smaller lower one with a crumbling fountain and to the long sea lawn beyond.

I closed my eyes and stretched my mind back. I could hear the lively music my mother preferred with trumpets and trombones, see the swishing beaded dresses flying up, and feel the bubbles of champagne in my mouth—before my father snatched the crystal glass away, saying to my mother, "She's seven, Cora," in an exasperated but loving voice. I saw her coquettish smile and how she looked at him, how she flirted with him, her husband.

My father and mother were dancing now, in my mind, all the guests gone or asleep. Round and round they spun as they gazed into each other's eyes. And around them Tess and I spun, dancing too, two sisters giggling, mimicking our mother and father as they waltzed around the ballroom. And to the side was it Mamie, who stood there, disapproval pursing her lips, with Aunt Laura cowering behind her? "There are things to do," Mamie was saying to my mother, who ignored her, ignored all of us in that moment, even Tess, her gaze fixed only on my father.

My eyes snapped open to the hushed room where music no longer played. All was still and quiet. The house was taunting me with the past, mocking me and saying in a voice like Uncle's: *You're the last one left.* I closed the door and rested my forehead upon it.

Sanctuary was familiar and real, a part of me, an eye or a bit of my heart. My memories of my childhood could be a comfort—all the carefree days of playing stone tag or hide-and-seek with Ben and Tess, flying up the stairs into the attic or over newly clipped grass on the sea lawn, looking for a spot they would not find.

Other times, though, my lovely memories twisted into me, plunging deep to a place rubbed raw by hurt and longing.

Something was here in this house, a presence that wanted me gone. I felt it keenly. It wasn't just Uncle's animosity. It was something more. I refused to believe it was Sanctuary itself. This was my home, where I'd been born and loved. But things were different now.

And I felt just as strongly that something outside of Sanctuary, in the graveyard, wanted me there.

That simultaneous pushing and pulling led me out the front door into fresh air I could breathe, beyond the portico, looking out at the dark lawn. Patches of clouds swirled here and there in the night sky, obscuring stars as they floated past. I was about to turn away when I glimpsed something in the trees by the stones.

It was a shadowy shape, quiet and suddenly still, as if it knew I was watching it. I stepped off the path and toward her, somehow knowing it was a woman, a young woman. Her hair was dark and long, like mine, but she wore long skirts that brushed the ground beneath her.

Something fluttered above my head, but I didn't look up. I had to reach her. She had something to tell me. She'd been waiting for me for a very long time. I wanted her to know I was sorry I left without helping her, that I'd only been a child and my aunt had banished me from the island. I'd had no choice.

A brilliant white shawl slipped from her shoulders as she held out her hand to me, closed in a tight fist. I reached for her, wanting to clasp her hand in my own and discover its contents. It was vital, urgent, not only to her, but to me as well. But I couldn't move quickly enough: Her hand opened, and specks of light rose out of her palm into the dusky air. My fireflies!

I hurried, desperate to catch the lights, angry with her that she'd released them.

But when I was but a few feet away, I stopped.

Where was she?

She'd dissolved. I'd seen her just there, at the edge of the line of trees. I had seen her. Maybe she was in the shadows, hidden from the moon.

But I couldn't move forward. Something wasn't what I thought it was.

A slow dread crept over me, fear prickling my fingertips. I closed my eyes, trying to center myself, not at all sure of why I'd needed to talk to this young woman. Opening my eyes, seeing no girl, no dark shape, nothing human or otherwise, I took a long slow breath. Pressing my lips together, I willed my eyes not to well up.

I am not my mother. I am not her.

Exhaustion pulled at me, the muscles in my shoulders sore and my eyes stinging and tired. Yesterday's long day of traveling and today's events had drained me. I looked again.

There was no one in the woods. I picked up the flashlight and the letter opener, which had fallen out of my hands into the grass, and hurried back inside. I lay in my bed thinking for a long time.

CHAPTER 15

I was in the kitchen the next morning when Mr. Bauer walked in. "Good morning," he said to Anna and me.

"Good morning, Mr. Bauer," Anna said. "Would you like some breakfast?"

"Thanks, Anna," he said. "Call me Eli." He sat down beside me, putting a newspaper on the table. "Are you all right, Miss Cross? You look pale."

"I'm fine," I said, trying to convince myself as well. I hadn't gotten much sleep last night. I'd ended up on the love seat in the library, drawn to the emotional comfort of the room, but my temporary bed was short and uncomfortable. I'd felt better when the streams of early morning light crossed the room, making the night before seem impossible and a trick of the shadows.

I tried to still my trembling hand as I drank my coffee. Mr. Bauer's eyes were on my hand as well. I put down my coffee, and it spilled over into the saucer. He looked at me in concern.

Glancing at the headline of his newspaper, I saw that it was the same one I'd seen in the library.

He saw me looking and tapped the paper. "A lot to read about Hitler's attack on Poland. England and France have declared war on Germany, you know."

"It seems so far away from us," Anna said, pouring his coffee.

"We'll feel it soon enough, I think," he said.

Anna served us poached eggs while the girls slept away upstairs and the sun brightened the kitchen, pushing the night's fears away. Everything seemed better in the day.

Mr. Bauer was absorbed in his newspaper. I was feeling kindly toward him for very rightly putting Uncle in his place last night.

Finally, I asked him, "What are you reading about now, Mr. Bauer?"

He looked up. "It's Eli." He gestured to the paper. "About British children being evacuated from the cities. They're worried Hitler will be bombing soon."

Anna looked up toward the ceiling as if she could see them falling from above.

Eli read out loud to us. In my mind's eye, I could see the children with knapsacks on their shoulders, carrying gas masks in their hands, boarding trains while their mothers wept and called out to them.

There we were surrounded by normal morning sounds, like the water pouring from the sink faucet or the rustling of the newspaper, and in other parts of the world, people were afraid bombs might be falling from the sky.

As I slipped looks at Eli brushing his hair out of his eyes—his particular habit—with a serious set to his lips, it struck me at how he made the quietness of Sanctuary seem companionable instead of cold.

"Good morning!" Mary said loudly, bursting through the door. She was smiling, fresh-faced, and full of energy, all directed at Eli.

"Good morning, Mary," he said. "You're in high spirits."

Anna mumbled something too low to hear.

"How are you, Mr. Bauer?" Mary asked, putting her hands on the back of the chair opposite from him. She pushed her full lips together and cocked her head to the right. Her color was high in her cheeks. She was a natural beauty, not strange or out of the ordinary. Elizabeth liked to say men married girls who were pretty and uncomplicated, and I thought now she must have meant girls like Mary.

"Call me Eli," he told her.

"All right, Eli," she said, her voice catching in a short pleased laugh.

"Are you leaving?" Eli asked when I stood.

"Taking a walk," I said, bringing my plate to Anna, who was washing dishes at the sink. Mary gave me a cat's smile as she settled down next to Eli.

Going out the back door, it was my intention to stay as far away from the graveyard as I could today. I took the path toward the docks but then, at its fork, went to the north end of the island, toward the old village. I was almost out of the trees where the island flattened back out for a short stretch.

"Miss Cross!"

I turned to see Eli coming toward me. "Are you following me again?"

"No, I'm asking if I can come along."

We were at a crooked turn of the path in a copse of low trees. I looked over my shoulder down the path and then back at Eli.

"I'd like to see more of the island," he explained.

I pointed at his feet. "Fancy shoes for a walk."

He looked sheepish. "I can change into boots."

"Okay, you run along and do that."

His mouth turned up in a half smile. "I can walk in these."

"Well, come on, then," I said, gesturing for him to join me.

He nodded in surprise.

"Mary must've been disappointed that you left," I said, slipping him a smile as we fell into step with each other.

"What?" he asked, meeting my eyes, then breaking into an embarrassed smile. He shook his head and glanced down the path. "Are you headed anywhere in particular, or just walking?"

"There's an old village on the island, long abandoned. My sister and cousin and I played there as children."

"Winship Island is so remote," Eli said. "It's different here—like going back in time."

"I didn't realize that until I left," I confessed. "We used to make trips into Lady Cliffs, of course." I didn't tell him that I'd always been uncomfortable with the way the townspeople looked at me there. "But that's a small place compared to a city like Bangor."

"Did you visit Bangor often while you were away at school?"

"Oh, no," I said. "But we would occasionally take day-trips. The first time I saw it—that was like a different time to me. What a surprise! With its trolley cars and automobiles and tall buildings. And shops."

The island village was very small, with no pattern, no main road running through it. Cottages—put up wherever was thought to be a good place— were huddled together against the harsh arctic wind the sea brought us.

The homes were very old, made of stone from the island, rock that endured. Still, they seemed to sag into the earth, lonely and forgotten.

We wandered through my favorite cottage, where I used to imagine I lived, just one room with a large fireplace with its single pot that the owners used for cooking. Tess chose one as well, and Ben said he'd just live with me.

"Not much bigger than the house I grew up in," Eli said.

"Really?" I asked as I opened the lid on the pot and peered in. "Dirt for dinner."

"We had a few rooms, but they were much smaller than this one," he said. "But we didn't have dirt for dinner."

We went back outside and sat on a stone step by the village well. I thought about asking him about his family. I wondered what they were like, if he was the oldest. I picked up a stick and broke it into two pieces.

"Open your hand," I said.

He looked surprised, but wiped his dusty hand on his pants and put out a palm.

I laid a stick in his hand. "Me." I was about to place the next one down, but after inspecting it, I broke it in half and put it in his hand alongside the other one. "Little child."

"Boy or girl?"

"It doesn't matter."

I put the last one down. "Mystery man."

He laughed, looking me right in the eyes. Pleased, I nodded at him and, without thinking, ran my fingers over the sticks, feeling how cool and tender his palm was as my finger slipped and touched his skin.

"Your stick family," he said, joining me in twirling the sticks.

"Tess was the one who wanted the big family."

"Not you?"

"I'm not sure I'd mind having a lot of kids, but I can't see beyond the first one."

"And the mystery man?" he asked in a teasing voice.

I felt a smile tickling my lips, against my will.

"Tell me, what is he like?" he asked.

I thought for a moment. "The best kind of friend."

He watched me, quiet. Then he looked back at the sticks. "Yes, I think that's it, isn't it?"

I took the sticks out of his hand and threw them one at a time at a cracked stone step, missing every time. "What do you think of the village?"

"Eerie," he said finally. "All of these abandoned homes."

"Yes, but also a haven from the big house for little children."

"When did they all leave?" Eli asked. "The villagers."

"In 1918. I think."

He laughed. "That's an exact guess."

Hearing a noise, I stood and looked at the woods behind us. I thought I saw someone in the trees, a bit of cloth of a shirt maybe. But then it was gone.

"What is it?" Eli asked.

I almost asked him if he'd heard the noise too, but I kept my thoughts to myself this time. "Nothing," I said, telling myself it *was* nothing, refusing to let it spoil my day. "I'd like to go exploring. It's been so long since I've seen the island. Do you want to go for a hike?"

He pointed at his shoes, giving me a quirky smile. "In these?"

I hid my smile from him. "They'll have to do, I guess."

"Lead the way."

I tromped north, both of us quiet as we walked through the woods. It was so beautiful and still. How I'd missed my island.

When we reached the flat rocks of the northern tip, I sat down, gesturing for Eli to sit beside me. He took a deep breath of the cold salty air. "It is stunningly beautiful. A bit of paradise."

"Captain Winship chose his spot well."

"I wonder," Eli said, "why he didn't build Sanctuary to face the east and the sunrise and the open sea."

"Maybe he wanted to see people coming from the mainland so he could blow their heads off."

"What about ships coming from the sea?"

"Good point. I'm surprised he didn't have cannons mounted on the back terraces of Sanctuary."

"What was it like growing up in that old manor?"

"For a long stretch, it was happy." Then I was quiet, remembering what came after.

"I grew up," Eli said, "with not a lot of money, especially once the Depression hit. We were all crammed into our small home, sharing beds, living on top of one another."

"That surprises me. Your manner and education . . . you don't seem to be someone with that background."

He looked at me. "You're a little bit of a high hat, aren't you?"

"What's a high hat?" I asked.

"A snob, darling," he said jokingly.

"Don't call me that."

"All right," he said cautiously.

"Darling. Don't call me darling," I told him, remembering my mother saying the endearment to me. "Anyway, I'm not a high hat," I said quietly. "Do you teach at the university? I thought professors were old and serious. But you're . . . not that."

He chewed on his lip as if something bothered him. "I graduated from high school early, and finished my undergraduate and graduate work fairly quickly."

I nodded. His presence was calming, almost lulling. I wanted to sink into it and let the sea wash away all the tragedy of my family. How fortunate he was to have a normal family, filled with all his brothers and sisters, alive and loved.

"What does your father do?" I asked him.

"He's a potato farmer, struggling to pay his mortgage now that potato prices have plummeted. A decade ago, he got two dollars per bushel." He paused. "It's not that anymore."

"You send them money, don't you?"

"Sure. Papa was disappointed when I didn't stay to work the farm. I hope he sees now that wasn't the path for me." He laughed, but as if his heart wasn't in it. "He probably doesn't."

"But he's grateful for the money, I'm sure," I said, trying to cheer him.

"He's proud and doesn't want to be supported by his son. He doesn't see that I want to help." His face was open and earnest as he talked. "They are very good people, my parents. I have been very lucky in my life."

"I imagine they feel lucky as well."

He smiled, but with uncertainty.

"To have such an honest, decent person as you," I said, feeling how much I'd misjudged him yesterday, "for a son."

Something passed over his eyes then that I couldn't figure out, a slight hesitation. "I'm not sure I deserve that, but thank you."

He was quiet again. Finally, he said, "Well, anyway, to see this place, your uncle's estate; it's different than what I knew. So I wondered what it was like growing up here."

"It was . . . well, it was all I knew. We children had a lot of freedom and ran the island like it was our playground." I shut my eyes, breathing in the warmth of the sun. "But it grew lonely," I said, thinking how things changed.

He hesitated. "Are you unhappy?"

"Oh, no," I said, "I don't think I am. Just trying to find my way."

"Why did you come back here?"

When I didn't answer, he continued, "The world has a lot to offer. You could attend college, or live in New York City, or travel to Hollywood to see where movies are being made. The world's a fascinating place."

"Have you traveled a lot?" I asked, trying to change the subject.

"Much of the United States, and in Europe too." He paused. "Although that's all changing, isn't it?"

"You think America will join the war?" I asked him.

"Yes, I do . . . Cecilia, why did you come back to Sanctuary?" he pressed, not willing to let the subject go. He gave me a careful look. "Are you so attached to it?"

"All those things you're talking about doing—traveling to Europe, for example—would be wonderful. I'd enjoy seeing the homes of great poets and writers . . . ," I said, thinking about John Keats's home on the Spanish Steps in Rome, "and places in America's West seem magical . . . the Grand Canyon must be a sight to see, but . . ."—I shrugged—"I don't have any money." I knew that wasn't all there was to it, but I could only tell him that much.

"Your parents didn't have any money?"

"My father lost his family's wealth in '29, along with the rest of the country. I was very young, but things changed after that. No more parties on the sea lawn."

"Your aunt didn't leave you anything?"

I looked at him in surprise. "Well, I don't know. Uncle hasn't said. But she wouldn't have had money. This is Uncle's house," I said, not able to keep the bitterness out of my voice, "as he likes to remind everyone."

Eli appeared distracted, deep in thought. "Are you all right, all in all?"

I opened my mouth to say I was fine, but I couldn't get the word out of my mouth.

"You're afraid of something," he said.

"I'm not," I said, pushing last night out of my head.

"Something's wrong, though, isn't it?"

"You think I'm mad?" I accused, wondering if Uncle had told him about my mother. I was sure he had. That was a secret Uncle would want everyone to know.

Eli looked startled, but I couldn't tell if it was because of what I'd said or that I'd said it.

"I'm sorry to snap at you," I said quietly. I was too defensive about my mother.

"No harm done," he said.

I hesitated. "Do you think madness runs in families?"

"I'm not sure," he said carefully. "Are you worried because of your mother?"

My eyes went to his. "Uncle told you."

"I'm sorry." He looked sheepish, and I wondered what exactly he was sorry for: that my mother was in an asylum or that he was talking about me to my uncle. "It must be very hard for you being the only one in your family left at Sanctuary."

I picked up a cold rock and turned it over and over in my hand. "I keep thinking of those children . . . those children in London going off from their homes."

I stood up then and hurled the rock as far as I could, watching it fly over and into the sea. "Ready to hike?" I asked.

"Of course," he said, standing. Looking at me, he reached toward me, and I leaned from him instinctively. He smiled with a gentleness in his eyes and put his hand on my arm, holding me in place, and pulled a stick out of my hair. Holding it out for me, he said, "Another child for your family."

Smiling, I took it.

The coast here was too craggy to be hiked, so I took him on a short trek into the interior before we went back out to the coast.

"Fascinating," Eli said as we walked past a cliff.

"What is?" I asked, admiring his neck, his chin as he looked up.

"A moraine," he said. "To think of all that it took to create Maine's striking coast and islands: glaciers, early volcanoes, the relentless pounding of the sea, rocks tumbling on rocks. See this wall of sediment and rock?" he asked, pointing at the cliff. "This is debris left when the glaciers pulled back twenty thousand years ago."

I was secretly fascinated, but I asked insouciantly, "Do you know everything?"

His lips curved up just a bit. "Yes, yes I do."

I smiled, and a light, sweet feeling came over me.

He turned back to the moraine. "Geologists could study this," he said, waving his arm at the cliff, "and find out things about your island's history. 'The present is the key to the past,' as Hutton said."

"I tend to think the past is the key to the present," I said.

He looked at me thoughtfully. "That too."

CHAPTER 16

"See that lighthouse?" I said, pointing toward a tiny rocky island off the coast of our larger one. "That's where we're going."

"We going to walk across the water?" he asked, nodding toward the sea before us.

I sat down on the rocky beach. "Just wait."

"Ah," he said, looking. "A sandbar's there. I can see it. So when the tide is low—"

"We walk over."

"What is that noise?" he asked, looking off.

"Gray seals."

"Spooky sound, reminds me of ghosts," he said, joining me on the pebbly sand.

I shivered. Sliding a glance at him, I asked him quickly before I changed my mind: "Do you believe in ghosts?"

He kept his eyes on me, so I looked away. "Do *you*?"

I didn't say anything.

"Have you seen a ghost?" he asked.

"Every old house has ghosts, doesn't it? Abandoned souls?"

He hesitated. "So Sanctuary has ghosts?"

"Ben thinks there is a ghost—a woman—haunting Sanctuary's graveyard," I said as indifferently as I could, as if my heart wasn't pounding in my ears as I spoke of her.

"He does?" he asked, bemused. "Has he seen her?"

"He said he hasn't." But maybe he'd seen her and was hiding it, not sure in the day's light if he had or he hadn't.

"I don't believe in ghosts," Eli said.

"Maybe you would if you saw one," I said more coldly than I meant to. "I'm beginning to believe my mother thought she saw the ghost of Amoret," I continued, softening my tone.

He visibly started, then tried to recover by asking, "Amoret?"

"Amoret was the wife of Captain Winship, a witch-hunter, as you pointed out. If anyone was to haunt Sanctuary, I suppose it would be her."

"Why do you think your mother saw her?"

What would he think of me if I told him I saw her too? It was safer to hide behind my mother's madness than to admit things I didn't yet understand. "Or maybe it was Tess," I said. "Or both of them."

"They told you that?"

"I don't remember," I said, shrugging. "They could have. They talked about her a lot."

"What did they say?" he asked.

I tried to think, to recapture their words. "Mother . . . no, it was Tess. Tess talked about her." Mother would stand behind my sister, her long fingers on Tess's shoulder. I'd felt her approval of Tess in that gesture. Or maybe it wasn't of Tess after all. Could it have been instead of what Tess was saying?

I glanced over to find Eli's steady eyes on me. I smiled at him tentatively. "I wish I would've paid more attention to them now." I didn't tell him I'd cared little about Amoret and had just been longing for my mother's attention. "But they were so possessed."

"Possessed? What do you mean?"

"No, no, obsessed," I corrected.

He paused. "Do you think . . . ?"

"What?"

"Well, that . . . your mother's interest in Amoret had something to do with her . . ."

"Her insanity?"

"Well, yes."

I felt very cold. I looked out at the sea, trying to pull in its strength.

After a moment, Eli asked, "Was she French?"

"My mother?" I asked, confused.

"Amoret. It's a French name, from *amour*."

"You're right! Of course! Love, it means love."

Eli was smiling at me. Suddenly I wanted to touch him, to feel his cheek upon my hand, for just a moment. His eyes changed, reflecting back at me what I hoped for, although I didn't even know what that was. Drawn to him, I saw his hesitation. We looked away from each other, but then our eyes caught. He smiled at me again, but it was more reserved, less inviting than before. And yet there seemed to be something that remained, that charged the moment, the space between us.

"Hear that?" I asked excitedly, pointing at the waves. "It's the rolling rattle of the pebbles in the waves."

"I hear it," he said with a smile.

We stayed like that, listening. I stole small glances at him, liking the look of his face and the thoughtfulness in his eyes. Once, he smiled a little, without glancing my way, and I wondered if he knew I was watching him.

"Time to go," I said, jumping up. He seemed startled out of his thoughts, but stood with me.

We walked across the now-exposed gravel path connecting Sanctuary to tiny Granite Island. The wind blew at us fiercely. I pulled my sweater around me tight as we walked across the sea. Eli was enjoying this. I was too.

The lighthouse was in poor shape, having been abandoned long ago. I wondered if some of the men on our island had taken turns manning it. We climbed cast-iron steps inside the tower, coming out onto the windy top. Granite Island was so small, we felt we were hovering about the sea, with wild waves crashing around us. I grinned at Eli, and he grinned back.

I hadn't visited the lighthouse in a long while, and even then, I'd always come alone. Tess hadn't been interested. Sometimes I'd see Ben standing off on the beach, watching me, probably worried I'd get trapped by the returning sea.

Being here with Eli felt very different.

After a while, we climbed down and out of the cold wind, and across the sandbar before the sea swallowed it back up.

We walked side by side on the path. "Do you have any talents, Eli?"

"I play the trumpet."

"The trumpet?" I asked in surprise.

"I'm not too shabby, actually," he said. "I sometimes play with a swing jazz band."

"I'd like to see you sometime."

"I'd like for you to see me," he returned quickly. We caught eyes, and my skin tingled, which caught me by surprise.

"Would you teach me to play?" I asked.

"I would like that."

CHAPTER 17

As we got closer to the house, Mary came out the front door, tucking a stray hair behind her ear, smiling, saying, "We've already eaten. Let me fix you a late lunch."

"Thank you!" Eli said. "I'm famished after our walk."

He looked at me, but I shook my head. "I'm not hungry," I lied, seeing his look of disappointment as we walked into the foyer. The truth was, I was starving, but there was something I had to do and I wanted some privacy. I slipped back through the library door.

Going to the case, I scanned the titles. Mary's comment about Tess's reading and also Eli's news about the captain's history reminded me of the books Tess was always lugging around.

They were about the French settlers Eli was talking about—the ones who'd been expelled from Nova Scotia—thousands of them, if I remembered right. Long-time French settlers the British pushed out, moving them to other places, during the French and Indian War in the mid–eighteenth century, about the same time Sanctuary was built.

Amoret must have been Acadian, then, because Tess was only interested in Amoret.

Mother had only been interested in a book if Tess was reading from it.

But Tess . . . for her, it was just Sanctuary, the island, Amoret, and her books. She hadn't always been so singularly focused. When we were younger, we explored the island and the sea together, never far from each other's side. But things had changed.

As I looked through the shelves now, I realized most of the volumes appeared to be in the same places I'd left them. I had my own system for organizing them, and I was pleased Aunt Laura had left them that way. I'd placed the ones Tess liked on the shelf closest to the inner wall, at the bottom. I had liked being in control of the books—the one who knew about them, who knew where they were, what they were.

Sitting on the floor now, I investigated the volumes on that shelf, but they weren't Tess's books after all. And things looked different to me. I thought hard, trying to pull the hazy memory from the past.

Looking to the shelves above, I realized there weren't as many books on them. Someone had rearranged them, I was sure of it. But why would Aunt Laura have changed these shelves only? Why would she have taken Tess's books?

Pulling out the books one at a time, looking at the titles, I saw they were all about the fall of the Roman Empire. When reaching for another, my fingers hit something behind them. I leaned down to look and saw that there were books behind the books, carefully placed so they couldn't be seen behind these larger volumes.

Opening one, remembering it, I ran my palm along its wavy pages, marred from Tess's bath, its title *Acadian Reminiscences: The True Story of Evangeline*.

Gently, I pulled another out. The cover was old, cracked leather, and its vellum pages, wrapped up by twine, were only loosely held together by fraying strings. It wasn't a book, it was a journal, written by someone named Dr. William Clemson. The name was familiar to me, but I couldn't remember where I'd heard it before.

I settled myself in my leather swivel chair, which was too large for the small desk, but comfortable. The book was handwritten, and the cursive words not easy to read. The diarist was on a ship, talking about the weather. Not a riveting way to begin.

I flipped the pages, and a yellowed piece of paper slipped to the floor. Picking up the fragile note carefully, I held it close to read the faded words. It was in two hands: the message on top not as practiced as the one precisely written below it. But the top message wasn't in English. The one below it was:

But I most ardently want to help you.

It was in the same handwriting as the diarist's.

Intrigued now, I perused the journal, still finding it dry and boring, catching words and phrases like "the angry sea," "dysentery and other ailments," "the captain," and "our dependable ship." I wondered if the captain was our Captain Winship.

Dr. William Clemson hadn't been a very enthralling storyteller, but he was a good artist, sketching members of the crew and various parts of the ship. They were a hard-looking, sea-worn lot. But the sketches brought their days to life more than the doctor's words did.

Then on the last page of the journal was a drawing of a young woman, about my age. The sketch didn't have the dry seriousness of old portraits. She was facing the artist, but gazed off with wild dark eyes, her hair unpinned and hanging over her shoulders, wisps of it wrapping about her neck. But a very small smile played about her lips, as if something pleased her. The tension that the artist captured—of a woman both delighted and haunted—was compelling.

Amoret, Tess's voice whispered.

The ghost in the graveyard, I said silently back.

The door opened, and I jumped, the note falling from my hand.

Eli was there, his hand on the knob, looking concerned. "Are you all right?"

"Yes, yes," I said, quickly picking up the paper. But I wasn't all right.

"You are so pale. Are you sure—?"

"I am." I tucked the paper in the pages of the journal, shutting the cover on the sketch. "I was just . . . intent on what I was reading. You ate quickly."

"I had to get back to my reading!" he said with enthusiasm. He settled on the love seat in the library, studying the books and writing in his notebook. I opened the journal again, trying to turn my thoughts from Eli.

As I studied the sketch, the woman's emotions came more into focus. Some past hurt pulled her gaze away from the artist, but her eyes also conveyed a dangerous rage. Yet there was something soft about the tilt of her chin and the subtle curve of her mouth that revealed a nature more naturally joyful—although very spirited, perhaps. Or was it an artist's hope that brought that out?

It struck me suddenly that he'd loved her, that William Clemson must have loved her, to capture her so clearly and closely. And the delight on her face, was he the cause?

At that realization—that the artist-diarist must have loved this complex woman deeply, for I felt strongly I was right—the journal itself became very enticing. I stumbled through the sentences as I tried to decipher the older English style and the elaborately cursive writing.

The doctor also liked to record all the ailments, no matter how small, of the crew. For such hardy seamen, they had many complaints. The sketches of them were intriguing—men with craggy faces and baggy pants, their eyes narrowed, but some with a glint of amusement. Underneath their pictures, the doctor had written their illnesses, not their names.

While reading, my thoughts strayed to movements on Eli's part. Once he got up to replace a few books on the shelves and to retrieve another, his body stretching to its longest as he reached for it. I swiveled quietly in my chair as if I were lost in my reading, glancing at him as he read still standing by the shelves.

It was possible he might be a little nearsighted, because he put the book up close to his eyes as he read. I caught a small smile on his lips and wished he'd read aloud what was amusing him. But then a feeling came over me that he knew I was watching him again and I immediately turned back around, a flush of warmth spreading over my neck. I pushed to plod through the journal.

While skimming over the dry recording of battles with the French in Nova Scotia and how much cannon the French had or who had the most prisoners, and the whippings of the crew for stealing food and rum, the name *Captain Winship* caught my eye.

"Aha!" I cried, thumping the journal with my fingers.

"Aha?" asked an amused Eli, still at the shelves.

I looked up at him, wide-eyed. "What?"

"Did you find something interesting?" His eyes went to the journal in my hands.

"Not really."

He laughed. "Tell me."

"Just go back to what you're doing over there," I said, waving my hand at him.

"I'd rather see what you're doing over there," he said, imitating me and waving his hand back at me. He had such a winning smile.

A strange feeling came over me—a strange, happy feeling. Turning reluctantly from him, I went back to the journal.

Captain Winship ordered the burning of a village and the loading of the women and children on the ship. Without commentary or emotion, Dr. Clemson wrote that this task proceeded smoothly. The detached description of the destruction of these people's way of life rattled me so much I had to stop reading. *Are you so sensitive?* Tess might have chided. But then perhaps she wouldn't have. She had been obsessed with these books. She'd have wanted me to know this.

If Amoret had been one of these villagers, how did she become Captain Winship's wife?

I picked up the other book of Tess's I'd taken from the shelves, the one on someone named Evangeline. Eli had moved back to his place on the love seat, settling himself there.

I skimmed the table of contents, then turned to the chapter entitled "A Night of Terror." This particular group of Acadians had tried to escape from the hands of the English by leaving their village in the middle of the night. But they were found and loaded onto ships.

> *We were huddled in a space scarcely large enough to contain us. The air rarefied by our breathing became unwholesome and oppressive; we could not lie down to rest our weary limbs.*

So, Dr. William Clemson, why not include these details in your journal?

> *With but scant food, with the water given grudgingly to us, barely enough to wet our parched lips; with no one to care for us, you can well imagine that our sufferings became unbearable.*

I turned back to William's journal, flipping through the pages, until I saw a change in his writing:

> *Only two days out, and I must confess the carrying of these souls is wearing on my own. They are packed into the hull of the ship. At the end of the day, when I lie in my cabin, their moans and cries haunt the night, turning us into a ghost ship.*
>
> *Clearly, we were overly concerned about the Acadians. Most were not supporting the French, despite their shared ethnicity. I see no great allegiance there. They were content to stay out of our war and live their lives in peace. It is—was—a close community they'd established, building it over decades. In only a few months, we dismantled it.*
>
> *A young woman is on the ship, the most beautiful creature I have ever seen, so unlike the women back home. Her eyes*

change and bring you in. She roams the deck and looks back toward Acadia, her face filled with grief, but rage too.

What tragedy have we begot here? How many generations have we affected? We have done a terrible thing, I fear—one for which History will not forget or forgive.

"Cecilia."

"What!" I said, jumping, staring up at Eli's smile.

"You do get engrossed, don't you?"

I smiled, shaking my head, looking up at him. He made me feel so light, even as I read this terrible account.

"Would you like to raid the kitchen with me?" he asked. "We missed dinner."

"I would."

CHAPTER 18

EVERYONE ELSE HAD GONE UPSTAIRS, SO WE HAD THE KITCHEN TO OURSELVES.

"Are you very hungry?" Eli said with a laugh.

I laughed too, without knowing why. I loved his laugh, and the way his face looked when he did. "Well, I am. But why?"

"The way you hurried through the dining room. I could barely keep up."

I smiled, pretending it was hunger that had me rushing through that room. I didn't like it in there. I lifted a dark blue towel to find a clay bowl filled with biscuits. "We need butter," I said, turning to the icebox.

"I'll be right back," Eli told me as he left the kitchen for the service stairs. I pulled out plates from the cabinet and two glasses as well, filling them with water. By the time Eli returned, our places were set.

"What is that?" I asked, gesturing to the can in his hand.

"Peanut butter."

"You carry peanut butter around with you?"

"Yes," he said, sitting down. He pulled the key off the bottom of the can to open it.

"Peter Pan peanut butter," I said, watching him smear it on one of Anna's biscuits. I sat down across from him. "I've never seen anyone eat a peanut butter biscuit."

"It's great on biscuits. Pancakes. Would you like some?"

"I've never had it before."

"Not really," he said, surprised. At my nod, he began making me a peanut butter biscuit. "You'll love it."

Our fingers touched when he handed it to me. The first bite was delicious. "It's both salty and sweet."

Taking a bite himself, he chewed like a happy kid.

I laughed, covering my mouth.

"What?"

I shook my head, still giggling.

"What?" he asked again.

I gave a small shrug. "You remind me of a little boy."

He raised his eyebrows and took another bite.

"What were you like as a boy?" I asked him.

"I collected turtles."

"I did too! I kept them in a box."

His eyes lit up. "I made a pen for them in the yard."

"Mine were painted turtles, only about six inches long. I'd kidnap them from a beaver pond and bring them back to Sanctuary to care for them. I fed them insects. I'm sure they were miserable."

"They are fascinating creatures."

"I envied them their shells."

He finished off his biscuit. "Will you show the pond to me?"

"We could go tomorrow."

"We'll need to bring a box."

"Oh, we can't do that," I said. "We should leave them to their pond."

"Quite right. Then we'll just watch them poke their heads in and out."

"And walk very, very slowly."

"It does make you wonder why we find them so fascinating."

"Perhaps we're still children," I suggested. I cocked my head, watching him. I liked watching him. "What else did you do as child?"

"Well, I was very curious. My father told me I wouldn't stop asking questions, that they tumbled out of my mouth one after another, sometimes without even a pause for the answers. I wanted to know everything."

"But you do know everything," I pointed out with a mischievous grin. "Isn't that what you said?"

"If I remember right, that's what you said."

"And you agreed."

"And I agreed."

There was a beat of silence as we held each other's eyes. Realizing simultaneously that we were both staring at each other, we looked away.

"What about you?" he asked, the first to recover. "Were you curious as a child?"

"The sea captivated me. The island too," I said, watching him make another biscuit. "All of its creatures and plants. The books in the library. Not just to read. Their pages. The way they are bound. The feel of their covers. And I liked to read stories too, of course."

"So the history of this house must've intrigued you?"

"A little," I said cautiously. "I knew it was built by a sea captain and that he and his wife are buried in the graveyard." I stared at the biscuit I'd just picked up and put it back down. "But I was born here. Sanctuary was my home, not a museum." But that was just an excuse.

Once I'd been talking to my mother and wanted her to pay attention to me like she did to Tess. So I made up something about Captain Winship in hopes of impressing her, of seeing her eyes light up like they did when Tess talked to her.

She'd laughed. "Oh, Cecilia. You are amusing. That's not true. Leave those stories to your sister." Her remark had stung. And so I had done as she asked.

"What are you thinking about?" Eli asked.

I smiled and shook my head.

We cleared the table of dishes, peanut butter, and biscuits and opened the books we'd brought with us. I found it difficult to concentrate. Eli was so close. If I reached out, I could touch his arm. I stared at the same page the whole time, not reading. I just listened to him, even though he was quiet. Excitement rippled through me. I felt something might happen. I wanted something to happen.

After a while, he looked over at me. "You haven't turned one page."

I smiled and gave a little shrug.

"What is it?" he prompted.

"Nothing, really." I could feel my face grow hot.

He studied me for a moment in silence. I knew because I kept looking up at him and then shyly had to look away. His eyes were so lovely.

"I didn't expect you," he said finally.

"What do you mean?" I asked him quizzically.

"I didn't expect . . . to meet someone like you."

"When you came to steal my books?" I asked softly.

"When I came . . ." But his voice drifted off. His eyes broke off from me and he leaned back in his chair. He glanced at me with a smile, then stood. My heart sped. Coming around to me, he reached for my hand. Without even knowing what he wanted to do, I put my hand in his.

"Shall we go back to the library," he asked, "and read our books?"

I nodded, disappointment washing over me. I wasn't even sure what I'd been expecting. Did I think he would kiss me? I'd never been kissed. I didn't know how it even happened, although I'd tried to figure it out. How did one go from talking to kissing? I didn't know what it felt like to have someone's lips on my own. I was blushing fiercely at the thought and not able to meet his eyes.

I picked up my book, and he picked up his. He let go of my hand as we left the kitchen. I sensed a sudden reserve in him, which confused me. I thought back over the conversation, wondering what was said that might've affected him. By the time we got back to the library, there was a distance between us that I didn't understand. I was a little embarrassed, thinking I'd revealed too much in my looks to him, and he thought of me as a silly girl. I pulled back into my own shell.

I sat down at my desk. Absentmindedly, still thinking of Eli, I reached for my journal. My head shot up. It was *gone*.

"What is it?" Eli asked as I looked frantically through the things on my desk and on the shelves. Uncle had taken it, I was absolutely sure.

"Nothing, nothing," I said, not wanting to involve him. Silently, I cursed Uncle, feeling he would do anything to keep me from learning the secrets of Amoret and the captain, and ultimately, my mother and my sister.

CHAPTER 19

I WANTED MY JOURNAL BACK.

That desire drove my dreams to be filled with frenzied images again, none of which I could identify in the morning. But I woke feeling as if all my nerve endings were sliced and exposed. The graveyard was calling me. Amoret's real, I thought. But she can't be. She can't be. *She is real.*

Forcing myself to get up and shake off the frightening feelings, I dressed and waited in my room until I knew Uncle was out of the house and Anna was in the kitchen.

I crept up the service stairs, intending on telling anyone who asked I was on the way to my old room to look for something. Jasper was nowhere to be seen, which was good because he'd only give me away. But as I climbed the stairs, I felt a tightening in my chest as if someone were pushing against it. I plodded on.

I slipped into the dark gallery of the second floor, but stopped, startled by the noise. Someone was singing in the guest bathroom at the end of the hall. It was Eli. His nice tenor voice calmed me a little.

Uncle and Anna's room was at the other end of the gallery, on the right, across the hall from my old bedroom. The upstairs felt strange to me, heavy and dark. It had been so long since I'd been up here. In the days I'd been back, I'd felt no compulsion to visit the second floor. I'd wanted to stay away.

But now I was overwhelmed by the memory of family. My father calling to us that Santa was dropping presents from a plane. Tess and I laughing so hard our stomachs hurt. I couldn't remember what we were laughing about, just that we'd been happy. But this used to be my home, where Tess and I ran the halls until we were told to take our wild behavior outside. I wasn't running now. I felt I was walking through a swamp of mud that sucked at my feet.

Doors to the unused rooms were shut, plunging the dimly lit gallery into shadows, with a gasp of light at its center flooding up from the open foyer. Here one could see the worn rugs and the paneling, scratched and chipped. It was a bleak place. I felt unwanted, as if the house itself wished to hurl me back down the stairs.

I was drawn to the door of my parents' old bedroom. Opening it, I found the room bare and sad. I remembered my mother sitting at her vanity facing the French doors, turning her head to look at me over her shoulder, her lipstick in the air. "What is it, my darling?"

"Are you getting ready for a party?" I had asked, feeling shy with her in her finery. She was as stunning as a woman in a painting.

"Why, yes, I am. How do I look?" She fluttered her eyelashes theatrically.

"You are pretty, Momma."

"Come to me," she said, waving the lipstick. Her dress was gold and swishy. "Now pucker for me, darling." Her elegant hand steadied my chin. I watched her eyes, so like mine and unlike Tess's, as she painted my lips.

Mamie was there, behind me. Had she been in the room this whole time? Or had she just walked in?

"This is where you were born," Mamie said, turning me around to face her, "right in this room. Childbirth is a very powerful thing, like a door to another world. And you, my dear, are connected to everyone born in this room."

"Mother!"

Mamie had looked up. "I want to teach my granddaughter what you should be teaching her." She grabbed a cloth off my mother's vanity and wiped off my lipstick.

"Go play, Cecilia," my mother said, her voice tense. "I want to talk to your grandmother."

Mamie had said something as I left the room, haunting words, words that Mother shushed angrily . . . but I couldn't find the words now.

Mother and Mamie dissolved before my eyes, leaving only a desperate emptiness threatening to yank me down some deep well of the past. There were so many memories here, so many moments of our lives trapped in the walls.

Each step toward Uncle's room was heavier than before. I passed the dreary, dark portraits of several men, thought to be previous owners of Sanctuary. Their stern faces had watched over the house since before my birth. One of the portraits had always been missing, obvious by the faded square on the wall where it had hung. Probably it was a woman, and Uncle had thrown her out.

I stopped in front of the last one in the row, the fierce Captain Winship, the witch-hunter. I wasn't sure how I knew it was him. I was struck by the intensity of his gaze. Slowly I moved toward the portrait, closer to his eyes, feeling drawn in. Such dark intense eyes. Are you still in this house, Captain? I reached my hand toward the portrait, hovering over it. I heard a whisper, "Cecilia," and jumped back. My eyes darted to the captain's mouth. It wasn't moving.

I backed away from the portrait. It must have been another's voice I'd heard, or some other noise I'd convinced myself was a voice. This was only a painting. But Winship looked so alive, as if he might jump out of the frame. I hurried down the hall.

I didn't stop at Tess's room, closed off now, or my own childhood room.

The moment I opened Uncle's door I felt cornered.

Whipping my head back and forth, I tried to figure out what felt so threatening. But no one was here. Just a bed, dresser, mirror, desk . . . nothing to cause the rising panic I was feeling, my every breath drawn short. There was violence in this room, in its walls. I collapsed into a chair beside the door, trying to catch my breath, feeling as if my lungs were being squeezed. A foul bitterness filled my mouth.

"Calm down, Cecilia," I whispered. "Breathe."

Standing, I shut the door defiantly, against my own imaginings or some sinister presence, I didn't know. But I was going to find Dr. Clemson's journal. Uncle wasn't going to keep me from it.

"I'm not afraid of you," I whispered to Uncle with my hands still shaking.

I opened the front of a pull-down desk. Papers, even loose bills, were everywhere. I sat in the chair, thinking how proud my uncle must be to live in the old captain's room and look out these fine elegant windows.

On top of the messiness were a ledger book and a mahogany letter box. I pushed those aside, as well as loose receipts for tools, boat parts, groceries, none of it filed or organized. I opened drawers. Paper clips filled one of them, nails in another. One drawer held an iron skeleton key, which I took out and looked at before shutting the drawer back up. Also in the drawer were bills of green, their eyes on me.

A large flat drawer held a silver-framed picture. I recognized my aunt immediately. There was something different about her, and I realized with a start that it was happiness radiating from her, breaking out of the old photograph.

She was in a hammock, not lying down the length of it but sitting with a familiar-looking man, both of them pushed together toward the middle. They were leaning back a little, but mostly leaning into each other, him more into her, but her arm was draped over his neck and the sides of their heads were touching. My aunt wore a contented smile, self-assured; the man's grin was open and pleased, and his bow tie was whimsically crooked. They were so relaxed and happy, and it hurt to look at their happiness.

I gasped. The man was Uncle. But it didn't look like him: His smile was . . . tender.

I heard a noise and jumped up, and the picture fell, whacking against the edge of the desk and hitting the wooden floor. I stared down at it, afraid to pick it up, frozen by the voices in the hallway. I cursed when I saw a crack in the glass. Scooping up the photograph, I started to shove it back into the drawer, but stopped.

Lying beneath the frame was a piece of paper with my mother's name, Cora Cross, written on it. Beneath her name, the words *Slattery Asylum* and an address in Bangor. I stuffed the paper into my pocket.

Footsteps were outside the door. It was too late.

CHAPTER 20

I OPENED THE DOOR TO THE BALCONY, SLIPPING OUT. NO ONE WAS ON THE lawn. I was frightened, finding it difficult to think.

Stone balconies ran along the front of the house, two on each side. I heard Uncle's voice just as I shut the door. I climbed on the edge of the stone wall. There was a narrow gap, less than two feet, between the balconies, but I had no choice. I heard Uncle's voice in the room through the balcony door and jumped onto the next balcony.

The French doors in the guest room took up most of the balcony, but I hid against a narrow wall of stone, where I couldn't be seen, for I heard noises coming through the glass door and then I heard singing again.

Eli.

I was confused. What was he doing in this bedroom?

I saw Ben coming up the walk and knew he would innocently yell out to me if he saw me. I opened the French door. Eli was shining his shoes while he sat on the bed. He jumped up, shock on his face.

Quickly, I raised my finger to my lips and shook my head at him. Then I pointed to the room next door.

He stood there, wide-eyed, staring at me. He had no shirt on.

I found I was staring at his bare chest. I flushed. "Why are you changing your shirt?" I blurted out. "You just came from the bath."

Red spotted his cheeks too. "I didn't like the one I had on." He quickly pulled his arms into a white long-sleeved shirt, yanking the sides together. "But I wonder what you're doing on my balcony."

"I thought you were sleeping in my bedroom," I said, flushing when I realized what I'd said.

"Yes, and I moved when I found out it was yours," he said a little too loudly. "I won't take your room from you."

"Shhh," I said, my finger to my lips again. "Do you want my uncle to hear and find me here with you?" My nerves were frayed, making me short with him.

His hands flew to the task of buttoning up the shirt.

I ran to the door, listening out in the hallway. Nothing. I put my ear to the connecting wall between my uncle's room and this one. I could hear rustling papers. My hands began to shake as I tried to remember the state of the desk when I had closed it up. If he didn't open the drawer . . .

"What are you doing?" Eli asked.

I held out one hand to silence him, my ear still pressed to the wall.

Only silence came to me from the other side. Finally, I heard someone (Uncle?) standing and shutting the desk back up. Uncle's bedroom door opened, then closed. I didn't hear footsteps for a moment, as if Uncle was waiting there, listening to me listen to him.

I jumped and almost gasped at the knock at the door. My eyes met Eli's. He gave me a reassuring nod. "What is it?" he called out.

Uncle's rough voice came through the door. "I want to talk to you about—"

"I'm dressing," Eli said. "Just had my bath. Can I meet you in the library in a moment?"

I stared at Eli suspiciously. What was all this business with my uncle? Of all people, Uncle.

"I'll be in the kitchen," Uncle said gruffly. Then I heard his heavy footsteps shuffling against the steps as he walked back down.

I reached for the doorknob, my heart still pounding.

"No, no," Eli said, stepping forward, not touching me, but still I drew back, now suspicious of him. "What was all that about?"

"It's none of your concern," I said, more testily than I meant to. I was still rattled.

He studied me for a moment.

"Are you angry with me?" he asked directly.

I hesitated, wanting to accuse him—accuse someone of something—but didn't know what to accuse him of. "You're here to steal my books," I said finally, the loss of the journal grating on me. Uncle's theft was a victory for him. I could imagine the gleam in his eye as he threw it in the furnace or something. I felt a pang at that thought.

"Not steal," Eli said quietly.

"They are my books, not Uncle's. He doesn't care about them. Your helping him with his theft is quite . . . monstrous, really. Taking the books from their home. They belong here. It's horrible, horrible," I said, working myself into a temper.

I went toward the door, but he was still in the way. He didn't move. I withdrew.

"Yes?" I asked. "Something more?"

"I'm sorry I upset you," he said.

His apology seemed heartfelt, but I couldn't let go of my frustration at him for not understanding what kind of man Uncle was.

"Cecilia, you don't seem well."

"I really must go," I said. "Could you please move?"

"Certainly," he said, agreeing and stepping back. "But may I say . . . ?"

I paused. My hand was on the doorknob.

"I won't take any of your books if you don't want me to."

I looked up at him then, seeing the kindness in his eyes. "But what about your university?"

He shrugged and looked guilty. "I won't take the books. But can I stay and look at them with you?" he asked. "We wouldn't be able to tell your uncle that, of course."

"I suppose that would be all right," I said, looking down at my feet.

"Really?" he asked, looking up at me by leaning down, cocking his head.

"Not if you keep going on about it, though."

"Then I'll be quiet on the subject from now on."

"All right, then."

His hands were in his pockets as he looked at me. "Monstrous?"

I won't be charmed, I won't be charmed, I thought, as I raised my eyes to see his teasing smile. "Horrible," I told him.

He continued to grin at me, and here we were acting awkward again, just as we had in our first meeting. But this time, there was something more added into it, because we knew each other a little now, had walked the island together, shared the lighthouse and some of our stories, even a private nighttime snack.

I glanced around his room, taking in its neatness: the lack of clutter on the oak dresser, the crisply made bed, the desk with books and papers neatly stacked upon it. He smiled at me as I moved to the dresser. I played with the row of pencils, running my fingers over them and thinking of him lining them up so correctly, ready for use.

"Like your sticks," he said, beside me now.

I nodded. "Yes."

I opened the black case on top of the desk. A silver trumpet with its beautiful twists and turns, and small buttons on top, rested on torn black velvet.

"May I?" I asked.

"Of course," he said, gesturing with his hand.

I lifted it out of the case, loving the sleek feel of the trumpet in my hands, trying to imagine him playing it, his fingers moving over the valves. He must be very attached to it to have brought it with him.

"Will you play it for me?" I asked, wanting very much to hear him.

"I would like that." He hesitated.

"If you'd rather not," I said, putting it back in its case.

"I wouldn't want your uncle to come looking for me and find you here. Not for my sake, but for yours."

"Yes," I said, moving toward the door.

He caught me gently by my hand. "But later," he said, "I will." He slipped his hand from mine, and my fingers felt cold and bare.

"Is that a promise, Mr. Bauer?" I asked very formally, smiling at him.

"A promise," he agreed as our eyes locked. And then I could do nothing but stand and watch him, taken in by him completely. Something was changing, deepening between us. I liked this man. I wanted to be close to him, to be near him. But the instant I realized that, the instant I wanted to abandon myself to it, I felt something else. A sense of disquiet, that these feelings emerging were very wrong. The thought was so strong I had to step away from him, back toward the door. And I saw in his eyes his confusion and his belief I was rejecting him.

"Okay," I said, my hand on the knob.

He looked disappointed, but he stepped toward me. "I'll teach you if you'd like."

"Teach me?"

"The trumpet," he said.

"I'd like that," I said, remembering the first time he mentioned the trumpet to me. Then, I smiled at him before slipping out the door. I checked the hallway below before going down the steps. I could hear Uncle in the kitchen, so I went into the library, still thinking about Eli. I heard him come down the stairs and his steps go toward the kitchen to talk to Uncle.

Uncle. My twisted uncle. If he found the broken photograph, he'd be livid. He'd looked almost harmless, lying in the hammock next to my aunt, love on his face. It was hard to put the two images of him together—what he looked to be then, what he was now.

But what bothered me most of all was not the love I'd seen in the photograph; it was the sudden longing I felt to have it for myself.

A dark thought flooded through me that only bad things would happen if I fell in love. When I tried to reason it out, I couldn't figure out why that would be so. Why shouldn't I fall in love with Eli? How could any great tragedy come from two people wanting to be together?

But some voice inside my head was telling me to stay away from him.

CHAPTER 21

I DIDN'T REALIZE I WAS WAITING FOR ELI, BUT I WAS. I COULDN'T KEEP MY mind on my search for the journal or Tess's secrets because Eli was ever present in my thoughts. I read—sort of—and walked around the room, picking up things off the mantel, books from the shelves, holding them, not really seeing them, putting them back. Still, Eli didn't join me in the library.

Then I saw them out the window, back on the path again: Mary and Eli. Tapping the glass thoughtfully, I found I didn't like it one bit. Eli wasn't mine. But hadn't there been something growing between us, or had I been imagining it?

Imagining is what crazy people do, Tess would have said. *It will get you into the insane asylum, locked up, for sure. You and Mother can have adjoining padded cells.*

I was so engrossed in my thoughts I didn't hear the library door open. I jumped when Patricia spoke: "She is rather annoying, isn't she?"

I pressed my hand to my chest and my thumping heart.

"I scared you," she said. "I'm sorry."

"It's all right," I said, turning away from her inquisitive eyes.

"You look so much like your mother," she said lightly.

"Do I?" I asked, looking back at her. "Do you remember her?"

"Oh, yes, I remember. I thought she was beautifully strange."

"What do you mean, strange?"

Concern flickered in her eyes. "Not strange, just secretive, and fascinating—like she'd lived an amazing life that I never would and had experiences that I would never have. There was a mystery about her."

"She was distant."

Patricia nodded slowly. "Yes. She was."

"She'd been a flapper when she was young, before there were flappers."

"I'd heard that."

"Dancing and living crazily in New York before she met my father." I paused. "And after."

"She seemed very happy with him."

"You remember him too?"

"He wasn't here as much."

"Because of his art."

"Yes, his art took him away," she agreed.

My father had been a wealthy man with family money, but also a professional artist with a respectable career. He was rarely with us at Sanctuary because he traveled the country frequently, as a paid guest of patrons. His work—focusing mainly on landscapes, particularly of wild, coastal Maine—had even been exhibited at a gallery in New York City in 1919.

"Your father was sweetly absentminded," Patricia said, "as if he was always thinking of the things he wanted to paint. Sometimes I'd see him looking out to sea, just staring at some spot on the horizon, and then the next day he would be out there painting whatever he saw." She smiled distantly, as if she were in a memory. "I'd watch him paint sometimes."

I looked at her in surprise. "I . . . didn't. I didn't know I could watch him paint."

Amused curiosity lit up her eyes. "What do you mean?"

Glancing away, a bit embarrassed, I said, "I don't know really. Just I never watched him paint. I don't know why, why I wouldn't have sought him out to see what he was doing."

"Well, you're much younger than I am," Patricia said kindly. "And it was many years ago." She laughed. "I had a schoolgirl crush on him."

"On my father?" I asked, incredulous.

"I know," she said, "it is ridiculous. But he was very talented. I've always been drawn to talented people, probably because I have no talent of my own."

"He used to read to me sometimes," I said. "In here. On this very love seat."

We looked out the window again, to see Mary giggle with her hand over her mouth and her eyes flashing flirtatiously at Eli. (Yes, Tess, I'm too far away to see her eyes, but I *imagine* they did that.)

"Come with me," Patricia said suddenly, grabbing my hand and pulling me toward the door.

"What?" I asked, resisting.

"Come, come," she said, and before I knew it, we were out the front door, walking toward Eli and Mary.

Seeing us, Eli broke into a smile, as if he hadn't seen me—seen us—for days. Mary turned to us, her back briefly to Eli. She scrunched her eyes and gave her sister an annoyed pout. Patricia ignored her and, still holding my hand, pulled us into their circle.

"Hello," Eli said.

"We thought we'd join you," Patricia said. "Are you going for a walk?"

Eli gestured toward the trees. "I was curious about the graveyard. Mary said she'd show me."

"Do you like cemeteries?" Patricia asked. I was mute, not able to think of a thing to say. I could feel Mary's eyes on me. She gave me a hard stare; then it disappeared and I wondered if I'd really seen it.

"I do, I do," Eli said. "Come with us."

Mary smiled at him then, and this time I was close enough to see her eyes, and they *were* flashing flirtatiously. Somehow, before I'd even seen how she'd done it, Mary had guided the two of them ahead of us on the path. Patricia gave me a wry look, and we followed them through the squeaky gate. The sun was out and bright, but once we entered the trees, it felt close and dark.

Nervously, I looked around for Sanctuary's ghost. But if I saw her now, then everyone else would see her too, and no one could accuse me of imagining her.

The path was narrow through the stones of the dead, so Patricia and I were stuck behind the other two. Eli listened to Mary, very intently it seemed to me.

I watched Mary, wondering if this was how to flirt. You put your hand ever so lightly on the man's arm. Somehow, you make your eyes twinkle, while your lips turn up into a slight, mysterious smile. Even your voice is different. It points its toes and twirls as you speak. It struck me as very contrived, but Mary didn't seem bothered by the artificiality of it.

"When I was growing up in Lady Cliffs," she was saying to Eli, "I never dreamed my aunt would now be the mistress of Sanctuary." That dancing, light-on-its-toes laughter spilled from her mouth. "I was in awe of *the big house*, as we used to say. Everyone in Lady Cliffs was, still is."

"Are they?" I asked. "I've always thought the town didn't like us very much. At least Aunt Laura thought so."

"Oh, they think you're all as mad as your mother. But they're captivated by the house and everything that's happened here."

I was silent, thinking how the tragedy of my family was only gossip to the town.

Patricia seemed to sense my thoughts. "Our cousin Mark," she explained, "told us the place was haunted by the old sea captain who built it. He'd tell us terrible stories, usually about a pirate with a hook." She smiled, inviting me to appreciate the ridiculousness of the tale. "When we were little, we'd be scared to death to visit Aunt Anna."

Mary wouldn't be deterred. "That's not what the town talks about. Your family, Cecilia, has given them much more interesting stories. After the cottage fire, your aunt told the police the arsonist was someone from town. That didn't go over well."

Eli glanced back at me, concerned. He seemed about to say something, but Mary exclaimed, "And now to think my family owns Sanctuary!"

Patricia looped her arm through mine and rolled her eyes at me.

And still Mary chattered on, with all of us quiet and listening, as we wandered through the land of the dead. "Of course, Patricia and I are helping Aunt Anna right now. But soon we'll get real servants and move out of the attic rooms into rooms on the second floor. I might move into Cecilia's room."

I stiffened. "There are other rooms you can have, Mary," I called up to her.

"The one I'm in is very nice," Eli said.

Mary stopped walking; we all stopped, in our little circle. "But Cecilia's room is the second-best room," she explained in a patient voice, "after my aunt's. Uncle Frank told me I could move in there."

"When did you start calling him Uncle Frank?" I asked.

"Yes," Patricia asked dryly, "when did you?"

"But he *is* our uncle now. And really, since Cecilia's aunt is dead, he's not hers anymore."

It so happened we were standing right by Aunt Laura's grave, looking new and fresh among the others. Mary had such a look—I don't know. It seemed to me she knew what she was doing, that she had led us here intentionally.

I couldn't stop myself: Although my stomach was sour, my eyes drifted to the headstone, with my aunt's name, *Laura Wallace*, carved into it.

So it was true. My aunt was dead. There was her death date—*August 3, 1939*—under her name. She had left me—along with Mother, my grandmother, my father, and Tess. I swallowed back grief. What made me think I belonged at Sanctuary without her, without any of them?

I left the graveyard then, back through the squeaky gate.

Someone followed me. I was surprised to find it wasn't Patricia, but Eli. He caught up to me and walked alongside me. I took deep breaths, thinking of calm things, like seabirds gliding over waves, their white wing tips stretched out tip to tip against the stunning blue of the sky.

Eli didn't say a word, just stayed beside me, step for step. He fit there, inside an empty space beside me, as if he should have always been there. I hadn't realized just how lonely I'd been. His presence brought tears to my eyes. Alarmed, I blinked them away. Why was it always kindness that made me cry?

We kept walking, through the trees, Eli following my lead.

When we came to the second graveyard—the villagers' graveyard—he still didn't speak. I thought he might reach out and try to stop me, as if this one might upset me too. But he didn't, and that was good. This cemetery was so unlike the other it didn't seem at all the same kind of place, and of course, it didn't hold my aunt.

There was no elaborate foundation at its center, and no benches to rest upon. The headstones were simple gray slabs, tilted, broken. They weren't arranged with any order or feeling of protection and care. The cemetery was out in the open, trees gone wild around it. The land here was rockier, and the graves harder to dig.

Eli began to wander through the stones, reading the names. As we went from grave to grave, our bodies drifted together, our hands briefly touching, our shoulders slightly brushing.

I'd noticed yesterday how he moved, the strength in his arms and legs, the self-assured set of his shoulders, the insouciant grace—a calm masculinity I was unfamiliar with. I hadn't known many men, many boys, but I would have noticed if they all moved in this way.

Shyly, surreptitiously, I watched him, embarrassed by the intensity of my emerging feelings. The feelings were familiar, however, and with a start,

I realized they were one of the things I sensed wafting in the air in the library.

Still, we wandered.

"What is it?" Eli asked me.

I pointed to the grave in front of us. The headstone was drab, with two words hacked inexpertly into the stone.

"Dr. Clemson," read Eli. "That's a strange way to remember someone, quite cryptic."

"I wonder why he's buried here."

"Was he the villagers' physician?"

"No, no, he was Captain Winship's doctor. He was on his ship with him." I still didn't tell Eli about the doctor's journal, holding the information close.

"He must have fallen out of the captain's favor."

"I wonder what he did." The missing journal began to grate on me again. It would have answers. Where had Uncle put it? And why had he stolen it? What could be so important now?

"What's wrong?" Eli asked.

Pulled from my thoughts, I looked into his eyes. "Just thinking."

He seemed taken aback, something suddenly shy in his gaze. My stomach fluttered very pleasantly.

After a moment, he grabbed my hand, and I could think no more of the journal as we walked back to the house, together.

CHAPTER 22

I STOOD UNDER THE PORTICO, HOLDING MY TOWEL CLOSE TO ME. IT WAS not yet dawn, but I'd been desperate for another swim. I stared at the gate to the cemetery, trying to keep myself from entering. I'd heard her calling me, and this time I hadn't been able to resist. The ghost in the graveyard wanted something from me.

She was out in the woods, waiting. I dropped my towel and went to find her. I wound through the gravestones in the moonlight, wondering about the people buried here. Were these all Captain Winship and Amoret's children? Were they Uncle's relatives? Was that why Aunt Laura, Tess, my father, and Mamie were in a different part of the cemetery, because they weren't Winships?

I found her in the shadows of the trees behind her grave. I wanted to see her face, but the harder I looked, the more shadowy it got.

"I don't know if you're real," I whispered.

She held out her hand toward me, clenched in a fist as before. I knew if I reached her in time, she would give me what was in her hand. The closer I got, the more her shape seemed to take form. She was wearing the same clothes, the same white shawl. It was the girl in Dr. Clemson's drawing. It was Amoret Winship.

There was a rage in her. I had to stop walking because her anger was so strong. I was stunned by the ferocity of it, unsure if it was directed toward me. I tried to break my gaze, but then heard my name. She wanted me. She needed my help.

"I'm here," I said, holding out my hand.

Walking forward, I reached out my fingertips, expecting the touch of warm flesh. Instead, an ice-cold feeling traveled up my arm. I tried to grasp her hand, but it wasn't solid. It felt whole, but not whole. It twisted into a continuation of my own body, as if my hand were a part of her hand. Her fist opened, releasing tiny lights that drifted up from our twin palms.

The fireflies swirled around us, resting in our hair, on our necks, brushing against our arms. We were perfectly still, but Amoret was mad and fierce. She was pulling at me, tugging on me. I felt my body changing. I shook my head at her. My throat began to close up, and I tried to catch breaths. I was losing myself.

The only way, she said without speaking. *The only way.*

With all my strength, I yanked my hand from hers and fell backward and to the ground, scratching my back on her gravestone. I scrambled to my feet as she stepped toward me. I found my feet and ran.

At the front door, I reached for the handle. It seared my flesh. I screamed and pulled my hand away. I tore through the woods to the one place I felt safe, my body feeling like it was burning. At my cove, I splashed my way into the seawater and dove under the surface. The cold water soothed my hot skin. I swam and swam. I'm not my mother. I'm not my mother.

Back and forth I went, swimming the length of the cove, trying to shut out the memories. I was on Sanctuary's cliff, my child feet at its edge, crying for my mother to come back as they took her away in the boat. I'd wanted to dive off, to follow her. Tess had been there, watching, a cold expression on her face. Mamie was there too, angry. "We have work to do, Tess," she'd said. "We have things to do." But all I cared about was my mother being taken away.

Now I wanted to swim out to sea and never come back.

Finally, when I'd figured out what I had to do, I struggled up onto the beach, my muscles spent, shivering in the cold. I made my way back to Sanctuary.

I went around to the kitchen door instead of the foyer, instinctively feeling that it was safer. Still, I hesitated before I grabbed the knob. No burning this time, but a deep unease settled over me as I walked past the kitchen table to the service hall.

I threw my suitcase on the bed.

I have to get out of here. I have to know.

The rush to leave was filling me up. Anna would be down soon, and I wanted to be gone. But at the back door, with my suitcase in hand, I found Jasper at my feet. I put down the bag and scratched his chin.

Talking to him, I pinned my hat on my head. "You must be quiet. No one must stop me."

I slipped out the door, my heart in my throat. I walked as quickly as I could down the dawn-lit path, not glancing behind me toward the front of Sanctuary, even though I knew she was there, waiting for me, not wanting me to leave.

At the harbor, I got in one of the boats, not Uncle's best, but one that looked reliable.

I started the motor. I'd often taken a boat out when I was young. No one had ever said anything about it or even noticed I was gone. That freedom had felt invigorating. I'd been glad to escape Tess and Mother, at times. And Mamie too. Mamie hadn't been one of those sweet-eyed grandmothers. "That woman could be a four-star general," my mother had said. "And she wants me to be one of her soldiers." Her eyes had flashed mischievously, charmingly. "But I want to *play*." "Me too, Momma," I'd said, giggling. "Me too."

I left my boat at the Lady Cliffs dock, avoiding the eyes of one of the elderly fishermen, who was sitting in his boat, working on a tangled line. He was gnawing on his lower lip, showing a missing tooth in the front, studying me. It wasn't a pleasant look. I thought of my grandmother's charred cottage and remembered my aunt's accusations about the people in the town. Although I had my own thoughts about who had caused the fire, I hurried down the pier.

The coastal townspeople in Lady Cliffs were leery of us. The internment of my mother and the fire and our family's tragedy, and all the rumors and stories about the island's early days, had made the coastal townspeople keep their distance, but as Mary had said, they were possessive of Sanctuary, in awe of it as well.

I took the motor coach, changing buses twice, from Lady Cliffs to Ellsworth, the reverse of my trip just days ago.

Switching to the train, I rode second class and watched out the window as we rattled down the rails through the countryside of pines, maples, and ash. The coach seemed tight and close to me, with a long narrow aisle, all of us in yellow seats facing forward. After the conductor collected the tickets, I pulled out a piece of paper from my purse.

Slattery Asylum.

CHAPTER 23

THE STATION WAS VERY DIFFERENT FROM THE ONE IN ELLSWORTH, BUSY and large and presided over by a tall clock tower. I took the trolley car down a wide street to the asylum. A little boy smiled at me. I thought to smile back, but he was off the trolley too quickly, pulled along by his mother. Glancing at my wristwatch, I was surprised to see that it was half past noon. I'd left early, but all the traveling—by foot, by boat, by bus, by train, and the waiting in between—had taken some time.

It was a short ride to my stop and a short walk before I arrived at the grounds of Slattery Asylum. Evidently, the town had not wanted to be too close to the patients.

The redbrick building was an imposing structure, with its high gabled roof and long wings on each side, so proud and sure of itself and its mission. I remained on the sidewalk, staring at it, for a long time. Nightmares at school had been filled with this place, although the asylum in my dreams was a Victorian house with boarded-up windows and endless halls with no doors. And I was always there not of my own volition, but trapped, trying to find my mother in an asylum with no rooms.

My body was trembling as I went up the steps to the front door. The reception hall was narrow with wooden benches and chairs against the wall and rugs on the planked floor. Just to my right was a door of two halves: The top was swung back and on the other side of it was a small office. When I'd entered the building, a woman at a desk behind the door had stood. "Can I help you?" she asked.

"Yes," I said, my voice quiet and shaking. "I'd like to see my mother, please."

She was looking at my suitcase.

"I'm not staying." I shut my eyes tightly and then opened them, trying to start again. "I mean, I have my suitcase because I came directly from the train."

She nodded at me, waiting. She had a long, thin face and eyes that didn't dawdle or imagine.

"My mother's name is Cora Cross."

Her serious eyes registered surprise for just a second. "I'll need to speak with the superintendent. Please sit down in the reception area."

I glanced to my side and back to the closed door just behind her. "All right." The chair I chose was just across from the doorway. I wanted to be able to see her when she came back out of the office.

No one else was about. It was awfully quiet. I'd been worried there would be screaming, but the patients must be kept far away from the reception hall. I wondered if they would let me in my mother's room or if there was a special room they'd take me to. Would my mother even recognize me? I was frightened to see her, anxious about what state she might be in.

I crossed my legs, folded my cold hands together tightly, and waited.

I didn't wait long. The woman was back at the door quickly. She opened the bottom half. "Miss Cross."

"Yes?" I asked, standing.

"Come in, please."

I was surprised, but did as she asked, entering into what seemed to be a private area. I hadn't thought they would let visitors in here, with the locked steel filing cabinets of patient files and secrets, and the important phone calls about the patients' well-beings and mental states. But here I was, back in the office, following the prim, efficient woman to a closed door.

She opened the door, holding on to the knob as she waited for me to go past her. The office was nice-sized, with a window that looked on to the automobiles out front, and a small man with a mustache sitting behind a mahogany desk with neat stacks of papers and a long row of pencils. He stood when I entered, and although he was reserved in his quick nod, I detected a slight eagerness in his eyes. Maybe he was lonely in his office and no one ever came to see him.

"So you're Cora's daughter?" he asked after we'd both sat down.

"Are you her doctor?"

"I'm Dr. Brighton."

I nodded, trying to be polite. I wanted to appear cooperative so I could see my mother. This man was the gatekeeper, and I had to get past him. I hoped he couldn't tell my secrets just by looking at me: that I saw ghosts and heard strange noises. I focused on keeping my face as composed as I could.

"And so, you are her daughter?" he asked again, his eyes considering me. He had an odd way of speaking, enunciating almost every word, but abruptly clipping the sentence off at the end, as if, really, he had more important things to do, and would I please hurry along with my answers. I wondered if he had learned that affectation in college. I couldn't imagine him running around as a child and talking like that.

"Yes, sir."

His mustache twitched. "You look like her."

"Yes," I agreed.

He continued to watch me, making me even more nervous, then his eyes went to the window. I followed his gaze. A trio of people were out in the parking lot, arguing. A younger woman was crying. A man and an older woman were trying to pull her toward the door, but she kept shaking her head, her short straight hair swinging.

When I looked back, Dr. Brighton was staring at me again, apparently not at all concerned he might be having another visitor soon, one who obviously didn't want to be here. "And you want to see your mother?" he asked.

"That's why I came all this way."

"Have you talked to your uncle about this?"

"Why would I?"

"Are you in contact with your uncle?"

"Yes."

I thought he might have smiled, but his lips hid behind his mustache. "I can tell he's your uncle. You both have little to say."

"He's not my blood uncle." This was important to me; I wanted people to know it.

Dr. Brighton's smile drooped. "Your uncle has forbidden us to give out any information about your mother."

"It shouldn't be his say."

He spoke firmly: "Your uncle was made your mother's legal guardian when she was declared mentally insane."

This shocked me. "He had no right."

"He has every right."

I twisted my mother's watch around my wrist. "She's not insane," I said, not liking that my voice sounded young and naive. I wasn't even sure why I said it. I believed she was insane. Didn't I?

"Has your uncle explained your mother's situation? I know you were a child when she was brought here."

I looked up quickly. He'd talked to Uncle about me. He looked a little flustered as I continued to stare at him. "Not so much a child," I finally said.

"I have your mother's file," he said, patting a dark folder on his desk. "Do you remember much about the day she was taken from your house?"

Images flashed in my head—my mother's twitching eyes that didn't recognize me, her screams at Uncle, her elegant hands gripping the doorsill. Wasn't there another man there? What had he looked like? Had it been Dr. Brighton?

I found the superintendent's eyes were on me. "I don't remember."

"Do you know why she was brought here?"

"She's not insane," I said again, this time more strongly. She was just very sad, and grief wasn't insanity, was it?

Startled for a moment, thinking I was hearing my mother's screams, I jumped out of my chair and looked toward the door.

Dr. Brighton cocked his head and looked at me. "Don't be alarmed. It's a new patient."

I realized it was the young woman from outside, now in the building. Her screams were horrid.

"Sit down, Cecilia," he said. "I'll be right back."

Still feeling disoriented, I did as he asked. But I realized he hadn't asked; he'd told me to. Was it because he was a doctor and had a fancy office that I was compelled to do as he said?

He shut the door as he left, but I could still hear the woman's screams. My hands were shaking, so I pressed them together, trying to relax. My body felt like a tight, tight ball of memory and emotion.

The screams finally stopped, very abruptly. I could breathe again, but my jaw ached from how hard I'd been clenching my teeth.

Dr. Brighton returned, not at all flustered, and sat across from me again and regarded me. "Would you like a cigarette?" he asked.

"What?" I shook my head. "I don't smoke."

"Isn't that what young girls like to do these days?"

I stared at him.

"You seem very tense, Cecilia. I thought it might calm you down."

"It's Miss Cross," I told him. "I really don't have a lot of time, Dr. Brighton. May I see my mother?"

He thought some more, and I waited while he did. If this was a test, and at the end of it I could see my mother, I would get through it. He scribbled something down on the paper in front of him, but it was hidden by a teacup and I couldn't see what he'd written. "Do you know what your mother told the doctors when she first arrived?"

I paused, not wanting him to see the eagerness in me. I did want to know. And I didn't. "What did my mother say?" I asked finally.

"That Sanctuary was a prison, that it captured people's souls."

Something frantic and true clawed at my heart. Tears welled into my eyes, and I stood abruptly and looked out the window. I wiped my cheeks, refusing to let this man see me cry. It would be like handing him power over me. I could feel him wanting to snatch it from me.

He kept talking. "We had to put your mother in isolation because her behavior frightened the other women. She would scream for hours, holding her head from headaches, yelling she needed to return to Sanctuary. She was worried for your sister, in particular."

Tess, Tess, Tess.

"What do you think of that?" he asked.

I tried to swallow down the tight fear that had my throat in its grip. I was frightened for my mother, locked away in here for years, and frightened because I wondered if Tess had been the one calling me home to save her. And if she was the reason I felt compelled to return now.

"Miss Cross?" Dr. Brighton asked.

I tried to give an unconcerned shrug as the trees in front of the building fought the wind picking up. Pulling myself together, I sat back down and looked at him with dry eyes.

He leaned toward me, his eyes ablaze. "But you agree that your mother cannot be sane if she believes these things?"

"I want to see my mother."

That disappointed him. He withdrew a little, scribbled something else down. How I wanted to pick up his teacup and shatter it against the wall.

He looked at me patiently. "I would like to explain something to you to help you appreciate our mission. We are beginning to understand things about the mind that we never knew before. The mind," he said, leaning forward, "is fascinating. Sometimes it doesn't work the way it should.

Sometimes we have—and we think this is passed from parent to child, a condition within families—a splitting of the mind, where it can't tell the difference between realities and the imagination or dreams or even memories." He continued to watch me. I said nothing, but my hands were grasped so tightly together I was hurting myself. He leaned back in his chair. "You mustn't think there isn't hope for people like your mother," he said, pausing and holding my eyes for a moment. "There are many useful therapies, some excitingly new and helpful, like inducing epileptic convulsions with drug injections, or electric shock therapy—"

"You can't do that to her."

"Don't alarm yourself. These are safe—"

"May I see her?"

He paused, clearly irritated. He pulled at his tie. "Come back in the morning, and you may see her."

I stood and picked up my suitcase.

"I've upset you." Coming around his desk, he gave me a handkerchief.

I stared at the white cloth.

"Your uncle said you were a sensitive girl," he said.

Alarmed, I looked up into his eyes. "He said that about me?"

He started to say something else, but I left his office quickly, the handkerchief fluttering to the floor. I went through the now empty outer office and out the split door. In the hallway, I literally ran into the efficient assistant returning to the office.

"I'm very sorry," she said briskly. She paused when she saw my face. "Are you all right? I am so sorry about your mother."

I looked at her, surprised at her tone. There was something not quite right about it: too nice, too concerned. Her eyes widened as if she thought she'd said something she shouldn't have. She turned and went back down the hallway and out of sight.

My hands were shaking as I left the building.

CHAPTER 24

I GAVE THE LANDLADY THE MONEY I HAD STOLEN FROM UNCLE'S ROOM. I'D never stolen anything before. But when I'd seen the money in the desk, my hand had gripped the bills tightly and stuffed them into my pocket. I'd heard Tess whisper *Thief* in my ear.

My room at the large boardinghouse had a window that looked out over a quiet street, with a bathroom down the hall to be shared by other boarders. After the landlady left, I plopped on the bed, facedown. Weariness sank my body into the mattress. I slept a dreamless sleep.

Waking, I flipped on the lamp. I stared at the ceiling above the bed, imagining a stain to be a sinking boat. I thought about seeing my mother, wondering what she would be like, what she would say when she saw me. My stomach felt sick. The sea, I miss the sea so much.

I closed my eyes, remembering my frantic early morning swim and how it had soothed me. I felt a hunger for the sea now. The desire was worse than when I'd first been left at the boarding school. Sanctuary pulled at me, calling me home. Or was it Amoret who called? She seemed to be lodged against my heart now, very close. My legs and arms twitched as I struggled to get this onslaught of feelings under control. I was frightened of going back to Sanctuary, but I needed to. The warring in me was so great I felt I might split in two.

I forced myself to get up and dress for dinner. I couldn't stay in this room alone with all my fears and thoughts. I'd go mad.

Dinner was crowded, with two large tables taking up most of the dining room. I sat in a corner and listened as people talked quickly and laughed loudly, as if they all knew one another well. They didn't give me too much notice. I faded into the background and watched their dinner show of conversation and friendship. They seemed more like a family than just friends.

A milkman tried to flirt with a shopgirl while she rolled her eyes at him. A middle-aged trolley car driver and a secretary had a quiet conversation amid the chaos. An ex–carnival worker told wild and funny stories that made me feel the narrowness of my childhood. Even a man with sad eyes laughed so hard he had to wipe the tears from his cheeks. I felt separate, apart. Uncertain on my feet, I climbed the stairs back to my room.

The door next to mine opened. A thin and bony man stood there, with tiny dots for pupils. "Hey, sweetheart."

His filthy smell made me take a step back, but he came into the hallway and blocked the way.

"Hey, I'm not going to hurt you. My name's Al. What's yours?"

"You look too sick to hurt me," I told him, noting his pasty face. "What's wrong with you?"

He looked taken aback. "I'm fine. I'm in heaven. What's wrong with you?"

"I'm being kept from my room."

"You're no different than me, girlie," he said, his tone changing. "You have the look, I know it."

"I don't know what you're talking about," I said. "May I pass?"

"*May* you? May you *pass*?" Dramatically, he stepped aside and waved his hand forward. "Please, my lady, do go past."

I eyed him as I went by quickly, catching another whiff of his sweaty skin. But I was distracted by his whisper. "You're an addict just like me," he said. "I know the look."

I shut my door and locked it.

CHAPTER 25

DR. BRIGHTON WAS AT HIS OFFICE WINDOW, WATCHING ME APPROACH. The sanitarium loomed in a threatening way. For a moment, it reminded me of Sanctuary, the mysterious part I didn't understand. Tess thought houses and buildings had lives of their own: their own moods, quirks of character, particular silences or noises, and even emotions. They should all have names, she'd said. *Slattery Asylum* fit this place. If this building were a person, I'd avoid him, not approach him.

What if Dr. Brighton meant to keep me here? I hesitated on the front steps, knowing he was watching. I faltered in my resolve and retreated to the bottom of the stairs. I put down my suitcase and paced, not able to care that Dr. Brighton watched. If I didn't pace, I'd run to the train. My fear of this place and of my mother's disappearance into it was balled up tight inside of me. I felt that ball would continue to pull the bits of me in— winding tighter and tighter until there was nothing of me left.

At school, when dark moods and fears descended, I'd disappear into the woods and walk the forest, not wanting the teachers to see how I couldn't control my feelings. As I crunched through fallen snow or leaves, I'd struggle with guilt. I felt responsible for what happened to my mother, and to Tess and my grandmother too. I'd been so taken with the island I hadn't helped them. Why hadn't I seen? I asked myself. As the years went by, that guilt had eased some. But right now, it rose up as irrational terror slamming against my heart.

Suddenly, I stopped, hearing my own voice from deep within me: *It's not your fault. It's not your fault.* I whispered the words, drawing strength from saying them. That conviction took me up the stairs, despite Dr. Brighton still at the window, watching me. Steeling myself, I grabbed the front-door handle and entered.

The receptionist greeted me and picked up the phone. I fixed my eyes on the door to Dr. Brighton's office, but it stayed closed. I gripped my purse tightly in front of me, feeling the tension in my neck. A nurse with black eyes was at my elbow. I jumped when I found her there. "I . . . I didn't see you."

She blinked her eyes ever so slowly. "This way. Leave your suitcase."

The stairs seemed excessively steep and narrow. I felt I was falling backward as we climbed. I held on to the railing tightly. Heavy doors, jangling keys, solemn looks, empty halls, my throat constricting . . . and then we were at a closed door. Black Eyes watched me carefully, silently, as she put the key in the lock, as if she thought I might run. What if they were locking me in? My mouth was dry. I needed water, desperately.

The room was small and windowless, feeling hot and close.

I sat in a large wooden chair that made me feel like a child. The only other furniture in the room was another chair like mine, positioned across from me. Nothing hung on the gray walls pressing in on me. Again, panic rose. Black Eyes shut the door, leaving me alone.

The last time I saw my mother's face was when they were dragging her down the stairs and out the door to put her away.

Tess and I were huddled in the foyer, alone. My father had been dead for a few years. Tears ran down my cheeks, but Tess's mouth was set in a determined line. She wrapped her arms around me and pulled me close. I leaned into that comfort, closing my eyes, not able to look. Then the front door shut, and my mother's screams grew quieter. I buried my face into Tess before I'd flung myself away and out the door, wanting my mother.

Tess had been kinder to me in that time between my mother's commitment and her death. I'd forgotten that until now. I'd left her arms and fled for the cliff, as fast as my legs could carry me, with her on my heels. I'd wanted to see my mother's face. I had to see her. But she was on the boat, too far away . . .

My thoughts were interrupted by the door swinging open. I sat up straight in my chair, my heart racing.

A man appeared, leading my mother by the arm.

I almost gasped when I saw her, she was so different from how I remembered. Her face still held remnants of beauty, but it was a haunted desperate copy of what she'd once been. Her white gown had small polka dots and hung on a thin frame. But her long, thick hair was brushed and tied back oddly with a bright red ribbon that felt as if it were more for the benefit of the visitor than the patient.

The man ignored me, not saying a word, and led my mother to the chair opposite me. She sat there looking at me, no recognition in her eyes. My heart was breaking.

I took a steadying breath, looking up at the attendant, who was standing behind her. "Can we be alone?"

"I have to stay with the patient," he said.

We sat in quiet for a little while, while I watched her. In the beginning her eyes were blank, but as the time passed, she became more alert.

Then she spoke. "Do you have a cigarette?"

"No," I said, "I'm sorry."

One thin shoulder went up. "I haven't had one in so long."

In the past, when I'd imagined this reunion, I'd hoped she'd reach out for me and hold me in her arms and say, "Cecilia, I'm here." But even as I thought those things I knew I was imagining a mother completely different from the one I had. And that any meeting between us would most likely consist of a quick kiss on the cheek at most.

But this was worse. This woman had no idea who I was.

My eyes wouldn't leave her. I searched her face, watched her hands fidgeting in her lap, while her listless eyes drifted about the room. I didn't remember her like this. They had done something to her, I knew it. Dr.

Brighton and his experiments had worked her over. My eyes burned, but I couldn't waste time on grief. I didn't know how long we had.

Acutely aware of the attendant, I tried to figure out a way to ask about the ghost at Sanctuary that wouldn't be alarming.

He caught my eyes. "Are you done?" he asked, in a bored voice.

"No," my mother and I said at the same time. Surprised, we looked at each other, and I saw a small smile play at her lips. She cocked her head to the side, scrunching her eyes. "Do you have a dog?"

"Yes, yes, I do," I said eagerly, hoping she was remembering. "His name is Jasper."

"Jasper," she said. "I never liked dogs."

I nodded. "You kicked him once."

She thought for a moment. "Did I?"

"He was in your way."

She looked sad. "I wish I hadn't done it. I wish I hadn't."

I leaned toward her. "Do you remember doing it, Mother?"

She scrutinized me then, looking closely, seeming more alert. "You look like someone I used to know."

Tentatively, I said, "I'm your daughter."

Her eyes lit up, just a little, showing some interest, finally.

Before she could speak, I said, "Cecilia," afraid that she would break my heart by saying Tess's name.

She nodded once very slowly. "You have such blue eyes."

"No." Tess was the one with blue eyes. "I have hazel eyes. Like you."

"Were you born in the sea? Sea babies have eyes like that." She laughed. "My mother used to tell me that. We took from the sea, don't you know? And then it cursed us for doing so."

We were cursed, I thought, but it wasn't the sea's doing. My beloved sea wouldn't do that. "I was born by the sea. In Sanctuary."

Her head snapped up. Instantly, her eyes were ablaze with something. She began to rock back and forth. "No, no," she said.

"It's all right," I said soothingly.

Her head shook back and forth. "She was leaning over the bassinet, that hair flowing down like black water."

"What bassinet? Who was?" I asked.

"James said he would keep us safe."

"My father did?"

She looked straight into my eyes then, hers widening, as if seeing me for the first time. "Who are you?"

"I'm your daughter."

"You aren't. You're someone else."

"Momma," I said, hearing my voice change, like I was a child again. "It's me."

Suddenly, she reached across the space between us and gripped my arm. "I have to get back to Sanctuary. I have to."

I waved the attendant off as he tried to pull her back. "Why? Why do you have to go back?"

Her eyes scrunched in confusion, frantic for an answer. "I did something I shouldn't," she said desperately. "Ooh, I can't remember." She began to tap the side of her head frantically. "I knew it once. But I can't find it. I can't find it. I can't find it."

The attendant ignored me now and took her arm. "It's all right, Cora. I'll take you back."

As he led her out, I followed them out of the room and down the hall. He was blocking her from me. I wanted to touch her arm, to see her face again. But I couldn't see her. He took her through a thick iron door, clicking the lock on the other side. I put my hand on the cold metal, wishing I'd never come.

CHAPTER 26

I WENT TO A BENCH OUT ON THE FRONT LAWN, UNDERNEATH A LONG-branched oak tree, positioned to look at the sanitarium. I stared at the windows, wondering which one was my mother's, if it was one of the barred ones or not.

Was this place where those who saw ghosts ended up, so they could be studied, their bodies shot up with drugs and shocked with electricity? A dull ache throbbed behind my eyes.

A woman with tight eyes and mouth, tiny hands clutching her handbag, sat beside me. Startled, I jumped. I was so lost in my thoughts I hadn't seen her approach. She darted a look at me, and I gave her a nod, wishing she hadn't disturbed my quiet.

"I have a friend in there," she said.

"I'm sorry to hear it," I said bitterly.

"Isn't that God's truth? I haven't seen her in a while. They say she can't have visitors, that she's in *isolation*." She nodded at me, looking at me right in the eyes. "Has to be by herself. But I sit here, right here, just in case she's looking out a window, so she can see me here. Because she's my dear friend. And I can't stand to think of her in there, that she might think I left her there." She glanced at me again, her little hands snapping and unsnapping her bag.

"I'm sorry," I said, feeling sad for this woman.

"My friend is your mother, Cora Cross."

Shocked into silence, I could only stare.

"The receptionist in there, Miss Tilly, is a nice lady. She called me and told me you were here."

"You knew my mother?" I asked, still incredulous.

"We were tight, your momma and me. Lived together in New York before she met your father." She smiled then. "We had fun. Gobs of it.

125

We ate New York up, the place to be before the Depression. Thank God that's over."

"What was she like then?" I asked, desperate to know my mother finally, looking for answers that the shell of the woman I'd just seen couldn't show me.

"Ah, she was different. Beautiful. Distant. Like she was from someplace wonderful and secret. She craved having people around her. Loved to dance."

"How did you meet?" I asked, anxious for details.

"We found each other on the train out of Bangor headed to New York. We both wanted to have our time in the city, like that poet Edna St. Vincent Millay. She was from Camden, you know. Cora and I moved into a tiny place in Greenwich Village."

"I thought that my mother was from New York, that both she and my grandmother were."

"What? No, no. She was from Nova Scotia. Didn't you know that?"

"What?"

"Oh, yes. Haven't you ever wondered about your looks? You look just like your mother—very different because you're a mixture of all sorts— French, Mi'kmaq, Basque, Irish, a blend of the world."

My heart beat wildly in my throat.

"Your grandmother followed your mother down to New York. That was when your mother changed. She and your grandmother got in some awful rows. Your mother was in love with James by then. So in love. Cora dragged me off with her for an errand, and I ended up witnessing their wedding at City Hall. Your parents moved into a grand apartment close to Central Park, your father's. His father had been rich as a Rockefeller. Then one day your parents packed up and left with your grandmother. They were meeting your mother's sister, Laura, who was married to your uncle by that time."

"Aunt Laura," I whispered.

She looked at me then. "I would have known you anywhere, Cecilia. Don't you remember me?"

For a moment, my confusion mixed with the strangeness of my life, making me think this woman was Aunt Laura coming back to life in another person's body. But no, she was nothing like Aunt Laura. "I'm sorry—"

She waved her hand at me. "Don't worry a whit about it. You were just a child."

I stared at her for a moment. "Miss Owens, my governess?"

"Governess," she repeated, laughing. "Isn't that funny? Your mother thought of that one. Otherwise, that nasty uncle of yours would never have let me live there. Didn't last long, though."

I continue to stare at her, amazed by this news. "That explains some things," I said slowly.

"I imagine. Which in particular?"

"Math lessons."

She stared at me a beat, then let out a loud whoop. She laughed so hard she held her stomach. I found myself laughing a little too, releasing the tightness in my chest.

"But . . . why . . . why did you come live with us?" I asked.

"I was in a bad way," she said, wiping the tears of amusement from her eyes, growing somber and more secretive. She sat still for a moment, and I was sorry I'd asked and broken the mood.

"Your momma helped me out," she said finally. "As you hit the rough spots in life, you'll find friends change. Those who abandon you," she said, shrugging, "you forgive, move on. Those who are loyal, who stand by you, when you're nothing, when you've got nothing, those are the ones you hang on to, Cecilia. And that's what Cora was for me."

"My mother was helpful?"

"She gave me money. She listened to me. She pulled me out of the dark pit I was in and set me back in the light of life."

"Okay," I said slowly, trying to reconcile this view of Cora with the one I had.

"And that's why when your uncle locked her up in this place, I moved back to Bangor to watch over her. My family held it over me, still does, how I went off to New York and came back with my tail between my legs. But I'm happy with my lot." She looked at the sanitarium. "Just not with Cora's."

I followed her gaze. "Is my mother insane, Miss Owens?"

"What? No, she's not insane. Your uncle stashed her away in here. He never liked her. I always thought he was jealous because Laura loved your mother so much and that took Laura away from him. Your uncle—ugly spirit that he is—always loved your aunt, that's for sure."

Relief filled me. I believed Miss Owens. My mother wasn't insane. "We could break her out," I said.

"Humph. Don't think I haven't thought about it." She gestured to my suitcase. "So where you off to?"

I paused. "Back to Sanctuary," I said finally.

"You were there?"

"For a few days."

"Your uncle?" she asked, her eyebrows raised.

"Still kicking," I said, mimicking the way this woman talked.

She laughed. "I bet he's kicking. Why go back if he's there? I could get you a job here, with me, working in the department store."

"I have things to do," I said, distractedly, looking for my mother's window still. "I don't like to leave her, though."

"I'll be here, right here. Hey, at least let me buy you a cup of coffee."

CHAPTER 27

My old governess was a talker. She gossiped about everyone at the department store. She was funny, though, and fun to listen to. She liked to laugh—and loudly—and didn't care much who heard her. I kept thinking how horrified the headmistress at the boarding school would be; she always lectured us to use our "lady voices" in public.

Miss Owens finally came back to the time she'd spent with my mother in New York. "Once Cora and I went off to a tearoom," she said with a wink.

"It wasn't really a tearoom?" I asked.

She laughed. "It was during the prohibition, so New York was jammed with tearooms, which were really speakeasies—you know, places you had to *speak easy* about, whisper about so the police wouldn't find you. Cora and I were there, flapping away with corsetless dresses, me with my short bobbed hair." She scrunched her shoulders. "I loved it. I felt free when I walked, like no one was pushing me and prodding me into something I wasn't, into a shape I wasn't. Not like at home."

"How old were you?"

"I was younger than your mother, only seventeen."

"Seventeen! You were my age."

"Sure," she said. "It was the high life. New York soared miles above the earth. The men were everywhere. So full of fun." She laughed. "So full of *themselves*. Cora had their number. She'd say something snide to them, but with a quirky smile, leaving them confused and off-balance. With a stealth wink at me, she'd start spinning some tale." Her laughter died to a sad smile. "She was something, your mother. Stunning. Men looked at her. And she had something else. Some call it confidence, and it was kind of that," she said, staring into her coffee as she stirred, as if the past were in her cup. "But it was also like she was testing herself. Pushing the boundaries—and not because she wanted people to admire her for it, nothing like that. She wanted to see if she could, to *know* that she could. She liked being on the edge of life, putting herself in that place where she could topple off if she stepped too far. She burned the brightest right there, jazzing it up at the edge. So bright she blinded everyone around her so that they wanted to be lost in the music with her."

I swallowed. "She's different now."

She looked at me sadly. "She's different now."

"How did she meet my father?"

"Ooh," she said, sitting up, enthusiastic again. "That's what I was telling you about. We were at this tearoom, drinking tea," she said with a sideways look and a laugh, "and all of a sudden Cora goes real quiet. I flick her on the arm and say, 'What's with your ears?' And still she ignores me. So I follow her eyes, and there's this man." She wiggled her eyebrows. "He's on a date with a wealthy young heiress who we'd seen around. He's drawing something for her on his handkerchief. She's bored, looking around, a little bent. When she catches Cora's eye, she doesn't like it one bit Cora's eyeing her fella. So she loops her arm through his, nodding like she's interested after all. Finally, he looks up, like he senses Cora there. And his eyes go to hers. This Jane, she stands up *on the table*, starts yelling at Cora to leave her man alone. Cora walks over, puts out her hand, and asks if she can see the drawing. He's entranced, your father. He picks up the handkerchief, has to pull it out from under his girl's shoe, and hands it over. By the time their fingers touched that heiress jumped off the table right onto your mother's back."

"No!" I said, shocked. "Not really."

"Really and then some," she said.

"Well, what happened? What happened?" I asked, trying to imagine my parents in a brawl.

"Awww, I don't know." She took a sip of her coffee, cold by now.

"But what do you mean? You have to know. You were there."

"The police raided the place, busted right through the doors. James led us out through an underground entrance. And then drove us home. I didn't see as much of Cora after that." She gave me a resigned but still sassy smile. "The girl fell in love. Then I fell in love. The good times were changing."

"What happened to Jane?" I asked after a moment.

She put out her hands. "Who's Jane?"

"The girl who jumped on my mother's back."

"Her name wasn't Jane; she was a Jane."

I shook my head, not understanding.

"Oh, never mind," she said, waving a hand. "She and Cora were friends after that. I saw her a few times. Not sure what happened to her, though. Mostly likely still rich. Probably hoping no one remembers her back in the day."

I grew quiet. "My father was rich too."

"Yeah, James was loaded. He didn't act like it, though. But he was lonely until Cora. He didn't have family. His father was older when he married James's mother. She died soon after James was born. He was an orphan when we met him. But one with cash."

"So I have no family left?"

"Not much, kiddo." One side of her mouth went up, as if she was sorry to tell me the news. "Your mother did have some family in Nova Scotia, I think. A few people."

"Who?" I asked eagerly.

She shrugged. "I'm sorry."

I nodded. "Miss Owens, did my mother ever talk about seeing . . . anything odd at Sanctuary?"

She shifted in her chair. "I don't know."

I could tell she knew something. "What is it?"

Her lips twisted thoughtfully. "You must never tell anyone this, Cecilia, because your uncle would use it against her. I still hold out hope we're going to get her out of that place."

"Tell me, please."

"Cora thought Sanctuary was haunted," she said, watching me as if this would disturb me. "It *was* a creepy place. One night I heard yelling and arguing, some big commotion, going on in your aunt and uncle's room. I thought he was roughing her up," she said with raised eyebrows, folding her arms tight. "It sounded like a fight. I tromped down there to put that man in his place. But through the crack I saw they were sitting on their bed. And he was scared. She was comforting him. It was strange." She shrugged. "I guess he was having a nightmare." She looped her finger around and around the side of her head. "Crazy man. Bonkers."

"But my mother, Miss Owens . . . what did she see?"

"She would make jokes about it, you know," she said, still slipping around the subject, like she didn't want to talk about it. "Just things she thought the ghost was doing . . ."

"Like what?" I prodded.

She fidgeted in her seat, played with her spoon. "Cora told me once the ghost wanted you." She waved her hand as if it was just one of Cora's funny games. "Your momma said it was like the ghost thought you were her own baby."

I was looking at her in shock.

"But," she said, seeing my look, "she was drinking when she said it. She was just making up one of her stories." She pressed her lips together, looked around the café, for the first time looking like she cared that someone might've heard her.

"Did she call her by name?"

That startled her. She gave me a quick look, but her eyes were scrunched in worry. "The ghost?" she asked, looking uncomfortable. "Yeah, it was that ghost everyone was looking for. Your grandmother. Tess. I don't remember her name," she said dismissively. But I thought she did.

We talked for a little longer until I needed to catch my train.

She dug into her handbag and wrote out her name and address. Handing it to me, she said, "Don't hesitate."

CHAPTER 28

IT WAS DARK WHEN I MADE THE CROSSING, WHICH WAS LIKE RIDING OVER glass, back toward home. I didn't believe my mother was insane. She was troubled, yes. She was depressed over the death of her family. But she was also drugged and shocked by Dr. Brighton. If I could get her away from him, I would, but I didn't know how to get her released—yet. She shouldn't be in there.

I was reluctantly returning. I felt the same pull on my heart for my home. But events were escalating. It was getting to be too much for my mind to understand and to bear.

A splitting of the mind. A condition within families.

I pushed Dr. Brighton's words away. Sanctuary *was* alive. And I was going back. I was frightened. I wanted to flee. I didn't know where I was finding the strength to return.

Amoret was calling to me too, her voice blending in with the call of the house. I couldn't resist. She wanted something from me. I thought about what Miss Owens had said, that my mother thought it was me Amoret wanted, even when I was a baby.

I was connected to Amoret in ways I didn't realize. I was Acadian. I was from a people torn from their country. Maybe that meant I'd always feel restless, always searching for a home and never quite feeling I had one.

Ben and Jasper were sitting in one of the boats at the dock.

"Cousin, it's late. Why are you out here in the cold?" I said.

"You're back," he said.

"Yes," I said, petting Jasper.

He took my suitcase, and the three of us walked up the hill in silence. When we reached the point just where we came out of the trees and could see the front of the house, Ben stopped. We looked at Sanctuary together. It truly was magnificent.

"I thought you had left for good," Ben said. "Again."

"No, just for a couple of days."

"Why did you pack all your things, then?"

"I don't know," I lied.

"You're my only friend."

I turned to look at him in the moonlight, most of his face in shadows. But I could see his eye was still bruised. "Ben," I said gently.

"Will you leave again?"

"Don't count on me," I said sadly.

"I do count on you," he said. "You're the only one I can count on."

I felt the weight of that faith on me and took his hand. "If I leave again, I'll take you with me."

He turned his head away from me, so I couldn't see his expression at all. I continued to stand there with him, wanting to comfort him in some way but not knowing how to do it. Neither of us had needed much from the other one over the years, just our mutual presence. We had grown up together, the two of us always here, except the times I'd left.

"Everyone is mad at you," he said.

I paused, looking toward the lit-up library. "Even Eli?"

He looked very serious. "He might be. We saw that you took the boat, so Eli went to Lady Cliffs and found out you took the bus to Ellsworth. He's packing to leave in the morning to try to find you."

I glanced up at his window and saw the light on there too.

"I'm not as stupid as you think I am," Ben said.

"What?" I asked, alarmed. "I don't think you're stupid."

"You don't listen to me."

"I don't listen to anyone," I told him. "It's not you."

"Don't get Papa angry," he said in a low, dark voice.

"I don't like him, Ben."

"He'll hurt you. Stay away from him."

"He doesn't scare me."

"He's done it before," he said, his voice changing. "Hurt someone."

"Do you mean you?" I asked quickly, angrily.

He waved a hand at his eye. "Not like this. Worse."

A chill went through me. "Who did he hurt?"

But his mouth was set in that stubbornness he had sometimes.

"Ben, who did he hurt?" I persisted.

"Our cousin," he said finally.

"Cousin? We have a cousin?"

"We *did*."

"What do you mean?" I asked him anxiously.

"She came to visit Momma, the year after the fire, after you went away. She was a distant cousin."

He went maddeningly silent.

"What happened to her?" I demanded.

"I saw Papa put her in the boat. She wasn't moving."

My blood went cold. "Are you saying he killed her?" I asked, horrified.

He turned to me then, looking me right in my eyes, something he never did. "Don't rile Papa." And then he walked away, Jasper following him, leaving me confused and with a pounding heart.

Uncle killed someone?

I didn't believe it. I didn't know any murderers, but I didn't think my aunt would have fallen in love with and married a killer.

Would she?

A cousin? Did I have a cousin? Was this the family from Nova Scotia Miss Owens told me about?

My throat was tight again. Almost stumbling, I took the path to the front of the house. I stood under the portico, feeling her in the trees. Not yet, I told her, ignoring the pull, feeling strength I didn't know I had.

Again, the door handle was hot to the touch, but it didn't burn me. It felt odd against my palm, as if I could feel the heat, but my hand was cool enough to receive it. The foyer was dark and still, but threatening too. *Witch*, the walls accused in a harsh whisper. *Sea witch.*

It was Captain Winship's voice. I didn't know how I knew it, but I did. This was a real presence, like the ghost in the graveyard. I wasn't sure how or why these spirits still clung to the house, but some dark thing had twisted them into the soul of Sanctuary.

The library was empty. I was disappointed at not seeing Eli, but someone else too. I couldn't think of who it would be. I closed my eyes, breathing in the air, feeling like I'd been gone a long time. This was a sacred room.

Eli's lamp was on by the love seat.

I switched on the light on my desk, noting it was undisturbed. I didn't have much here: a couple of letters my father had sent my mother, postcards my mother had mailed to me when she was traveling through Europe, and some small sketches my father had done of the sea and cliffs on our island.

Standing in front of my lovely bookshelves, I stretched out my arms, leaned forward, and put my body against the books, which ran floor to ceiling, wall to wall, all books, all our books. These books were my imaginary friends, especially after Tess had died. "I missed you," I said. They whispered comforting words back to me. I was safe.

I turned around quickly when the door opened.

CHAPTER 29

"I'm glad to see you're all right," Eli said, shutting the door behind him. He put his hands in his pockets and said nothing else.

My heart flew with joy at the sight of him. But he seemed so far away. I hesitated. "Are you angry with me?" I asked finally.

He looked taken aback. "What? No." He took an exasperated breath. "You left without a word," he said, gesturing with one hand. "I didn't . . . we . . . no one knew where you'd gone."

"I didn't feel the need to tell you my plans." He looked so dejected. "You and I have only known each other for a few days," I said, quite reasonably, but also thinking we were more to each other than that implied. Weren't we?

Disappointment showed in his so-very-blue eyes. "Well, yes, when you put it like that, I suppose you're right. But I had thought . . ." His voice trailed off, and he gave a feeble laugh. "You've put me out of sorts, I'm afraid. I hadn't known I would be so . . . so worried." He turned from me abruptly, going to the window and looking out.

But there was only blackness out there. The window was a mirror, and I saw his reflection in the glass. The look on his face—concern and relief both—made me step toward him.

"Please don't do that again," he said with emotion, looking at the glass still. "Please."

"I am truly sorry. I didn't mean to worry you."

"I thought that you had disappeared into the world," he said, turning toward me, "and I would never see you again." He looked utterly miserable when he said it.

"I wouldn't . . . ," I began, but then I stopped. Wouldn't I?

"Yes?" he prompted.

"I wouldn't have liked it either," I said quietly, "if you'd just left without a word."

He stepped toward me so that we were just a foot apart, so close but not touching, but almost. "I wouldn't do that. I won't do that."

Filled with emotion but holding back, I gave him a silent nod. I didn't believe him. So many in my life might have made that same promise, trusting in it, and now they were gone.

He put his hand on my cheek lightly, and his gentle touch felt shocking to me, his skin against mine. I covered his hand with both of my own, feeling like I was sinking. And I didn't know if he was pulling me down or holding me up. But whichever it was, I wanted it.

Again, I heard a whispering coming from the walls around us and felt keenly that Eli and I had stood in this spot before, touching each other. The room spun in delightful circles as his eyes kept me centered upon him. But I realized they were different eyes, not blue but a deep brown. Confused, I stepped back, almost falling back. His hand was on my arm, keeping me steady.

"What is it?" he asked, alarmed.

I looked at him again, almost afraid to look, but relief rippled through me at the sight of his eyes. *His* eyes. I tried to give him a reassuring smile— because how could I tell him these tricks of my mind? I didn't understand what had just happened. "It's nothing," I told him. "It's nothing."

CHAPTER 30

I COULDN'T RELAX ENOUGH TO SLEEP. I STARED UP AT THE CEILING, thinking of my uncle. Did he really murder someone? Ben tended to get things mixed up. But there was a rage in my uncle that was dangerous and volatile.

The sheets twisted around my legs as I turned first to one side, then the other. I'd straighten them out only to toss and turn and twist them again. Amoret's words were twisting inside of me as well. It was like she was talking to me. She was different now from the ghost in the graveyard. It was the same woman, but more whole, still angry, but it didn't slice as deep, not yet. Her dark hair was blowing in the breeze of a sea wind as she climbed up a ladder onto a ship . . . her eyes flashed . . . I saw they were hazel like mine . . . sea eyes . . . but there was something different about them . . . I tried to look closer . . .

They are taking us from our home. My eyes drink in the sight of Acadie before I help my sister Aimée down the ladder. The captain of this wretched vessel is loading us into the hull, like cargo. There are twenty-four of these prisons, including the naval warships of the British. Thousands of us have been taken. We rock on the waves of Minas Basin, our cottage and fields so close. We were separated from Papa, Pierre, and Andre.

We are sailing away, leaving Acadie . . .

My beloved sea tosses us like rag dolls, not wanting us to go. She slashes the ships with howling winds and high waves, but our captors do not turn back. We huddle in the ship's hold, an unnatural dark place. Salt water soaks our clothes. There is little space, not enough for us all to lie down. We take turns sleeping. Many are sick, including my little Aimée.

"I'm scared," she tells me. Her eyes are large in her petite face.

Maman wipes Aimée's forehead with a wet salty cloth. "It's all right, my love."

"Will it be?" she asks, her voice raspy and weak. "All right, Maman?" She is so frightened.

Our mother forces a smile. "Amoret is here, isn't she? What is it that Amoret can't do?" She means it as a joke. It is what Papa always says. But she also believes it. It is like heavy stones tucked in the folds of my heart.

But I say, "I will take care of you, Aimée. You know I will."

The ship's doctor comes through the hatch. I grab his fine sleeve. "Help my sister," I say, bringing him to her side. "The doctor's here for you, Aimée." A tortured cough comes out of her, wracking her small body. I hold up the lamp for the doctor, gesturing for him to do something.

He tends to her but his mouth is grim. He asks my mother in French, "Do you have any more children?"

"If you can swim across the sea to one of your other ships," I snap, "you will find my two younger brothers and my father too."

He stops and looks up at me. I notice how young he seems, although he must be a few years older than I am. "The soldiers were told to keep families together. I heard the order given."

"Then I must be a liar. A liar who also saw our men and boys over the age of ten locked in our church at Grand-Pré for weeks."

"Amoret," Maman chastises.

"What? Am I to be polite to the men who took us from our home?"

The doctor looks at me in the light of the swinging lamp with eyes a deep brown. Warm, kind eyes. I turn from his shallow kindness.

Anna's bed rocked as I woke. I gripped the sides, feeling I might roll off into the raging waters of the sea. Staring into the dark of the room, I waited for the sensations and images to pass. So vivid. I had seen them all so clearly: Amoret, Aimée, Maman. The doctor too. Those eyes of his. I had seen them before, just last night in the library. And how did I know Amoret had a sister? Nausea like a seasickness overwhelmed me.

I held my head as reason battled what I thought to be true. "A dream," I whispered. "Only a dream." I'd created the eyes of the doctor, Aimée, the concerns of Maman . . . and Amoret herself.

The Amoret in my dream was different from the one in the cemetery. I might believe there was a ghost, but she was *not* inside my head. She was a presence out among the stones of the dead. Slowly, I breathed more easily. Nightmares had haunted me all my life. These were new ones I had to adjust to.

The next morning, Eli was in the kitchen, leaning against the sink. He was drinking his coffee, contemplating something so deeply he didn't hear me come in. But then he looked up, his eyes a clear blue. "It's good to see you," he said. There was an awkward, lovely moment between us as we studied each other with shy smiles, just wanting to look and look.

"Care to go for a walk?" I asked.

I brought him to my beach. I took off my shoes, although Eli kept his on, and we climbed up the small cliff. The sea looked so inviting I was tempted to jump in for a needed swim.

I caught Eli watching me as I struggled with my hair in the wind. "Why are you looking at me like that?" I asked, smiling under his gaze.

"No reason," he said with a smile.

"What is it?" I prodded.

"You are . . . very . . . I am . . . ," he said, his cheeks turning pink. "Your voice is . . . just enchanting," he said finally. "I've never heard another like it."

My cheeks grew warm with pleasure, and I lost my words. I looked at my bare feet. If only I'd had more exposure to the outside world, and to young men, and to what a girl was supposed to say to them. But this giddiness filling me lifted me up high and sweet, like I was flying. When I looked back at Eli, he was smiling, so it was all right after all.

"Would you like to see something else?" I asked, wanting to include him in my secrets, to bring him closer, hoping that showing him a part of me would do that.

"Yes," he said eagerly.

I took a glance at the sea below and then back at Eli.

"You're not going to jump?" he asked in disbelief.

"I do it all the time," I said, taking the hem of my dress and pulling it up.

He was stunned into silence, his eyes fixed on me. Then he seemed to breathe easier when I discarded my dress. "You're wearing a swimsuit."

I walked to the edge of the cliff and looked back at him.

"It's too high, too dangerous, Cecilia," he said in alarm, stepping toward me.

"It's fine," I told him, putting my arms over my head and diving into the air.

"Cecilia!" I heard him yell.

The water felt good and sweet against my skin. I came up out of the water and waved to Eli. I couldn't see his face, but he didn't wave back. Instead, he made his way quickly down the cliff. I met him on the beach.

His face was white. "Here are your dress and shoes," he said quietly, then left me on the beach to put them on. Once dressed, I joined him on the path back to the house, but tried to stop him.

"Eli."

He kept walking.

"Eli, please stop. I'm sorry."

When he turned back to me, I saw the concern on his face. "Why did you do that? Do you know how much that frightened me?"

"I do it all the time," I said, reaching for his hand, grasping it in my own. It was cold and shaking.

Suddenly, he drew me in, placing his forehead against mine. I could still feel him shaking. "Cecilia, please be careful."

"Don't worry, Eli," I whispered. "I've jumped off that cliff more than a thousand times. I know what I'm doing. I won't be hurt."

"Cecilia," he said, pulling back to look at me, rubbing his hands up and down my arms. "You can't give the appearance of . . ."

"Of what?" I snapped, pulling away from him.

He hesitated.

"You think I'm crazy," I accused.

"I think you're kind and brave," he said. "But please think about how others perceive you."

"I don't care what others think of me."

He looked off, almost speaking, then stopping, finally saying, "You're not eighteen, Cecilia."

"I'm almost eighteen."

"Just be careful," he said again.

"Do you know something you're not telling me?" I asked him directly.

He shook his head. "I'm . . . just worried about you." He held out his hand to me.

I stared at him for a moment, but he kept his hand out. Finally, I took it. "Don't worry about me, Eli. I'm quite all right."

We walked back up the path, hand in hand, and returned to our library. When I sat at my desk, he looked at me from his place on the love seat. "Will you sit beside me?" he asked.

I nodded and took my books over to where he was. We spent the rest of the day like that.

In the evening, we went for a moonlit walk on the beach, looking at the stars.

"'Bright star! would I were steadfast as thou art,'" Eli quoted.

"You like Keats," I said with a smile.

"Do you know his poetry?" he asked, obviously surprised.

"He's the only poet I read anymore. My mind flits about when I try the others."

He smiled into my eyes. And we had this moment of pausing there and nothing happened but us looking at each other. I'd never had these feelings before, of wanting someone to look at me like he was looking at me now, of wondering what it would be like to kiss someone—no, not just someone, to kiss him, to kiss Eli.

Did a girl have to wait for the boy? As I watched him now, I couldn't think of why that would be.

CHAPTER 31

I STOOD BEFORE THE GATE, KNOWING I WOULDN'T GO IN. COMING BACK, I thought I was strong enough to face her again. But I knew I wasn't.

I didn't see her, but I saw the fireflies. One of the lights broke off from the others and floated toward me. I followed it into the graveyard. The firefly hovered before my eyes, this small bright light, and I held out my palm. It drifted down into my hand, filling me with sadness and yearning when it touched my flesh. I closed my eyes against the pain. When I opened them, the light, all the lights, were gone.

I realized I was standing on Tess's grave. I felt the loss of my sister, a deep well of emptiness inside of me where she had once been. It hadn't been only my mother's attention I'd sought. It'd been Tess's too.

Had Tess seen Amoret? I tried to think back and remember. But the harder I thought the more slippery the memories became. My friend Elizabeth suggested to me once that I blocked them out, that it was all too much—the loss of mother, father, sister, grandmother, aunt, and the loss of home.

But I thought I hadn't been paying attention, that my childhood was defined only by what I saw. Everything else—conversations, ghosts, feelings, voices, strange tales of the past—slipped through my mind as easily as a breeze through a field of summer grass. I hadn't latched onto it. I'd just let it slip away.

But I was beginning to remember. When I was eight, I thought the books greeted me in the morning. At night, I would take turns sleeping with different ones so the others wouldn't get their feelings hurt. On my tenth birthday, I asked to blow out my candles in the kitchen because the dining room didn't feel quite right to me. Many times, I woke from the same ending of my dream, that a woman was leaning over me, a woman with flowing black hair.

But I hadn't seen her then. Not like I saw her now. I had never seen her in the graveyard, no matter what Tess said. Amoret had been the woman in my dreams, an elusive, hazy creature that I barely remembered when I woke and that drifted quickly into Sanctuary's air as I bounded out of bed.

Had Amoret pulled my grandmother, my aunt, and my mother to the island? Was it no coincidence that Aunt Laura married the man who owned the estate?

This would all be much easier to figure out if I still had the journal. I was determined to search the house for it in the daylight. Sanctuary sat there, in all its glory, taunting me with its size. It wouldn't be easy to search.

Maybe there was someone in Lady Cliffs who knew the history of the island. I doubted it, but I could try to find out.

CHAPTER 32

Our neighbor Mr. LaFontaine and his Celeste died yesterday. As the sea took their bodies, Maman's eyes brimmed with anxious tears. "Your sister will do something," she tells Aimée. But I don't know what she thinks I can do.

I am frantic for a place to quiet my own heart so she won't see my doubt. There's no place like that on this ship. So I bite my fist at night in the dark where she cannot see. Fear creates more fear. Papa taught me that.

The captain struts by on his long legs, lashing out at his crew. We are his cargo. He is angry when we die. I heard one of his men say the captain will be paid by the number of Acadians delivered.

Aimée struggles with a deep cough and pain in her chest. I tell her she is so brave. I watch Dr. Clemson, who is kind to her, to all of us. Still, he is one of them, friends with the captain. I don't trust him.

He feeds my sister hot chicken soup. I think he steals it from the kitchen, saying it's for himself. He is trying to get Aimée to smile by telling her a ridiculous story about a pig in a lady's hat and a goat that always checks his pocket watch. I am pulled into their foolery too—despite the watch, they are late for everything—listening intently. I have suspicions that Dr. Clemson is making up the story as he goes along.

Behind us, two of my friends are talking about the captain. I shush them. But it is too late. Dr. Clemson has heard the name we call Winship: Jambes du Diable.

We all become very still. My eyes blaze at the doctor, daring him to tell the captain. Instead, he laughs and says in English, "Legs of the Devil."

My shoulders relax. "It is a good name," I say. His eyebrows lift. I turn away, angry with myself for revealing I speak English.

Some days I want to climb onto the railing and return to the sea. My desire for Acadie burns so strong inside of me I think it would carry me home.

The villagers say I came from the sea. Papa found me in the sand of a cave. "The waves brought her to me!" he tells anyone who listens. Cautious Maman always laughs and says loudly it's a silly story. My parents most likely died. "It doesn't matter," she tells the neighbors. "We are Amoret's parents now."

But I know I was abandoned or from the sea.

Jambes du Diable has noticed me.

I woke, straining to see in the darkness as if I were trying to find the sea's horizon. I closed my eyes, waiting for the room to stop rocking. Poor Amoret, I thought as the dream faded. I had seen the way her mother had looked at her, the way she relied on her.

These weren't just dark dreams. Amoret was telling me her story. The need to know burned inside of me now. These supernatural happenings had been Tess's domain. I'd push away her ghost stories and turn to things tangible and real. But now, I understood Tess's obsession.

I felt brave and reckless. I wanted the journal.

Grabbing a flashlight, I took the service stairs down to the basement, a floor of the house I rarely visited. When I was a child, the servants had shooed me out of the rooms filled with laundry, bottles of wine, and boilers, and a large pantry that seemed to my child self a cook's secret place of jars of jelly and herbs hanging from the ceiling.

But the basement was also a man's world too, with a dusty room crowded with rusty tools, cabinet hinges, and automobile parts. "Not a place for you," I'd been told, but it was where everything happened, all the things that kept the household running. I'd been banished enough times that I'd grown used to not going down into the house's darkest floor.

I wandered through the rooms now, turning on lights and finding it dreary and sad, a reminder of how active the house had been so long ago. I searched high shelves and through dusty drawers, only coming up with dirty hands for my trouble. Two hours later, I was washing my hands at the kitchen sink, fighting off sleepiness.

149

Forgetting myself, I walked through the dining room. I'd avoided the room, especially since I'd returned from Bangor. A black feeling came over me as my eyes were drawn to the head of the table, where my father used to sit. Uncle had deferred to my father, even though it was Uncle's house, because it was my father's money that kept Sanctuary afloat. Neither my uncle nor my father sat at the table now.

The room seemed an otherworldly haze. I blinked twice, but the distorted images remained. At the head of the table was a man from another century, dressed in a long silk coat of dark green and black. Stained white lace protruded from his cuffs, matching the cravat sloppily tied around his neck. I recognized him from my dreams, from the portrait upstairs: Jambes du Diable. He was gripping the arm of someone. I felt like it was my arm, that I was the woman beside him, even as I stood there watching them. She yanked away, her cheeks wet, looking more vulnerable than she had in my dreams. Black circles rimmed her sea eyes, sunken in her pale face. Her despair took me aback. And her words dripped with hate: "I know you"—her voice caught and I thought she might not go on—"I know what you did."

Smug satisfaction curled up the edges of the captain's lips as he took another bite from his silver fork.

"Your own husband's brother." She spat out a French word that flamed the captain's face with anger. He slapped her with the back of his hand, sending her head twisting on her neck. My hand flew to my own throbbing jaw.

She jerked back straight, staring into his eyes, her hands still on the table before her. "We did nothing wrong."

"I saw," he said. "I saw the way you looked at each other, and I knew. I know what women are."

Slowly, she leaned back in her chair. I wondered why she didn't leave, but she seemed to be waiting for something.

My arm was tender. I looked down and saw the bruise. When I looked up, I was alone in the dining room.

My legs shaking so much I could barely walk, I made my way to my sanctuary. I sank down onto the love seat, not able to think or move for quite some time. Finally, I realized I was rubbing my arm, remembering the feeling of being grabbed, only to find there was no longer a bruise there. My eyes fluttered closed, as I tried to recall the sensation of seeing Winship in the dining room. Was it possible that he was here, in this house? Sanctuary was seeping into me, even deeper now, anchoring me to it whether I wanted it to or not.

A splitting of the mind.

I shook my head. The only way is forward, I thought.

These images and odd things were very real. As much as my mind tried to reason against it, it was the only explanation. I could leave again, desert Ben, leave Eli behind. Abandon my mother to Dr. Brighton. Just start anew, afresh. Like my mother had tried to do in New York. But I couldn't do that. I loved them all. I understood how Amoret felt about taking care of her mother and her sister. I felt that too.

Sanctuary was holding me fast. I felt responsible for its past, its future. I felt complicit in its tragedies. I felt guilty for still being here, when so many of my family were gone.

Slowly, I got up and began to take the books out and look through them. I was consumed with the need to understand, the need to know. As quietly as I could, I went through all the shelves, looking for books hidden behind books or notes tucked into pages. The physical certainty of the thick covers and delicate pages brought back not exactly my confidence, but at least a feeling of being on solid ground.

"What are you doing here?" asked Patricia, poking her head through the door.

"Dusting the books," I said, showing her the rag in my hand.

She rubbed her eyes. "At this hour? The sun's barely up."

"What are you doing awake?" I asked.

She laughed a sleepy laugh. "That is probably the greater riddle. I couldn't sleep. Want some coffee?"

I put down the rag. "Sure." I was ready for company, wanting to be in the presence of people.

I was quiet, but found our morning breakfast calming after all the strange things that had been happening to me. Mary chattered on about something while Anna bustled around as usual in the background. I was distracted, but tried to join in the conversation. Jasper nestled against my feet. When Eli joined us, I gave him a happy relieved smile.

Our party was broken up by Uncle coming through the door. I immediately got up, taking a sweater off the hook, and went outside, Eli joining me.

CHAPTER 33

WE HEADED TO THE SOUTHEASTERN TIP OF THE ISLAND, A PLACE I RARELY visited. The village, the cemetery, and the docks were located on the northern part of the island, the smaller "half." I thought of the island as halves, with the house in the middle. The southern portion was much fatter and wilder. The farther we walked from Sanctuary, the more I felt the dark, heavy feelings leave me.

All I thought of now was Eli.

"What are you smiling at?" he asked playfully.

I shrugged, not saying I had many reasons not to smile, but being with him made me happy, giddy almost. Even after only three hours' sleep, I felt invigorated, like I could do anything.

I could feel something on the island trying to rush me, pressing on me as if time was precious and I shouldn't be wasting it with Eli. But I ignored the feeling.

"Are you all right this morning?" he asked. "You look tired."

I just nodded at him, giving him a reassuring smile.

We traipsed through the dying grasses of the meadow. Winter would soon be here, and this walk wouldn't be as pleasant. Plunging into the shadows of the thick eastern forest made me shiver. The trees stretched high and full over our heads, darkening our path, which had now begun to rise upward.

There were no wide, cleared trails here, so we carefully made our way through scratching branches and bushes. The forest was peaceful, though, with the rustle and calls of its creatures.

We came to a place where the trees weren't so close and tight. As we walked side by side over a soft carpet of pine needles, Eli took my hand, as if we did this all the time. We continued to walk together as my skin tingled. I wanted him closer, as close as I could get him. The feeling was intense and scary. I didn't want to be parted from him, ever. I squeezed his hand, wishing for more. In response, he smiled at me, and in his eyes, I thought I glimpsed my own feelings.

"Do you ever want to go home?" I asked.

He was surprised by the question. "To my parents?" he asked. "You mean to live?"

"To live."

"No, not really." He thought for a moment. "There are times when I feel a strong desire to see my family, and I miss them very much. And then," he added, "when I'm home, I look out across our land and it's . . ." His voice drifted off.

"What?"

He raised a hand in a helpless way. "I don't know. There *is* something about it. I can't really articulate it. But something feels right when I'm there, like things are clicking into place. But then, after several days of it, I want to leave."

I nodded.

"Is it the same for you?" he asked.

"In a way. But more intense."

"Intense to return? Or intense to leave?"

"Both." I mulled it over for a moment. "Yes, both."

"My parents miss Germany. They are appalled by what's happening there, and deeply sad. And in public, they denounce it, probably to protect themselves from their less kind-spirited neighbors."

"Oh, Eli, are they treated cruelly because of the war?"

"Sometimes," he said. "It bothers my mother a great deal. But my father handles it well enough. My father is a patient man. His philosophy is to live your life being true to yourself and to God, and let that guide all your decisions and behavior." He gave me a wistful smile. "It's been difficult to follow in his footsteps."

"It seems to me you live your life that way," I said.

His face grew very serious. "I've found life is more complicated than I thought it would be."

"In what way?"

He smiled at me. "You've been a surprise."

Pleasure swept through me. "A good one, I hope."

"A most excellent one."

We kept looking at each other for a few moments as we walked. Suddenly, he grinned at me.

"What?" I asked, grinning too.

"Nothing."

"Your ears are red."

He laughed and took a breath. "What were we talking about?" he asked, looking desperate to change the subject. "Oh, my parents and Germany."

I nodded, happy to listen to him.

"When they talk about their childhoods, and their homes there, and their cousins, and the lush green of it, a longing creeps into their voices. I can hear it and know how bereft they are they won't see it again."

"Why did they leave?"

"The Great War. They didn't want to be a part of that."

"Maybe the longing for home is worse if you have to leave but don't want to."

"Yes," he said. "I think it would be."

A surge of panic went through me at the thought of that forced separation from Sanctuary. Again. "Our souls seem rooted to the place we're born. We'll always feel that pull back."

"Perhaps," he said, then a quirky, gentle smile crossed his face. "But can't we put down new roots?"

"Perhaps," I agreed, wanting that to be true.

But it was more complicated than that. I'd put down new roots at the boarding school and felt that gentle pull back to Elizabeth and our classmates and our school in the woods. But what I felt toward Sanctuary was different. As if—beyond my control—Sanctuary was yanking me back.

It wasn't that on the island I felt a sense of belonging, but rather that I was a possession: I belonged to it, or to something that remained here at least.

CHAPTER 34

AS WE STARTED BACK ACROSS THE LONG GREEN EXPANSE OF THE LAWN toward Sanctuary, I slowed and slowed until we finally stopped.

Uncle was on the roof, Ben on a ladder, handing new shingles to Uncle. My eyes stayed on Uncle and the way he went about his task, handling the shingles as if they were precious. After he finished hammering, he ran his hand over the roof, then patted it with a strange tenderness. I felt a warring inside my soul, yearning to reach out and caress the house as well, but also to take Uncle's hammer and smash it into the roof.

"Cecilia?"

I turned to Eli, my eyes not really seeing him.

"Are you all right?" he asked.

I nodded, then looked back at Uncle, who was scowling at us now.

"Will you go into Lady Cliffs with me?" I asked Eli, not wanting to be parted from him. "I need to do something."

"All right," he agreed.

I found an empty spot at the Lady Cliffs' dock. It was comforting to have Eli by my side as we walked into town. Still, I avoided everyone's eyes, not wanting to catch those baleful stares, while Eli nodded at people we passed, giving them a polite but reserved hello.

A few cars lined the street, and quite a few people roamed the sidewalks for a small town. The main points of interest were Turner's Store and the one brick building (a bank), but the dress shop, sweet shop, drugstore, post office, café, and filling station were also getting customers.

We made our way to the one-room library with a long front walkway and small gabled porch and two small windows on either side. Two older people, maybe in their sixties, looked up from their desks in the library, reading glasses perched on their noses. They faced each other on either side of the door.

The woman stood. "Can I help you?" Her glasses dropped, hanging from an amber chain around her neck. For the briefest of moments, her eyes registered recognition as she took me in. The man bent back over his papers with his pencil busily scribbling.

Because she didn't give me the Town Stare, I plunged in. "May we look at the Lady Cliffs newspapers?"

"Recent papers?"

"A few years ago. Late 1929 to 1935 or 6."

The man's deep voice interrupted. "Look in the files," he said, pointing to the oak cabinet. "The town had only a weekly back then."

"You aren't going to find a lot from the early thirties," the woman added. "The paper was discontinued for a while after 1930." She nodded at a table before sitting back down at her desk. "You can use that area."

In the second drawer of the filing cabinet, we found the files, but there were only three for the period 1931 to 1935.

"What years did you want?" Eli asked.

"I need articles from September 1934." I looked at him soberly. "The month of the fire. And from 1935 too."

I also wanted to find anything about my father's death, sometime after the stock market crash of 1929. The crash—Black Thursday—took place in October, taking Uncle's money, Papa's family money, everyone's money, and ruining Sanctuary. But that would have to wait. "The other time period is late 1929, maybe early 1930."

Eli retrieved several more files for me. When I pulled out one of the chairs at the table, a loud screeching noise filled the room, but the man and the woman were still quietly huddled over their books and papers.

"What are you looking for?" Eli whispered, sitting down and putting the files beside me.

"Hmm?" I asked, flipping through the one-sheet papers from 1935. Not much news to report in Lady Cliffs: notices of deaths and children's birthday parties, Boy Scout meetings and family picnics, and even a short news item about a woman who received a postcard from her daughter on holiday in Florida who said she was lonesome.

"Cecilia," Eli asked, "what happened in 1935?"

"A murder."

He stopped. "Whose?"

"What?"

His hand was on mine. I looked up at him. "Whose murder?" he asked.

"A woman. I don't know her name."

"Who was she?"

"My cousin."

"And you think she was murdered?"

"Maybe."

I was startled by the woman at my shoulder, looking down at me. "You should ask Joe Reed about that," she said.

Eli stood. "We should have introduced ourselves. I'm Eli Bauer, and this is Cecilia Cross."

She nodded. "Rita Scott. That's my husband, Pete." I glanced back, but the man didn't look up. "Joe Reed used to work for the Coast Guard before he retired. He found a woman's body a few years ago. I'm almost certain it was in the summer of '35."

"Summer of '35?" Eli asked me.

"It could be," I said quietly.

Eli continued to look at me, but when I didn't say anything else, he turned to the woman. "Where can we find Mr. Reed?"

"He lives outside of town, but most likely he'll be at Turner's Store. He spends most of his days chatting with Earl." She looked at me. "You know, Earl Turner, the owner."

I nodded, remembering the grocer with his wiry mustache and cold stare. The few times I'd visited his store as a child, he took my money as if it held some evil taint or magic.

"I remember Joe finding that body. But I'll let him tell you the details." She hesitated, watching me. "You think she was your cousin?"

"I—I don't know."

"I don't think anyone in Lady Cliffs knew that." She kept looking at me. "Your aunt used to come in here. Your mother too, sometimes.

"Your mother was always urging your aunt to leave when the two of them were in here, and most of the time your aunt would do what your mother said. Cora Cross was clearly the leader. But both of them liked to look through the folders, like you're doing now, and learn more about your island."

"Did they ever bring me with them?" I asked.

"No," she said. "This was before you were born."

"Do you remember what years exactly?"

"It was a few years after the Great War. Maybe 1921? I remember their visits because people from Sanctuary usually kept to themselves." She pressed her lips together. "Still do."

"Do you know anything about the history of the island?" Eli asked. I went back to flipping through the weeklies, listening while I did so.

"As I said, the Winship islanders have always been . . . private people. We had some information . . . old land deeds, a family Bible with a list of names and births, and a fascinating article someone from Lady Cliffs had written about it in the late 1800s, mostly fanciful stuff. You know how they were then, all superstition and ghosts and contacting the dead." She hesitated, and I looked up to find her eyes on me. "All of those things went missing. Your aunt stopped coming in about that time." Her face flushed.

There was an uncomfortable silence. So my aunt was a thief like I was.

If those things were at the house, if my aunt had taken them as Mrs. Scott was implying, they would be very useful to me.

Finally, Eli said, "Do you remember what the article was about?"

"Sure." She laughed nervously. "But it was nonsense."

"What exactly?"

She cleared her throat and scratched her neck. "Every outlandish thing that could be thought of was thrown in there. What I remember most were these claims that two separate groups of women had visited Winship Island over the years," she said, leaning forward and saying quietly, "and were never heard from again." She pulled back, thought for a moment, and then flushed again.

Eli and I exchanged a look.

"Do you remember any more from the article?" Eli asked.

"They also brought up the old stories about the original captain—or maybe this article was the source of the old stories, I don't know."

"What stories?" I asked.

"You've heard them?" she asked.

I shook my head.

She stared at me for a moment longer. "The old captain and his young wife died on the same day under mysterious circumstances."

"Captain Winship and Amoret?"

"Yes, yes. There was talk of murder . . . or . . ." She broke off, looking at me, turning red again. "No one knows what happened." She looked back at her husband. "I'll leave you to your work," she said.

"Thank you," I said.

"I'm glad to help."

I shut the last file from 1935. There were no newspapers at all for the summer of 1935, and only one that fall, and it had no mention of a body being found.

I flipped through the weeklies from 1934, easily finding what I was looking for: an article about the burning of my grandmother's cottage. Scanning over the first paragraph, I could tell it was written in an ostentatious style that had probably created more of a rift between the people of Lady Cliffs and Sanctuary. A slow, sick unease swept over me, so I broke off reading and glanced at the other articles on the page: a short biography of my father and his career as an artist, and a brief history of the island, complete with pictures of its first inhabitants.

My hands shook as I studied Captain Winship, the man in my visions and dreams looking like he might jump out of the page and slap me. This was his portrait at Sanctuary, showing a man with a large, grim face and cruel eyes that stared condescendingly out of the frame. He had not been handsome or kind.

My eyes went to the other one I recognized: It was Amoret Winship. It stunned me a little, seeing it. Every image I saw of her revealed some other side to her. Her ghostly self was angry. My dreams showed her vulnerability.

But the artist had captured a different view of her. Amoret had no affection for the painter, so I doubted William Clemson painted these. Her hair was piled perfectly on top of her head, not a strand out of place, and dark eyes looked to the side. Her pose was almost relaxed, with an arm draped over a round upholstered edge of a couch, but her rigid posture belied that sense of calm. It was her beautiful face that truly revealed her disdain, her pretty mouth set angrily, keeping her from looking empty and sad. Had the captain forced her into this painting? If we could look underneath her fine clothes, would we see bruises?

The portrait alone would have been enough to spin tales, even without the rumors of murder.

The third picture was of a man whose portrait wasn't in the hallway of Sanctuary. I knew who he was before I even saw his name: Dr. William

Clemson, with dark handsome looks and kind eyes. He too had visited my dreams. I felt as if I knew him a little. The newspaper said that Dr. Clemson had been murdered by one of the villagers on the island. But after my vision of the scene between Amoret and the captain, I wondered if that was true.

The day following Dr. Clemson's murder, the bodies of Amoret Winship and the captain were found in the dining room at Sanctuary. My heart sped as I thought of all the vileness I felt in that room.

Their deaths were a mystery. Amoret had bruises on her body. The cause of the captain's death was not known. Stories began to circulate that the spirit of William Clemson had murdered them both.

There was maddeningly little detail about the matter.

I braced myself before I began the article I most wanted to read, but was still not prepared for what I discovered:

Tragic Fire on Winship Island

Two people, one only a child, died tragically yesterday when a French-style cottage on Winship Island was consumed in flames. Mrs. Lancaster and her granddaughter, thirteen-year-old Tess Cross, were sleeping in the two upstairs bedrooms at the time of the blaze.

Jess Turner, the stable master at the estate, awoke to the smell of smoke and the "extreme agitation" of the animals. He alerted the household, but it was too late. The cottage was completely consumed in less than an hour. In a miraculous stroke of luck, the heavens opened up as the cottage dissolved into ashes, releasing a heavy torrent of precipitation, extinguishing the devilish flames and sparing the remaining estate and its inhabitants from perishing in the horrible inferno.

Mrs. Lancaster's younger daughter, Laura Wallace, and granddaughter twelve-year-old Cecilia Cross were asleep in the main house at the time of the incident and are in shock, according to an unidentified servant at the estate. Mrs. Wallace, married to the owner of Sanctuary, Mr. Frank Wallace, had to be sedated by Lady Cliffs' own Dr. Wilson.

This family has had its share of tragedy. Mrs. Lancaster's daughter (and Tess's mother), Cora Cross, was confined to a sanitarium a few months ago after prolonged grieving for the loss of her husband, the renowned artist James Cross. In 1929, on Black Thursday, Mr. Cross—whose inheritance allowed him to pursue his art—shot himself in Sanctuary's graveyard. His body was found by his wife.

The police have not yet discovered the cause of the fire, but this reporter has it on good authority that they suspect arson. Despite rumors to the contrary, it is not to be believed that any of the good citizens of Lady Cliffs could be responsible for this horrendous deed.

Townspeople of Lady Cliffs and inhabitants of Winship Island have a long history of being suspicious of one another. A wealthy English captain settled Winship Island in the mid-1700s, long before Lady Cliffs was established. Those who have lived there tend to be recluses or to seek the company of well-to-do people not from Maine.

My vision blurred. With shaking hands, I stuffed the papers back into the folders and walked out of the library.

CHAPTER 35

"Are you all right?" Eli asked, catching up to me on the sidewalk.

He leaned toward me, and I felt his hand on my back as if he were steadying me for just a moment.

I looked in his eyes, but I only saw my father's eyes.

"You're so pale," Eli said, taking my arm.

We found a bench at a little park across from the shore.

"I saw the article," he said. "I'm sorry about your father."

I nodded.

"Did you know how he died?" he asked gently.

I shook my head.

He took my hand, and we sat and watched the tied-up boats bobbing in the harbor. It was midday and there wasn't much going on. All the fishermen were resting, preparing themselves for the next journey out to sea.

The sun was out. It was warm. It should have been a nice September day, a glorious day—one to enjoy the weather, spread out a blanket, and have a picnic before the cold set in.

"Do you miss your father?" Eli asked finally.

"Miss him?" I asked absently. "I barely knew him." Images came to me. "I do remember his hands, moving, working over a canvas, colors and things popping out of the blankness." I looked at Eli in surprise, and my eyes stung. "I didn't see that until now. Could I have just imagined it?" Had it been triggered by Patricia's memories of my father, or was I just stealing hers because I had none of my own?

"I wouldn't guess so," he said. "Memories are tricky things."

"Memories are little devils," I snapped, but then glanced at him with an apologetic look. "Forgive me."

"Cecilia," he said gently. Then he did something so delightful it shocked me. He kissed the back of my hand. For that split second, my thoughts turned from my father and my family, and I didn't trust myself to look at him.

"How did you find out about your father?" Eli asked slowly.

I turned to him, lost in his eyes for a moment. "I can't remember. Mother was a mess. She was always a distant kind of mother"—except with Tess, I thought—"but after his death, she was not there anymore."

"She loved him," he said simply.

"She adored him," I said bitterly.

He looked puzzled. "Doesn't that feel right, though?"

But that adoration ultimately took her from us. She loved him so much she couldn't find her way back to us when he died.

So, yes, I thought, she adored her husband, doted on Tess, but kept me out of the family. And here I was left, alone.

"I hadn't known my father was so sad," I said urgently, as if he were still alive and we could still save him, save Mother, save Tess.

He squeezed my hand gently. "A lot of people took their lives that day. It must have seemed the end of the world."

"It was only money," I said fiercely.

"He didn't feel he could provide for his family, perhaps."

"He wasn't much use to us dead either."

Eli nodded.

"And his death took my mother away too. So he made me an orphan."

"You're angry with him."

"Yes," I said, surprised. "I guess I am."

"I would be too."

He looked like he was about to say something else, but then he didn't. I was glad he didn't. I didn't want anyone to try to make it better or excuse what my father did or try to understand it. Right now, I just needed to be mad about it. I drew strength from that anger.

"It can't be easy," Eli said gently, "delving into the past. It would be a lot for anyone."

"But I've been living with it for a long time," I said, looking at him. "Some of this is bringing back memories. But they're so sketchy and vague, I can't grasp them." I paused, thinking, staring off into the past. Finally, after all these years, I wanted to speak the memories.

"I remember some about the night of the fire: the yelling, running out into the grass, the bright wicked orange of the flames, the horror of knowing that Tess"—I felt my throat catch—"and my grandmother too, of course . . . but especially Tess."

I thought of her quirky smile, with her crooked front teeth. Her hair, as straight as a board, always cut at odd angles because she cut it herself. Tears pricked my eyes. "And then the rain on my cheeks, the rain that put out the fire." I looked at Eli. "I'd been angry that night. For a long time, I thought my anger had caused the fire. Silly, I know."

"It's the way children think," he said gently. "That they have more power than they do. Why were you angry?"

"Tess was supposed to stay with me that night, in the main house. The cottage was being repaired that day, but the roofers finished earlier than they thought they would. Our grandmother, at the last minute—at least that's how I remember it—said she and Tess, and Tess only, had to go to the cottage. I was seething. And I felt so guilty about it later."

"Have you ever told anyone that?"

"I'm telling you," I said.

He squeezed my hand. "I'm sorry."

Eli was getting a glimpse into my world, and I had to wonder what he thought. His eyes were so gentle I felt I could tell him anything. I'd never known anyone so kind or as attractive—

"Cecilia?"

"Hmm?" I asked, continuing to look at him and seeing the hesitation in his eyes when he realized I was studying him.

I reached toward him, and he became very still, and I kissed him on the cheek. "You make me feel calmer," I said.

He seemed at a loss for words.

"I'm ready," I told him, "to go talk to Joe Reed."

CHAPTER 36

TURNER'S STORE WAS LONG AND NARROW, AND OVERLY WARM, AND THE wood-planked floor was dusty. When Eli shut the door behind us, the room went quiet. Earl Turner looked up from his place behind a tall glass counter and twisted his lips in distaste. Shaking his head, he went back to scribbling something down on the pad of paper in front of him.

A stout woman in a dark apron was sweeping in the back of the store. Two men watched us from small wooden chairs in front of a shelf of neatly stacked cans, one of them wearing a black hat. When he touched his hat in greeting, I was encouraged and stepped toward them.

"Do you know Rita Scott at the library?" I asked.

"I know Rita," the man in the black hat replied.

"She said we could find Joe Reed here."

"You found him."

"That's you?"

He nodded.

"She said you found a body in 1935."

His friend seemed even more interested in our conversation now, but I could tell he wasn't surprised.

"That I did, Miss Cross."

I was a little surprised, but not very, that he knew who I was.

Eli stepped forward and introduced himself. "You did, sir?"

"I found that woman the year before I retired from the Coast Guard." He scratched his ear with his little finger. "I had beach patrol."

The man beside him let out a short bark of a laugh. "You did not like beach patrol, Joe."

Mr. Reed slid his eyes over to his friend, then back to me. "It was about ten o'clock, almost at the end of my shift. I was about to go up and trade with the guy in the tower when I found her. She'd been in the water for a few days. Not a pretty sight."

"Did they find out who it was?" I asked.

"Not that I know of," he said. "You believe you knew the lady? But you must have been a child."

I swallowed. "Were there any clothes left?"

"Sure." He thought for a moment. "You know, she was wearing a bar pin, one of those brooches you women like. It was about this big," he said, holding his fingers a couple of inches apart. "Long and narrow and green, and it had these small pink and blue flowers on it. Miss Cross, you don't look well. Do you want to sit down?" he asked, starting to stand.

Eli grabbed my elbow.

I shook my head. "Was an autopsy done?"

"The coroner said she drowned. She'd been drugged with Luminal, quite a bit of it, maybe twelve or thirteen grains, if I remember right. It would have knocked her out for a while. Someone threw her into the sea, and she never woke up.

"Are you sure you're all right?" Mr. Reed asked me.

I nodded.

"Would you like a glass of water?" Mr. Reed asked. "You don't look well, girl."

"No, thank you."

"You knew her, did you?" he asked. "You need to go to the police."

"I need to go to the police," I repeated, not knowing what I was saying. Eli was looking at me; everyone was looking at me.

CHAPTER 37

AFTER WE DOCKED BACK AT WINSHIP, WE TOOK A WALK TO THE NORTH TIP of the island, far away from Sanctuary. Eli was deep in thought.

"I knew the pin Mr. Reed described," I said.

"You seemed to recognize it."

"It was my aunt's."

"Oh," he said, understanding coming into his eyes. "So you're convinced it's your cousin?"

"It must have been. My aunt must have given her the pin. What're the chances someone else would have the exact pin?"

"It is possible, Cecilia, that this woman killed herself, overdosing on the Luminal and jumping into the sea. But you're convinced someone murdered her?"

"I am," I answered, making my way over a cluster of rocks.

"Who?"

"Uncle."

"You're not serious."

"But I am," I said.

"You actually believe your uncle is a murderer?" he asked incredulously.

"Ben told me he did it."

"Ben." He laughed a little. "And you believed him."

"Why wouldn't I?" I asked defensively.

"Don't get me wrong," he said gently. "I like Ben. But he is different."

"You mean slow."

"I'm not sure I'd rely on his opinion."

"Why do you think so highly of my uncle?" I asked angrily.

"I don't think highly of him. He's an arrogant, unpleasant sort of man. But it's a leap to think he's a murderer."

"He's violent."

"I haven't seen that side of him," he said.

"What about Ben's eye? You don't call that violent?"

He paused. "Ben fell," he said slowly.

I shook my head in frustration. "Ben did not fall. Uncle hit him. I'm amazed at your trust in Uncle's words."

"Anna was the one who told me Ben fell, not your uncle."

"Anna!" I rubbed my hands across my face. We were silent for a moment and I wouldn't look at him. Finally, I said, "Uncle hit Ben because he took the window frame apart when Uncle told him not to. Uncle admitted it to me."

Angrily, I turned from him and continued to walk across the rocks. I took us on the most difficult trail possible so that we had to walk single file, climb up steep embankments, and at one point step across a small cove using rocks just beneath the water. The hike required concentration and exertion, and took away some of my anger.

It didn't matter if Eli didn't believe me. I was going to pursue this case against Uncle. Not only did this murdered woman deserve justice, but if I could get Uncle put away, I might be able to get my mother released. Then my mother, Ben, and I could all live here again, and this time without Uncle. But something caught at me, made me hesitate in rejoicing in this fantasy. Sanctuary wasn't the same as before. None of us were.

When we arrived at the point, Eli dropped to the ground, leaning back against a white boulder. He held out a hand to me, looking at me with a remorseful face. I took it, although still put out, and joined him against the boulder.

We sat in silence for a while, watching the waves, with their caps as white as the clouds drifting overhead. I closed my eyes, putting my head back against the cold stone, hugging my sweater to me.

With a bit of a pleasant shock, I felt Eli's fingers on my face, so strong and cool, then running through the strands of my hair, brushing lightly against my scalp, taking away my anger, sending a sweet tingling across my skin. I opened my eyes to find him looking at me.

"You deserved a different life, Cecilia."

Lulled into quiet by his touch, I watched him. I wanted to say, *But you're here now*, yet I didn't. So I continued to keep my eyes on his, desperately hoping he would stay close, keep touching me. It felt so nice, so calming, but at the same time it opened up a yearning in me for it to go on and on.

Our eyes locked, and he seemed to sense my desire. His touch changed. I felt his fingers caressing my neck. He leaned toward me, his eyes dropping to my mouth. His lips were soft as they grazed lightly against mine. One small kiss, and then another, his lips parting my own. Eager now, I pulled him to me, closing my eyes and losing myself in the moment. He wrapped me tightly in his arms, and I wrapped him tightly in mine. We kissed again, and again, tender kisses that took our breath away.

Pulling back to look at me, he gave me a slow smile. I returned it. To our left, the sun was low over the dark mainland. I cuddled close to him.

We stayed like that for a while, looking at each other, then the sea and the sky, and then back to each other, with the sound of the sea below us. I barely knew him, but after our long days together, I felt closer to him than I did to Ben or to Anna or even to Elizabeth. The thought of him leaving me alone at Sanctuary made me feel empty. More than empty. I realized with a shock that it would devastate me.

"Will you go back soon?" I asked.

He smiled. "Do you want me to?"

"No."

"No?" he asked in a teasing tone.

"Why would I?" I asked.

"So you could have your books to yourself."

"There is that."

He gave me a crooked smile. "I can't tell when you're playing with me. For all I know, you really do want me to leave so your books will be unmolested."

"Have you known many women?"

"What?" he asked, laughing nervously.

"I mean, have you ever been really serious with a girl or engaged or anything like that?"

He withdrew a little. "Not engaged, no."

"But close to someone?"

"There was someone for a while."

"What was her name?"

He looked at me. "We've been over a long time."

"So you've forgotten her name?"

He laughed. "Helen."

"Hmm," I said. "That's a terrible name."

"You think so?"

"I'm not so enamored with it. She sounds . . . ," I said, hesitating.

"Well, don't stop now."

"I don't want to offend you."

"It's not *my* name," he said.

"Like she's a bit of . . . a high hat."

He laughed. "You haven't forgiven me that, I see."

"So why didn't you marry Helen?"

He thought for a moment. "We weren't right for each other."

I smiled at him, and he kissed me tenderly.

"Did she hurt you?" I asked, my hand on his cheek. I didn't want him to be hurt.

"I'm afraid I hurt her."

"That's not good."

"No," he agreed.

"What happened?"

He hesitated, rubbing the side of his face. "She wanted me to give up something for her. And I couldn't do it. Although I loved her"—I felt a stab of dislike for Helen—"I looked at my parents and realized I didn't love her the way they loved each other. That *I want to be with you forever* way."

"That's good, that you didn't," I said, hugging him. He kissed my head. I looked up at him and asked, because I had to know everything about this Helen, "What did she want you to give up?"

"My career. She wanted me to be a family doctor in our small town. That was her dream. I couldn't share it."

"She had quite a particular dream."

"What about you?" he asked.

"What?"

"Did you have a beau?" he asked.

"No," I said, shaking my head.

"I would be jealous if you did." He was smiling at me.

"I'm jealous of Helen," I admitted.

He studied me. "Do you like me a little, then?"

"A little, perhaps."

His smile widened into a grin, and he looked away.

"You're blushing!" I said. Which only made him turn redder and look so charming and endearing, I felt giddy. Me, giddy. What would Elizabeth think of me now?

He pulled me in closer to him. "Cecilia, what are you doing to me?"

Something sweet and fine soared within me. I wanted him to elaborate because it sounded wonderful and with such promise. Instead, I fumbled around, finally saying insensibly, "Yeah."

He was still for just a second. "Yeah?"

I burst out laughing. Catching his eyes, seeing his confusion, I laughed harder, patting my knees, even though it was not really that funny. It was like there was this well of joy and laughter inside of me, and suddenly it had been tapped. Eli began to laugh too, at me laughing, I knew. And we didn't say anything because nothing needed to be said. Instead, we laughed together, and it felt *magnificent.*

Our eyes caught again and again, and finally we settled down and into each other, more at ease with each other than before. I was snuggled into his shoulder, so happy, when I turned to look at him, and he put his hand on my cheek and gazed at me. I wasn't embarrassed by his attention.

"I like you, Eli Bauer," I said.

He smiled into my eyes. "That's a relief, Miss Cross, because I like you too. Very much."

I was content, quiet.

"Very, very much," he whispered in my ear, his breath warm and pleasing.

I put a hand on his chest, wanting him nearer, and we stayed like that, watching the sea together. I thought it might be cold, but I couldn't feel it.

Uncle gave us a long, hard stare when we returned to the house. I felt a light touch on my back and realized Eli was guiding me away from Uncle. He came into the service stair with me, stopping before my door. He glanced back toward the kitchen, through the open door, at Uncle sitting at the table. When his eyes returned to mine, I saw a momentary flicker of worry before he blinked and then smiled at me.

"It was a good day," he whispered, "because we were together."

CHAPTER 38

When I closed my eyes to go to sleep, my thoughts were filled with Eli. I wasn't prepared for Amoret. When she visited my dreams this time, I wasn't watching her anymore. I *was* her.

Yesterday, one of the crew grabbed me around my waist, saying ugly things in my ear. I yanked him even closer and whispered in English, "Die." He is now ill and vomiting. The crew is frightened of me, whispering "sea witch" when I am near. Fools.

Maman is thin and frail, her worry wasting her away. She fainted yesterday. As I rushed to her side, Dr. Clemson trailed me, pushing me away to tend to her. I like that he is forceful when he is helping people.

The doctor persuaded the devil to let us visit the deck. I steal small moments to look out to sea, pulling in strength from its ancient power. It has always been here. It always will be.

The captain appears at my side. "Hello, Amoret."

I stiffen. I don't like that he knows my name. I don't say anything to him, which I think angers him.

"Is your little sister hungry?" he asks.

My head whips around to look at him. I think he's threatening us. He pulls at his nose in that unpleasant way he has. Yank. Yank. "I can make things better for your family."

I hesitate for a moment, thinking of Aimée. He leans toward me in that hesitation. I walk away, not too fast, not wanting him to think I am afraid.

I find Dr. Clemson in the hold, tending to one of my neighbors.

"What is your given name?" I ask him in French.

"William," he says, looking surprised I am speaking to him.

"I heard you arguing with the captain yesterday."

He laughs. "I do that daily."

"It was on our behalf. I do thank you, William."

His smile is wide and sincere.

I want to keep him close. He could help us. It is true he is handsome. The captain chides him for his kindness and how it makes him weak. Perhaps it does, but I like that he is kind . . .

Finally, we reach Virginia. Staring at the shore, I breathe a sigh of relief. I don't know what life will be like here. But it doesn't matter. We'll be returning to Acadie soon. When Aimée is well, I will find us a way home. And I'll find Papa and my brothers. We'll be a family again.

The crew is unloading us onto boats taking us to shore. The people in the town don't want us here, so the captain is abandoning us like cargo on the beach. I will breathe easier when I am away from his dark eyes. I know his kind. He is both suspicious and tempted, his own desire crafting his fear.

We wait our turn to get in one of the small boats. I approach William, who is sitting on a pile of thick rope with his book in his lap. I want to thank him, but I struggle with how to do it. I look down at his sketch.

"You are gifted," I say.

He stands immediately.

"May I see?" I ask.

He hands me the journal, and I study the drawings.

"None of me?" I ask him, teasing.

He blushes so fiercely, I wonder if he has some hidden away.

We stand at the railing together, staring at the wild coast of Virginia. He is very quiet and seems nervous. Finally, I ask, breaking the silence, "Why didn't you keep all of us together? Would no town have us all?"

He hesitates. "They feared you could be a threat to the Crown."

"We've lived in peace in Acadie for more than a century," I say, still shocked by the beliefs of the English. "Why do you see us as your enemy?"

"Because you wouldn't agree to be our friend."

"That document you asked the men to sign? They agreed to be neutral in

your war with the French. Why isn't that enough?" I sigh, weary from the sense-
lessness. "It should have been enough."

"I agree."

I look at him, liking the look of his chin. Not soft, but one with strength and
character. Papa always says you can know a man from the set of his chin.

I lean toward him, which startles him. "Then why are you on this ship?"

"I'm a doctor. I'm duty-bound to help the injured or sick."

"You burned our cottages."

Shame reddens his cheeks. "So there would be nothing for you to return to."

"You are fools if you think that will keep us from our home." I look at him
steadily, so he knows I tell him the truth. "We will return to Acadie. We will
not rest until we do."

Maman is waving at me. "Amoret! It is time."

I hesitate. I do not dislike him as much as I did before. In other circum-
stances, we might have been friends. "Good-bye, William," I say, still not able
to say thank you.

He struggles for words. I smile, which makes him more flustered, and finally
leave his side. My reluctance to leave him confuses me.

Aimée is very weak. I yell at the crew to be careful with her as they lower her
into the boat below. I jerk away from the man trying to help me down. When
I feel a grip on my arm again, I shake him off, thinking it's one of the crew.

"Not you," the devil says, and pushes me back.

Alarmed, I lunge for the side, the railing biting into my palm. One of the
crew grabs my waist and holds tightly. I see my mother and sister in the boat
below, looking up at me.

"Amoret!" Maman screams. She tries to get back in the ship, but the oars-
man pushes the small boat away.

"Maman!" I yell. "My mother needs me!" I say to the men restraining me,
as if they could understand. I kick them fiercely in the shins. The shorter of the
two slaps me, the sting burning my cheek.

The captain lashes his whip at the short man's legs and hips. "You're not allowed to hit what's mine."

I hear William's voice trying to reason with the captain. I hear Maman yelling. I hear my own voice scream and scream. "Maman! Maman!"

I flew up out of my bed, thrashing, sending the lamp to the floor. I thought I was screaming. I expected to see the sea before me, Maman's face looking up at me, but I only saw the shadowy dark of Anna's room. My heart was feeling, remembering, pounding. Amoret's anguish at hearing Maman's screams became my anguish at hearing my mother's when she was taken from Sanctuary.

I closed my eyes and waited for the sense of terror to leave me. *I'm not there, I'm not there.* I began to breathe more easily, steadying myself.

In my dream, what Amoret saw, I saw. But I knew her better than she knew herself. She didn't know what she felt for William. She was drawn to his kindness and his decency. And there was more—a desire to be with him, to listen to his voice, to hear his thoughts. I knew what it was to feel these things.

I righted the lamp and crawled back under the covers, thinking of Eli.

For me, it was more now. I had an intense yearning for Eli that shocked me. I lay in bed for a while thinking of him, until I could stand it no longer. I had to see him. But I took care in getting ready. I scrubbed my face and brushed my hair one hundred times. I put on a nice skirt and blouse and went into the kitchen.

Mary and Patricia were busy with Anna cleaning up after breakfast and didn't notice me because they were so involved in their conversation. I stepped back into the service hall, listening.

"I can't believe her!" Mary was saying. "Going off every day with him like that! Walking all over the island—I saw them traipsing across the lawn back and forth—and then off in the boat toward Lady Cliffs yesterday. It's not proper."

My face grew hot.

Patricia was laughing. "Since when have you worried about such things, Mary?"

"I don't go off with boys," Mary said indignantly. "Oh, why does she get him anyway?"

"Ha!" Patricia exclaimed. "You've lost your eyes. She's stunning and with that wavy, silky hair, just like her mother."

"There's something odd about her," Mary insisted, "I've always thought so. Especially her eyes, the way they change colors—sometimes dark gray, sometimes green, sometimes brown. And the way she looks at you when you talk to her, and she doesn't say anything, just stares."

"That's called listening, little sister," Patricia said. "Something you know nothing about."

"Oh, she's very odd. I don't like her at all. In fact, I dislike her most strongly."

"Really? Most strongly?" Patricia asked in a mocking voice. Mary didn't notice.

"And neither does anyone else. In town, they talk about how strange her family has always been—her, her mother, her sister, even her grandmother. The whole lot of them! I don't see what Eli sees in her."

"I most certainly do."

"And he's been very kind to me," Mary said. "Did you see how he looked at me when I gave him his plate at dinner the other day? The way he thanked me for it extra politely?"

"He's like that with everyone," Patricia said. "Mary, you need to just leave them alone. I've seen you sneak out after them. You're spying on them."

That stunned me. I remembered the feeling I'd had of someone watching me, but I didn't think of Mary. I thought, if anyone, it was Uncle.

"So what if I am!" she said, not the least bit embarrassed. "And where is the princess now? Still asleep!"

Impatient for their conversation to end, I finally went into the room, sitting myself down at the table and scooping up Jasper for a kiss. Everyone was now quiet.

"Am I too late for breakfast, Anna?" I asked.

Patricia gave me a plate of cold ham and cheese, saying, "Good morning," while Mary shot me irritated glances.

"Good morning, Patricia."

I hugged Jasper and put him back on the floor, glad that at least he was glad to see me. I ate my breakfast in the tense silence, which was only broken by Mary banging cabinet doors closed and clomping loudly about.

When Ben came into the room, I asked him to step outside with me for a moment. He pulled his jacket off the peg by the door, and we stayed close to the house out of the whipping wind. The temperature was dropping now, snatching summer from us.

"Tell me about our cousin, Ben."

"I told you already."

"You said that Uncle got rid of her." His eyes slid away from mine, and I put my hand on his arm. "Look at me. Did Uncle hurt her?"

"I didn't help him."

"What did he do?" I asked quickly.

He clamped his mouth shut, but I could see the truth in his eyes. Ben couldn't easily hide things.

"Ben."

He looked off.

"You tried to warn me about Uncle. I want to know just how worried I should be."

He gave me a sullen look. "I saw him put her in the boat, Cecilia. You need to stay away from him."

A chill went through me. "Was she dead?"

"She was trying to hurt us," he whispered.

"Ben," I said, frustrated with his suspicion, put there by Uncle.

"She was sleeping, I think. He carried her." His eyes watered. "I didn't hurt her, Cecilia."

"Of course not," I said.

"Don't tell Papa I told you."

"Uncle can't just get rid of people. You understand that?"

He was quiet for a moment. "Are you going to tell the police?"

"We must. Don't you see?"

"I'll say you're lying."

"Ben," I said softly.

"I'll say I never saw Papa with the lady."

"We have to report it and tell the police what we know."

"I remember when they came after the fire. They don't like us."

"That was a long time ago," I said.

"I don't like the Lady Cliffs people," Ben said. "They aren't . . . nice."

"Have they been unkind to you?" I asked quietly.

He wouldn't meet my eyes. "I'm not dumb."

I paused, thinking. "I remember one day years ago I went down to the harbor and you were sitting on the pier, with one of the motors to the boat, and all these pieces were everywhere." I laughed. "Do you remember?" I prodded.

He shook his head, eyes to the ground.

"And I said, 'Oooh, Cousin, you are in so much trouble.' You explained it was broken, and you were fixing it. By afternoon, the motor was working again." I shrugged in disbelief. "You couldn't have been more than eleven years old."

He still wouldn't look at me, but I saw the grin breaking out on his face, and he looked eleven again.

"Let's go back in," I said, looping my arm through his, resting my head on his shoulder for just a moment, the affection so unlike me it must have surprised him. "It's cold out here."

CHAPTER 39

P ATRICIA HAD LEFT, BUT M ARY WAS STILL IN THE KITCHEN WITH A NNA , peeling potatoes over one of the stone sinks. "I cleaned your dishes," she said, looking up, the knife hovering over the potato.

"Thanks," I said.

"You left your dirty dishes on the table." She glanced at Ben, but he avoided her eyes and sat down.

"I would have done it, Mary," I said.

"You would have left them there, like you always do. You could help out around here. Everyone works but you."

"Let me do the potatoes, then," I offered.

She grunted and turned back to the sink.

Anna glanced at me, and then turned quickly around, not wanting to get involved as usual. I was put out with her for lying to Eli about Ben's eye, especially because she was protecting Uncle.

I thought of how Anna had been here when my mother was taken away, when the fire had happened, when my aunt had sent me away. She'd been here through all of it.

I heard someone in the dining room and—despite all the unsettling things going on—felt twinges of excitement at the thought of seeing Eli. When he came into the kitchen, my stomach did giddy cartwheels.

His eyes brightened. "Good morning."

"Good morning," I said, wanting to go to him, but staying where I was.

He put his hands on the back of a chair across the table from me.

"Can I get you anything, Mr. Bauer?" Mary asked.

"No, thank you," he said, keeping his eyes on me.

"Maybe a drink of water?" she pressed.

"No, thank you," he said, giving her a quick smile before turning back to me. "I want to show you something. Will you come to the library?"

A smile played on his lips.

"What did you want to show me?" I asked from across the library, feeling the spines of my books brushing my back.

"Nothing," he said with a shrug of one shoulder.

My face must have been beaming with pleasure, plain for him to see. I shuffled my feet and looked up at him. "Mary has a crush on you."

"I don't want to talk about Mary." He patted the seat next to him. "Will you sit by me?"

I gave him a slow smile, but didn't move, my eyes not leaving his.

He grinned and broke his gaze, letting out a laugh. "You are stubborn."

"You're bossy."

"Shall I come to you, then?"

"No," I said, "you stay right where you are."

He laughed again, and when his eyes caught mine again, the humor in them changed to softness. "What shall we do today?"

"Get out of this house."

And for the next several days, that was what we did. I packed us cold sandwiches and hot coffee in a thermos. We took long walks and ran through gentle tides, and investigated caves I used to play in as a child. At night, my dreams were free of Amoret, or at least I didn't remember them the next morning. I also was able to push my fears about Uncle out of my mind. It was like Sanctuary was giving me a reprieve.

One day, Eli and I went to the beaver pond and spied on a turtle basking on a rock in the sun, his neck stretched out.

Lying on our stomachs while we hid in the grass, we whispered back and forth to each other so as not to disturb him.

"I'm itching to pick him up," Eli said, his eyes gleaming, "and bring him back with us."

"We can't," I whispered.

"We could."

"But we won't."

"Did you know," Eli said, still watching the turtle, "that some sea turtles will migrate back to their place of birth?" When I was quiet, he looked over at me. "What are you smiling at?"

"Why do they?" I asked, still smiling. "Tell me."

"Well," he said, a little bashful at being studied so intently. "Well, they return to have their eggs. Sometimes they are thousands of miles away and they swim back."

"But why do they?" I played with his hand beside me. "Swim back?"

He kept looking at me, watching me like I'd watched him.

"You're not answering me," I said.

"No one knows," he said, stroking my cheek. I closed my eyes and he caressed my eyelids too. "I guess they want to go home," he said softly.

I forgot about turtles.

Another day, I showed him a small trickling waterfall at the south tip. We brought blankets and books and lay in the sun, the sound of the water burbling from the shadows.

"Doesn't the university miss you?" I asked.

He hesitated for a moment. Something passed over his eyes that I couldn't read. Finally, he glanced over at me. "The university doesn't miss me."

"Well, good," I told him.

He read passages to me about long-ago kings or goddesses, sometimes translating from other languages, stopping to add asides about the various histories or mythologies. I grew more impressed with how much he knew, but sometimes just let his dreamy voice lull me into bliss.

"I don't think you're listening to me," he said.

I was on my back, he beside me on his stomach. I opened my drowsy eyes and turned my head to look at him. A lock of his sandy hair had fallen over his brow. I brushed it away to touch his skin warmed by the sun.

"Tell me something else about you," I said.

"What do you want to know?"

"Everything," I said.

He fidgeted with the book, looking uncomfortable.

"What is it?"

"I don't talk about myself very much usually." He smiled at me. "But I find I want to tell you things."

"Why do you?" I asked.

"I want you to know me. And I want to know you."

"I don't usually confide in people either."

"I know you don't," he said. "So when you tell me things, I . . . am . . ."

"What?" I prompted.

"It means a lot to me that you trust me." But he looked unhappy when he said it. "Cecilia," he said, very serious now. "I've never felt this way about someone before."

"I haven't either," I whispered, thinking this must be what love felt like. With one finger, I traced his eyebrows, his nose, his cheekbones.

His look changed, his eyes dropping to my lips. "If it's all right," he said, leaning in, very near, his lips whispering close to mine, but still too far, "I'd like to kiss you."

"I think that would be all right."

"You think so?"

"Yes," I said, raising my head toward him.

He pulled back. "You're sure?"

"Come here," I told him, pulling him to me. Desire swept over me, and he responded. His arms wrapped around me, mine about his neck. He pulled me to him and pressed against me, and the kiss went deeper and longer. Our lips came apart, but our eyes were locked.

He pulled from me a little, but I drew toward him.

"Just a moment," he said, withdrawing again, "give me a moment."

I sat there, watching him, doing as he asked and giving him his moment. But then I pulled him back, and he kissed me again.

He whispered into my lips, "Read to me in your lovely voice."

"Read what?" I whispered.

He put Keats in my hands. And while he kissed my neck, my shoulders, my ears, I read—slowly and haltingly—the first two stanzas of "The Eve of St. Agnes."

Not able to stand it any longer, I put aside the poem and pulled him to me, cupping his face in my hands, kissing him like he'd kissed me. My hands went to his chest, and I could feel his racing heart. I was lost in his kisses as he lowered me to the ground, his body on mine, his heavy weight pressing down on me, the kisses never ceasing.

Abruptly, he broke away from me, and I wanted to cry out. He untangled himself from my hair. I reached for him again, but he sat up and put a palm out and looked away, off someplace else, far away from me.

"Eli."

"Wait."

"But—"

"No" was all he said. Then he stood and walked away from me.

"Eli?"

He looked at me then, his eyes still filled with passion. "You're so beautiful," he said in a voice that made me reach for him again. "No. Stay there."

"What are you doing?"

He gave a small laugh, as if to himself alone. "I don't know." Then he looked at me, gesturing for me to stay on the blanket when I tried to get up again. Finally, finally, he came back to me.

He gave me a wary smile.

"And are you feeling better now?" I asked.

"I wouldn't say better," he said.

"Shall I read to you again?"

"No, I think I better read to you," he said, kissing my nose.

I lay down on the blanket, listening to his voice, falling into dreams.

"You shouldn't love me, William."

He is putting a book on the shelf and turns to look at me. "But I do love you," he says simply. My eyes travel to the door. "Amoret, don't worry about the captain."

"I'm not talking about him. I am a wild thing, William. The boys in my village knew it. They stayed away from me. The crew, the other men on the island, they know it. Don't you see? I'm no one to love." He looks at me with such sympathy I have to explain further. "Don't misunderstand me, William. I don't say this in sadness. I tell you because it is the truth. It's what is." I must be cursed. I want to tell him, but don't.

He sits beside me. I stare down at our hands, so far apart. Although I long for it, he never touches me. Sometimes I imagine the feel of his hands. But I dare not reach for him.

"But see, it is too late," he says, "I already do love you."

"Nothing good will come of it."

"Only good can come from these feelings I have for you. They are true and sure. I've never loved anyone like this. It is a feeling . . . I can't even describe. I know our obstacles. But I love you and will care for you as long as I live. And I think you love me too."

If he knows of my love, it'll only be worse. But I tell him, "You are the finest man I have ever known." He smiles at me. It hurts to look at his goodness.

Papa would have liked him. The thought of them never meeting, never laughing together, fills me with sadness I don't have time for. I hide my face from William so he won't see my trembling chin. I can't feel my papa, my

maman, my Aimée, Pierre, and Andre inside of my heart anymore. I fear . . .
I fear . . .

I hold William in my heart at night when I must endure the devil. It gives
me the strength I need. I fight him every time. I let my nails grow long and mar
his face with scratches so his men can see. The devil rages at me, saying I
bewitched him. He twists my fingers so hard I think I hear them break.

I am dying inside. Am I so weak? Fierce Amoret of the sea. I could not save
my little sister and my mother. I see their faces everywhere I turn, the way they
looked up at me from the small boat, wondering how I could let this happen.

Our neighbors in Acadie were afraid of me. But they also sought me out,
telling me I was strong and endless like the sea and always knew what to do.
They had small problems with simple answers they could not see. It was an easy
thing to tell them what to do. No, you should not buy Mr. Landry's cow; she
does not give milk. Yes, you should ask Danette to marry you (because she loves
you, you oaf).

Even Papa confided his worries to me so as not to burden Maman.

But that Amoret lives no more.

"Cecilia. Cecilia," Eli was saying. His hands were on my face as I
thrashed about. "It's just a nightmare."

I looked around, trying to figure out where I was. Trees. The sound of
water. I'm on the island. I'm with Eli. I'm not Amoret. I'm Cecilia. "Sorry.
Sorry."

"Are you all right?"

"Yes," I told him.

He pulled me into a tight embrace, and I let him, feeling Amoret's
agony deep within me.

CHAPTER 40

When we returned that evening, Eli went upstairs to shower, and I to the library, but through the breakfast room instead of the dining room.

I was still shaking. My dreams were vivid and so real. When I woke that afternoon, it hadn't been easy for me to separate my feelings from hers. I wondered what happened to her family. I wondered if Aimée survived. She loved them so much.

I froze at the sight of the envelope on my desk, immediately recognizing my aunt's stationery. Her letters to me had always come in this same thick ecru paper. I knew when I opened the letter that the matching paper would have her name in cursive at the top, with only *Sanctuary* printed beneath it.

With shaking hands, I read. The handwriting was my aunt's, but faint and wobbly.

> *Dearest Cecilia,*
>
> *How are you, my beautiful niece?*
>
> *I wanted to tell you this in person, but I've waited too long and now am too weak to travel. I've been ill for a while, and the doctor said there is nothing more to be done. So this is a good-bye letter, and one I tearfully write. I had wanted to see your face once again.*
>
> *There is much to say, but I no longer have the strength to say it. It exhausts me thinking about trying to explain it all. When what I really want, rather need, to tell you is this: Don't return to Sanctuary. I know I have said this to you many times, but you must understand the seriousness of it. Your*

uncle is not the man he used to be. It's too complicated to go into now, but he would not be kind to you.

This is difficult for me to write because I worry about my sweet Ben being left alone here with his father. But he loves his father, and the part of Frank I loved that still exists loves his son.

But you would be in danger.

Instead, I suggest you go to Blanche Bouchard in Grand-Pré, Nova Scotia. She'll take care of you.

I hope you find love in your life, Cecilia. Know that you were loved by us.

Always,

Your aunt Laura

I turned the piece of paper over, hoping for more words, more time with her, but there was nothing else on the back. Oh, Aunt Laura. Why hadn't I received this letter weeks ago? And who had left it for me to find now?

Another piece of paper caught my eye. I picked it up. It was a page ripped out of Dr. Clemson's journal. Frantically, I looked through the desk to see if the journal was there, but it wasn't. Only this page:

June 30, 1756

My money is gone. My blackmailers warn me they will tell the captain. If he sends me away, I can't help Amoret. He calls her a witch, a temptress, and says she lured him into marriage.

I must sell my books for money because my father has refused to send me any. I tell the men to be patient. But I see their eyes and know they think they will make their fortune from me and my love for Amoret.

Eli came in. "What is it?" he asked anxiously.

I took a steadying breath. "I need to search the attic."

He closed the door behind him. "Are you looking for something?"

"Peace," I said flippantly, my aunt's letter still in my heart.

He came to me. "How can we get that for you?" he asked gently.

"I wasn't . . . serious," I said dismissively.

He put his hand on my shoulder, trying to look into my eyes. "What do you most want?" he asked, not letting it go.

"What do you mean?" I stalled.

"It's not wrong to want things in life—happiness, love, doing what you love . . . *peace*."

"When you want something it's taken away." His eyes were sad, so I turned from him. "Maybe it's only in my family. We're cursed, I think. And I'm the only one left to feel the effects of it. So what do I want? I want the curse to go away."

"All right, then. How do you do that? How do you make the curse go away?"

I shook my head, at a loss. "Find the answers, so find the journal."

His brow furrowed. "What journal?"

I didn't answer him.

"Cecilia."

I looked at Eli, not seeing him for a moment. "I need to help Amoret."

He was very still. "The captain's wife?"

"She was more than that," I said firmly, as if I knew it, but again I felt that warring inside of me—two strong feelings clawing at each other, ripping my insides apart. Fatigue came over me, and I sat at my desk, shuffling papers, stacking them, putting things in order, trying to calm the franticness inside of me.

He was behind me. He leaned over and stilled my frantic hands with his steady ones. He swiveled my chair around and knelt down before me, taking my hands in his. "Do you believe you'll have peace if you figure out the past?"

I talked through the pressure I felt pushing on my chest. "I want to know why they couldn't have peace, why they couldn't just leave the past alone and be a family."

"Your mother and your sister?"

"Something was so powerful it consumed them."

"Something?"

I gave a quick nod. "Something on the island."

He looked down at our joined hands for a moment, then back at me. "Amoret?"

"You don't believe me."

His hesitation gave me the answer. I broke off from him and went to the window, looking out toward the graveyard. "I've seen Amoret. I've seen her." *She's in me. I feel her.* I didn't turn around. I didn't want to see the disbelief on his face.

He was quiet for a while, but then was beside me, looking out the window too. "You've seen her ghost?" His voice was sad.

"She wants something from me, like she wanted something from my mother and my sister."

"And they didn't share it when you and Tess were children?"

"I was excluded, yes."

"Because you were younger, perhaps."

"That wasn't the reason. Tess was only a child herself."

"Do you want to figure out the past because you think it'll give you the answer to why you were ignored by your mother?"

My head whipped around to him, and he looked at me directly. I started to leave, but he gently grabbed my hand, releasing it when I stopped to look at him. "Please don't leave because you don't like what I'm saying. Talk to me."

My eyes stung. Still facing him, I turned to look out at the graveyard again. When I returned to his eyes, I saw only kindness and concern. "Will you . . . help me look for the journal tomorrow?" I whispered.

"Yes." His hand cupped my cheek. "Yes," he said again, looking at me just as William looked at Amoret.

CHAPTER 41

W<small>E MET IN THE LIBRARY WHILE EVERYONE WAS HAVING BREAKFAST IN THE</small> kitchen and slipped by the kitchen door to the tower service stair. The third-floor attic was an empty, ghostly place with many closed-off rooms once occupied by Irish and English servants. We passed Mary's and Patricia's doors, closed, but I knew they were downstairs. I'd heard their voices.

The door to the unfinished part of the attic creaked loudly. We stepped into the attic space and shut the door.

There was no electric light up here, but sunlight strained through the lone window in the center of the wall. With a bit of a shock, I registered that many things were missing.

"What does the journal look like?" Eli asked.

"It's small, brown leather, very old."

The black trunk in the center of the room I recognized. I'd always referred to it as the photograph trunk. Someone had thrown dozens of loose ones in, not bothering to put them in a book or even write names on the back. I'd always enjoyed looking at them even though I didn't know who the people were.

Deterred from my mission, I swung open the lid with greedy anticipation, sneezing as dust flew into my nose, opening my eyes to find the trunk empty except for bits of paper and a lone dirty handkerchief. Swaying back to my heels, I cursed, thinking of pictures now lost, knowing Uncle had gotten to them, but not understanding why they would have bothered him so.

"What's wrong?" Eli asked, beside me.

"The photographs that were in here are gone." My mind mentally clicked through them, and I felt so sad I didn't have my father's skill to re-create the images, to be able to move my hand about and draw what I could see in my mind's eye. I thought of the photographs of my mother and my father together, just a handful of those, and of others in the family.

"Who would have taken them?" he asked.

"I can only guess," I told him, not wanting to talk about Uncle.

"Any place in particular you think the journal might be?" he asked, looking around the room.

I waved an arm. "I'm searching everything."

A stack of boxes and old lamps and toys were stashed in a corner. Eli sat on the floor and began going through all of it.

Smiling at memories, I went to a trunk pushed to the corner and threw open the lid. Reaching in, I pulled out dresses and hats. As I was pulling on some elbow-length lace gloves, I caught Eli watching me.

"Already taking a break?" he asked with a laugh.

"Tess and I used to play dress-up in all these old clothes. They must have belonged to all the women who lived at Sanctuary over the years." I pulled out a long dress, standing and holding it up against my body.

"Your favorite?" he asked.

"Tess's," I said softly. I went back to the chest, folding the clothes neatly as I pulled them out, putting hats in one stack, dresses in another. When I got to the bottom, finding no journal, I put them all neatly back in the trunk.

We searched for a long while. I found an almost empty chest that once held my mother's things. Only one thing remained, lying at the bottom.

"What is that?" Eli asked.

"A book of drawings." I turned the pages over. "It was my father's."

The sketches were all of Mother, of Tess and me, Aunt Laura, my grandmother, and Ben. "I think he must have loved us," I said quietly.

Eli kissed me tenderly on the lips. We studied the drawings. The best one was one he did of Mother. He made her utterly beautiful, with large wide-set eyes, a long thin neck, and full but fragile lips. There was also a nice one of Tess and me with our arms thrown around each other, our cheeks pressed together. We'd only been a year apart in age, but she'd always seemed so much older.

Putting the illustrations aside to take them to my room, I began to pick up everything, although there wasn't much to do. Eli and I had both been organizing as we searched.

"Let's eat," Eli said. "Are you hungry?"

"Why don't we search the other rooms?"

"All right," he agreed. "How many are up here?"

"A few. But I'd like to search Mary's and Patricia's rooms while I have this chance."

He paused. "I don't think I'll be joining you."

"Never mind," I said, shaking my head.

CHAPTER 42

Late in the day, I looked for Ben, who hadn't appeared for lunch. Anna had told me that Uncle and Ben were still working on the roof, but Uncle came in for an early supper. While Eli sat down to eat with Uncle, I went outside to find Ben.

Afternoon was waning when I thought to search the cemetery. I had been avoiding the graveyard after finding out my father died there. But it was still light, and that made me feel less anxious, so I went into the trees and heard Ben's voice. He was sitting cross-legged in front of his mother's grave reading *The Tale of Peter Rabbit* to her.

I sat down beside him and placed the letter on the book.

He picked up the envelope and pulled out the letter. "You found it," he said sadly, tapping the letter on his foot.

"Didn't you put it on my desk for me to find?"

"No."

"All right," I said, disturbed by that news. "But you've read it."

He sighed. "Momma asked me to send it to you from the Lady Cliffs post office. But when I got there . . ." His voice drifted off.

"What happened, Ben?"

"There were some boys from town there, standing on the sidewalk in front." He paused. "I thought I'd go back later, but then I thought about how it would be if you would come back and stick up for me like you used to."

"Did I?" I asked. "I don't . . . remember."

"Once when we were in town, one of the Lady Cliffs kids pushed me down, saying I was too stupid to know how to stand up." He grinned. "You mouthed off to him while Tess helped me up."

"What did I say?"

He laughed. "Crazy stuff."

"Like what?"

"Like they had better be afraid of you because you were crazy like your mother and who knows what you'd do. It was after Aunt Cora was taken to the asylum. Don't you remember?" he asked.

I shook my head. "That time after . . . all of it is hazy."

"That was why I didn't mail the letter. I wanted you to come home."

Closing my eyes for just a second, thinking about home and loss, and if I had ever had a home to lose, and knowing that I did, I finally asked him, "How did the letter get on my desk?"

He shrugged. "Maybe Mary put it there."

That stopped me cold. "Why would she?"

"She doesn't like you."

"I've figured that out," I said, picking up the letter. "But how could giving me this hurt me?"

"Maybe she wants you to be scared so you'll leave."

"Why do you think that, Ben?"

"Because I heard her say it to Anna."

"To Anna," I repeated, feeling a little stab in my heart. I put the letter back in the envelope. "Did you give the letter to Mary?"

"A few days ago, after Mary changed the linens on my bed, the letter was gone."

"Do you know if she also has a journal? A very old journal?"

"I haven't seen it," he said, shaking his head slowly.

"Maybe in her room? Have you seen something like that in her room?"

"Mary never lets anyone in there. Not even Patricia." He looked at me. "Are you going to leave again?"

"I have some things to do," I told him.

He was about to say something, but then pressed his lips together.

"What is it?" I asked.

"You know how Mama was pregnant with me when she had that sickness."

I nodded. "The influenza. The year the villagers all left."

"Is it my fault Mama died? In the letter, she talks about how she's weak. And Anna told me once that Mama was never the same after she had me, that she was very weak."

I took his hand, glad he didn't pull it from me. "No. It isn't your fault." I didn't have any idea what sickness Aunt Laura died of, but I wasn't going to let Ben carry that guilt around with him.

"But—"

"There are no buts," I said, taking the book from him. I began reading it out loud to him. When I turned the last page, he asked if I'd stay and read it to his momma one more time because he was hungry and had to go inside.

"I always read it three times. Exactly."

"Sure." I was reading the book when he walked away and still reading when I heard footsteps behind me. I smiled, looking up. "I told you I would . . . oh, hi, Patricia."

She plopped down beside me. "Just what are you doing?"

I smiled. "Something for Ben."

"Ah," she said, picking at some grass.

I closed the book. "Everyone finished with supper?"

"Your uncle has," she said, "if that's what you're really asking."

"Your uncle too now."

"Hey, I guess we're cousins of a sort."

"Cousins," I said, thinking of the cousin I hadn't even known. Did I have even more? Patricia was looking at me, waiting. "Do you like living here?" I asked her.

"Not really. But Mary does. She has grand plans." We both stood, then sat on a bench by the dry fountain. "But when I was growing up, the kids in town would pepper us with questions after we returned from summers helping out Anna. It gave us a dangerous celebrity at school and in town, and Mary liked that. I think even Anna liked it."

"Anna? She doesn't seem the type to be into all that."

"There's a lot more going on with Anna than we know, I've always thought." She slid a glance at me. "You know your mother wasn't kind to her."

I let out a bark of a laugh. "My mother wasn't kind to anyone."

Her brow furrowed. "She was kind to you. She loved you very much."

"*My* mother? I don't think so."

"But, Cecilia, I could see how much she loved you. I mean, sure, she talked to Tess a lot, but the way she looked at you, I always thought she adored you."

"That's not the way I remember it," I said, distracted by an image to my right. Slowly, I turned my head and saw the faint outline of Sanctuary's ghost. I could feel her presence in the air. I grabbed Patricia's arm.

"What's wrong? What is it?"

"Don't be alarmed," I said. "But look in the trees, just there." I pointed, looking at my lady ghost. When I turned back to Patricia, she had a puzzled look on her face.

"Are you trying to scare me?" she asked with a laugh. "It was always your sister who played those games."

"Look there, Patricia. In the trees, there."

She stood then and walked over to the trees, approaching the image with no hesitation in her step. She peered so closely and the ghost just hovered. When Patricia looked back at me, I saw alarm there, but I knew it was for me, not because she'd seen something disturbing.

She couldn't see Amoret. Or at least she said she didn't.

But it didn't matter because I knew Amoret was there.

CHAPTER 43

THE NIGHT PRESSED IN UPON ME. I WAS IN THE KITCHEN, ALONE, LOOKING out the window into the darkness, seeing nothing. I'd been dreaming of Amoret and William again, but when I woke I was left with only a vague remembrance of soft words spoken. In the daytime, the dreams, ghosts, and images receded, as if they couldn't coexist with the bright light of day. Our simple conversations about meals or if it might rain were somehow loud enough to drown out the elusive frightening things haunting our minds dusk to dawn. My mind. Haunting my mind.

Tess had always been fascinated by the supernatural or the past or anything you couldn't grasp in your hands. For me, it was the opposite. It was rocks and water and animals and books. For both of us, it was Sanctuary. But for me, it was the house itself: the exquisite elegance of the archways, the solidity of the stone . . . Tess wanted to know the house's stories created by those who roamed its halls, alive and dead. That had been a scary game to me, one I didn't like to play. She hadn't seen it the same way. The things that disturbed our mother and me hadn't weighed on her soul.

With each day at Sanctuary, I felt as if the house itself were falling apart and bit by bit someone was heaping its rubble of marble and mahogany on my chest. My breaths seemed short and shallow, as if I was afraid to take a full gasp of air into my lungs. The only easing I felt in the pressure was when I was with Eli. He was becoming so important to me, almost vital to living. The need I felt for his presence was disarming, but thrilling too.

But right now I needed to be alone, really alone. I never felt alone anymore, even in my dreams. I dressed and took a flashlight and went out. I traipsed through the dark woods, going away from the house. The night was dark; heavy clouds hid the moon.

At the deserted village, I walked through the cottages, thinking of Tess. Even in our childhood playground, I wasn't alone. I was with my sister. The memories were so acute and fine they were a sweet hurt. But still I couldn't turn from them.

Memories were tricky. You shape people in your past by what you remember. But your mind latches on to certain things, gives some words, some events, more meaning than others. Some moments are pushed down so deep you don't remember them, or if you do, you don't even know if they're real. Did you see it in a photograph? Did you dream it? Was it someone else's memory that was told to you? And could you trust that?

Now, after weeks back at Sanctuary, I finally found the Tess I'd been looking for. She was right here beside me. Not a ghost like Amoret. Not images like those I saw in the dining room. Memories I thought must be real. Must be.

I settled on the dirt floor of my favorite cottage, remembering Tess brushing my hair. "You have nice hair, Cici," Tess had said to me. "Like Momma's." She piled it on top of my head, letting some of it fall to my shoulders. "You could be a mysterious sea princess."

I sensed something in her voice I didn't recognize. I turned to her, facing her, our young knees touching. "Your hair is like silk."

She laughed that confident laugh she had. It was direct and open, no secrets there in her laugh. "You mean flat."

"No, soft and fine." I ran my hand down the side of her head, stopping at her chin. She had short hair. She always took scissors and cut it off herself, saying it got in her way. But maybe she cut it because she didn't like it.

She studied me then. I worried a little because when Tess got thoughtful she was planning a scheme I wouldn't like. Something involving séances or the cemetery or reciting strange words I didn't understand.

"No," I'd told her that day in the cottage when I saw that look.

"No, what?"

"I won't do it."

"Do what?"

"Do whatever you're thinking."

She grinned. "Yes, you will, Cici. Because you always do."

I folded my arms together angrily. "I won't."

She'd wrapped me into her arms then in an unexpected hug. "But you do because you know I'll always look after you." She caressed the top of my head. "You are my sister. And sisters are special."

"Why are they?" I asked suspiciously, pulling away.

"Sisters have a spiritual bond," she said, repeating words Mamie used, losing my interest. I knew she was about to go off on one of her speeches. "We know what the other is thinking."

I looked away, not wanting to know what she was thinking.

"Cecilia, we are part of each other. We won't be separated."

But Tess had been wrong. Very wrong.

A noise yanked me into the present. A swaying light moved across the glassless window. I caught a glimpse of a shoulder, a hand, not much more. Quickly, I stood, accidentally kicking my flashlight, the light spinning, spinning. "Who's there?"

Things were quiet, but it seemed a forced quiet. He was off to the side now, whoever it was. But I could still see the light out the window.

"Ben, is that you?" I called out, down on my knees, grabbing for my light, while looking up toward the door.

It flew open. My light illuminated heavy shoes. I looked up the large frame to see my uncle's face staring down at me. Grabbing my flashlight, I scrambled backward until my back was against the wall. "Why are you here?" I yelled up at him. Raindrops began hitting the roof of the cottage, plop, plop.

Uncle blocked the door, not saying anything, as I stood, gripping the light, my hand shaking. "What are you doing here?" I asked again, my heart speeding.

"Following you."

I had nothing to defend myself with. "What is wrong with you?"

He scrunched his eyes. "I see you. I know who you are."

"Of course you do," I said, too scared to add *you fool*. The words felt like Amoret's. My eyes darted past him, desperate to see my cousin there. But Uncle was alone. "I'm Laura's niece, Uncle, her blood," I said, trying to connect with this man so he wouldn't harm me. "You've known me since I was born."

It was the wrong thing to say. "Do you think you have any right to this place because you were born here? Sanctuary is mine. Do you hear me?" He stepped toward me again. "Mine!"

The rain was harder now, some of it dripping into the cottage through holes in the roof. Water trickled down the wall, dampening my back. "Yes," I said, trying to calm him. "Yes. It's yours." I would fight him. He wouldn't throw me dead into the sea without going in himself.

"It's time for you to go," he said. "Do you understand me? It's time for you to go." But he was still, not moving toward me. He didn't have anything other than a lantern in his hand, looking at me with venomous eyes in the swaying light. He reminded me of Winship, something in his eyes, his expression. Physically, he didn't look like him. But the contortions of his face arranged his features to be like Winship's. That similarity stunned me. I repositioned the flashlight in my hand, gripping it tightly.

I had this odd feeling he was afraid of me. I drew strength from that. "Move, Uncle, and I'll go back to the house, then."

"I mean—girl, witch—whatever you are: You're to leave Sanctuary."

"If that's what you want, then I will."

"You're to leave now."

"You know I can't do that, Uncle." I wasn't going to let him get me anywhere close to a boat. "Everyone will wonder where I am. Eli will wonder. He'll see my clothes and suitcase. He'll think something happened to me. He'll involve the police."

Something flashed in his eyes. I saw it in the light. He seemed lit from within by something else. Again, I thought of Winship.

His voice changed, became less possessed, more sure. "I'm taking you off the island. Right now."

And I knew he intended to throw me into the sea, along with my cousin.

He was reaching into his pocket. I whipped the beam of my light directly into his eyes. His hand went up. I tried to rush past him, but he grabbed me easily in the small space. His grip was strong. I fought against him, but he held me fast with only one hand. Like Amoret, I scratched my attacker's face, going for his eyes. Vile words flew from his mouth, strange words in the way they were spoken, as if from another time.

Then I saw them, the lights. Fireflies were all about us, swarming around Uncle, stabbing him in his eyes and face. He swung at them, his voice frightened, yelling, "Off, demons! Off!"

I flew out of the cottage, the rain stinging my face. Outside the door, I slipped down into the mud, dropping the light again. I got to my feet and left the light. I didn't look back. I tore through the trees until I was back at Sanctuary. Through the kitchen door, I went, tracking mud along the way. I yanked a drawer open and grabbed two very sharp knives. I went to the library, the only place I felt safe in the house. I locked the door and went to the love seat. My heart was pounding. Eventually, I heard the kitchen door slam. I thought about how the tracks of mud would lead Uncle to the library.

Silently, I went to the door, standing on the inside of it, waiting, a knife in each hand. My throat was so constricted I didn't think I was breathing. But I could hear him on the other side of the door.

"Frank?" came a voice, making me jump. "Frank, what is it?" It was Anna.

He cursed loudly. I listened to him cuss some more. She kept talking to him, trying to reason with him. Finally, I heard him follow her upstairs.

I collapsed on the love seat, watching the rain until it stopped. I stayed in the library, not sleeping, until the room was lit by morning light.

CHAPTER 44

I heard Anna bustling through the house. I cracked the door, listening intently. When I heard Mary's and Patricia's voices in the kitchen, I crept quietly up the service stairs and went to the attic. I felt time was growing short, that I didn't have long to discover the secrets of Sanctuary. I had to know if the journal was in Mary's room.

I slowly opened the door, peering inside, making sure the room was empty. I shouldn't be trespassing in Mary's room, but I hardly cared anymore.

The small attic room was filled with nice things: a brand-new bedspread, an elegant green glass lamp I recognized from one of the guest rooms, and a dresser top covered in jewelry. I studied the pieces, recognizing my aunt's and my mother's, feeling a surge of anger. Looping a gold necklace of my mother's around my hand, I cursed at Mary. How could she?

Hearing shouting voices, I looked out the circular window toward the sea lawn. Eli and Uncle were arguing, or rather Uncle was. He grabbed Eli by the arm, and Eli jerked away, leaning in and saying something that made Uncle step back. Uncle stayed where he was as Eli went back into the house. Then Uncle stormed off.

I sat on Mary's bed, feeling ill, my heart in my throat. Eli, I thought. What were you doing with Uncle? Perhaps he was scolding Uncle for hitting Ben. Maybe it was about me, that Eli had found out about last night. But how could he have unless Uncle told him?

And then I saw it, the journal, on a lower shelf of the bedside table.

I took it, turning it over in my hands. Mary had stolen it, and my mother's things, my aunt's things. I guessed she wasn't going to wait until Uncle allowed her to move to the second floor to have a nice room of her own.

I read through Dr. Clemson's descriptions of Amoret, watching him fall in love with her in these pages. Finally, I got to the part in the story I wanted to know.

December 25, 1755
We are back at Sanctuary. They are married.

January 2, 1756
Winship keeps her locked in their room.
Last night at dinner, Winship barked at me, "For God's sake, stop that tapping of your fork!"
I put it down; I had not even realized I'd been doing it.
"How long will you keep her a prisoner?"
"None of your affair."
"It is wrong."
He took a bite of his roast and shrugged. "It's my island. I decide what is right."

January 5, 1756
I woke to her screaming at him. I stormed out of my bed-chamber and banged on the door.
"Go away, William!" the captain shouted.
I put my shoulder into it, ramming the heavy door. It wouldn't budge.
Finally, he threw it open, his face contorted in rage. I tried to see beyond him into the chamber, but he blocked the door-way, pushing me out into the hall. I threw him a punch that landed on his jaw. But he quickly straightened and came at me with one solid blow to the stomach, sending me to the floor.
"You were never a good fighter, William."

January 8, 1756

The captain's father is dead. Winship is sailing to England to tend to his family's estate and see to his young daughter, who is also my niece. Winship was married to my sister Isabel before she died of consumption. My mother and father care for my niece. Winship has no need for a daughter. He wants a son.

He warned me not to let Amoret out of his bedchamber.

As soon as his ship sailed, I went to visit her, not having seen her in weeks. She is much changed.

She was at the window, pale and listless, looking out at the bay. She barely registered surprise at seeing me, saying in French, "I wish this wretched house faced north. Instead, all I see is that." She pointed to the coast. "A foreign soil and the sun sinking at the end of the day."

She looked behind her at the open door, giving me an odd smile. "Have you come to help me escape, William?"

"I'd like to show you my library."

She nodded. "How is your stomach?"

I was confused at first, thinking she thought me ill.

"You saw the captain send me to the floor with a punch?" I felt heat creeping up my face. "I've never been a man of violence. The captain is correct—"

She interrupted me, calling the captain an ugly French word.

February 14, 1756

I am teaching Amoret to read English. She mocks the captain, the way he pronounces things. She does his accent very well.

The captain's men grumble about me disobeying him. One of them warns he will not be punished for my sins.

Amoret eyes the boats, but she is closely watched. I am closely watched too.

April 28, 1756

Winship has returned and is in a black mood. His father had gambled away much of the family fortune.

The men are threatening to tell the captain I spent time alone with Amoret, blackmailing me for money. I am low on funds and have written home to my father to see if he'll send me money. It shames me to ask for it.

May 1, 1756

Finally, the captain has freed Amoret.

She and I spend time together in the library, but are careful. It is dangerous, and I shouldn't write these words, but I love her. I believe she is fond of me and loves me as well.

I thought of the sensation I'd had in the library of lovers whispering and the scent of longing. I believed she loved him too. I felt her love for him.

Last night, at dinner, the captain couldn't keep his eyes off her, but rather from fear or desire, I couldn't tell. I wanted to knock the look off his face.

"The men are afraid of you," he said to her. "What have you done to them?"

She narrowed her eyes—bold and calculating—and leaned toward him. She knew what would frighten him: "I am a witch of the sea. Stab me and watch the water flow." He drew back from her, pale. He could not hide the panic in his eyes, quickly replaced by rage that she would speak to him so.

He stormed out of the room, and she stared out the window, turning inside of herself.

May 3, 1756

Amoret is with child. The baby will be born in September. She wants to have the child in Acadie. She confides in only me. And perhaps the servant girl too. They are close. The girl seems to worship Amoret, following her around wherever she goes.

"If you left this island," I asked Amoret carefully, "wouldn't you rather go to Virginia to find your family?"

"They would never stay away from Acadie. They have gone back, I'm sure of it, to find one another."

June 15, 1756

Yesterday, as Amoret tended her garden of herbs—tansy, yellow iris, lovage, foxglove, lavender, and thyme—she chatted to me about her two little brothers. She seemed happy as she worked in the soil with her sleeves pushed up.

I knelt down and took her arms. "What is this?" I asked, putting my fingers on the bruises.

She pulled away. "It's all right, William. Didn't you see the scratches on his face?"

I came to the page that was torn out of the journal, running my finger down the frayed edges.

July 2, 1756

Amoret is in a quiet, pensive mood. Only to me, she shows that tender side of herself. She cares so deeply for her family.

Yesterday, she brought out a small white pipe and a brass thimble that she keeps hidden in her dress. "Papa's and Aimée's," she explained. "I took them quickly when the soldiers came." Her eyes were moist. "I wanted to see Papa's eyes light up when he saw his clay pipe. But I haven't seen him since they loaded him onto the other ship with my little brothers." She turned the thimble over in her palm. "And Aimée was too sick." She looked at me then with beseeching eyes. "Do you think Aimée is better? Do you think they're treating her kindly where she is?"

"Your mother is with her. They have each other."

"Maman is with her," she said, rolling the thimble on her palm.

July 23, 1756

Her condition, I believe, is what has brought on her deep thoughtfulness. She confides in me about her life in Grand-Pré.

"Some of the villagers were frightened of me."

"Why?" I asked.

"Because of my temper," she said, "but also because of this."

She stopped and pointed—

I was startled. I lowered the journal to my lap and stayed still so the bed wouldn't squeak. I heard Mary's and Patricia's voices out in the hallway. I looked around frantically, trying to find a place to hide. There was a small space on the other side of the fireplace. I stepped lightly across the floor, hoping they were going into Patricia's room. But they sounded like they weren't moving from the hallway.

A board moaned under my foot. I stopped, watching the door. My heart thumped so hard I put my hand over my chest as if I could soothe it. I listened. They were still talking. I made my way to the hiding place and tucked myself in.

I still had the journal in my hand, but thankfully the bedside dresser was in order. But if they came into the room, they would see me.

I heard Patricia's door open and the voices faded. I could hear them through the wall. They were in Patricia's room. As quietly as I could, I made my way to the door, turning the knob. I peered out into the hallway. Patricia's door was open, but they were inside her room. I slipped out the door and down the stairs. I heard Anna in the kitchen and went into my room and shut the door, collapsing on the bed.

I read again.

> She stopped and pointed to her eye. A small portion of her pupil was a different color, a reddish-brown color. I'd noticed it.
>
> "Did you injure it?" I asked.
>
> "Ha! But how did you know? Some think it's the devil eye!"
>
> "I've seen it before. How did you do it?"
>
> "Curiosity. And a stick." She laughed, putting her hand on her growing stomach protectively.
>
> "But didn't the villagers see your eyes when you were born?"
>
> She grew secretive and gave a little shrug. "It may also be because I like fire."
>
> I looked at her sharply. "What do you mean?"
>
> "People at Grand-Pré would say, 'Start a fire and Amoret will come running to stare in the flames.' I do like the beauty of it. Such color, like the sun setting."
>
> "Tell me what else you like."

"Things in nature. The Mi'kmaq believe that everything, including people, animals, trees, and plants, hold the Creator within them," she said with a smile that was sure and knowing. "They respect the land, as do the Acadians. We are called défricheurs d'eau, those who reclaim land from the sea." She was thoughtful. "I am like the land of Acadie because I was reclaimed from the sea."

I love the way her lips move and her hands fly as she talks.

"When we arrived in Minas Basin," she continued, "the sea covered the great meadow. Our men built dykes and turned the salt marshlands into useable land. Rainwater washed out the salt. We grew corn, peas, wheat, barley, so much the earth gifted to us in gratitude for releasing it from the domain of the sea. We remember what the earth gives. We worked for it, but we remember it, as the Mi'kmaq do."

A smile lightly touched her lips. "Once my papa reached over and pushed my hand into the wet soil. I shouted at him, for I have a wicked, sharp tongue I can't control. As I tried to rinse the mud off my fingers, he grasped my wrist. 'Amoret, we are part of the earth, part of the soil. It owns us, and we own it.' Then he released me. So, you see, Acadians can never be parted from our land. And that is how I know we will reclaim Acadie."

Her face lit up with hope. When she was like this, it wasn't easy for me to remember the fierce slant of her eyes. But then her head would turn slightly, and I would see it again.

September 12, 1756

I delivered a baby girl. Amoret was in great pain. But thankfully, the baby arrived quickly and is healthy and pink, with a shock of dark hair. *The first time I have ever seen joy on Amoret's face is when I put her daughter in her arms. She gazed at her with such love. She squeezed my hand. "Thank you, William. Thank you."*

"What will you name her?" I asked.

"Aimée," she said, her eyes brimming with tears. "Yes, Aimée." She looked up at me, that love still in her eyes. "If she were a boy, I would have named her William."

I was deeply moved. "Winship wouldn't have allowed that."

"It would have been a secret name."

Winship is livid the baby's not a son. "I've been tricked," he mumbled to me. "'Greedily she engorged without restraint, and knew not eating death.'"

"What do you mean?" I asked him cautiously.

"I've seen how all of you look at her. She's a witch! I've been ensnared, caught. I know how witches weave their spells. I've hunted them down. They tricked others, but couldn't hide from me. But now, I have fallen to temptation. Amoret has the devil in her."

I am planning our escape. I'll take Amoret away. ~~I only hope Winship will not~~ I don't care what he does. We're leaving.

September 29, 1756

There is something different about Amoret now, quieter, even fiercer. I can't seem to reach her anymore. She adores her baby, even if it is the captain's, but it is more than that. She spends less time with me, huddling with her servant girl, who is devoted to Amoret and her daughter.

I tell her to be patient. We will leave on October 14, 1756,
when Aimée is one month old. I don't have any fortune of my
own, but I hope to convince Amoret to come to England with
me to live and to find her mother and sister and bring them
there. I'll care for her and little Aimée.

The handwriting changed, and the language went from English to French. It looked familiar to me, as if I should be able to read it, but I couldn't.

I pulled Mamie's once-white handkerchief out of my suitcase. "Keep it safe," she told me one Christmas. I'd seen her eyes shift to my mother and knew this was our secret, the only one we'd ever shared.

The lace on the handkerchief had long since ripped and frayed. But the three initials embroidered in its corner were still there: MEL. My grandmother's name had been Marie Elizabeth Lancaster—at least, after marrying my grandfather, who she'd said was of English descent.

I unfolded the soft cloth, revealing the little clay pipe. I stared at the white pipe in the sea of white of the handkerchief. I was certain I knew whose pipe it was. How did Mamie get it?

CHAPTER 45

THE LIGHTS IN THE KITCHEN WERE ON, BUT IT SEEMED SHADOWY AND gloomy. Mary was at the table with Eli, laughing at something he said. He had an amused look on his face, was pushed back from the table, his arms folded, an empty plate in front of him.

Patricia was smiling beside him. Even Anna was seated at the table, wearing an agreeable expression. Ben had his head down, eating.

I put the journal down in front of Mary.

She picked it up. "Oh," she said, looking up at me. "How did you get this?"

"How did you get it?"

"Someone left it in my room."

"Just left it in your room?"

"Yes," she said. "What were you doing with it? Did you go in my room?"

Thief, Tess whispered, but I didn't know who she was talking to.

Eli was regarding me. I knew he thought I was in the wrong because I had gone into Mary's room. But I wasn't in the wrong if she was the one who had stolen it from me. And I had my own questions for Eli.

Patricia looked from Mary to me and back to Mary as if she was trying to figure it out.

"This is mine," I said, grabbing it out of her hand, feeling like a child, turning back into a child in our childhood kitchen.

"It's not yours. It belonged to a doctor who once lived at Sanctuary, so now it belongs to Uncle Frank." She waved at it. "But have it, if it's that important to you. Just please don't go in my room again."

I narrowed my eyes. "You don't fool me, Mary."

"It was me," Anna said abruptly, folding her arms tightly. "I saw the book when I was cleaning the library. I thought Mary would like to see it."

I stared at her. "Why would Mary like to see it?"

"Because," she began, seemingly reluctantly, "Sanctuary is her home now. Maybe she wants to read the books in the library like you do, to find out about her new home."

I was struck dumb by this speech, while Eli was looking at me with concern in his eyes. Finally, I thought of my retort, only to be stopped by the loud footsteps racing down the stairs and Uncle's voice bellowing, "Anna! Where are you?!"

Alarmed, Anna pedaled back from her chair to the sink, and Eli stood.

Uncle burst in, pushing past Eli and heading straight to Anna. "What were you doing in my things?" he screamed at her.

Her eyes were large and frightful as she stared at him, frozen, one hand clutching the counter behind her. Her mouth moved, but she said nothing.

"Get away from her, Uncle," I said, coming toward him.

Eli reached around to grab me, but the slap came hard on Anna's cheek before we could do anything to stop it. Patricia called out as Anna went down, her head hitting the counter with an awful crack. She crumpled a little, and I lunged for Uncle. He turned toward me, dropping something to the floor as he pushed me back with both hands on my chest. I fell against Eli, who was trying to get to Uncle too. Together, we stayed on our feet.

Anna was now beside the fireplace, holding her head. I saw the blood there, matted in her hair. "Are you all right?" I asked her frantically, my eyes darting toward Uncle to make sure he didn't approach her.

Eli charged toward Uncle, but Ben draped an arm around his chest and pulled him back just as Uncle grabbed a knife off the counter.

For a second, we all froze. Then Uncle stepped back from us and glanced down. I followed his eyes and saw Uncle and my aunt staring at me from the broken frame. Uncle whisked it off the floor.

"I was the one who broke it!" I told him.

"You," he said, understanding slowly appearing in his eyes. "You broke it." Then: "You!" he yelled, shaking the frame at me. "You were in my desk?!" His face grew red, and the knife shook in his hand. "You were in my things!" Uncle cried out again.

"Put the knife down," Eli said evenly, trying to wrestle away from Ben, who held him firm.

"Who the hell are you to tell me what to do in my house?"

"You're just a coward," I said, my breaths coming fast, "beating up people who don't fight back."

"You're just like her," Uncle snarled.

"And you locked her away, didn't you!" I screamed at him.

I felt Eli's arm come around me. Out of the corner of my eye, I saw Patricia trying to tend to Anna, moving her to a chair.

Uncle's face was contorted, and a deep anger seethed beneath the surface. "You shouldn't have come back here," he said through clenched teeth, suddenly eerily quiet and fierce. "You shouldn't have come back. I know how to deal with your kind."

My heart thumped wildly. "Like you did with my cousin that you threw into the sea? Like you did with my grandmother and my sister?"

The blood left his face then, leaving him ashen. "Your sister and grandmother were witches, trying to attempt some devilry," he said, waving his arm. "They killed themselves and deserved it too."

I shook my head back and forth. "No" was all I could say.

His eyes still blazing, he pressed his lips together then, as if he'd said the wrong thing.

I leapt on that weakness, spurred on by the anger I felt over my family's demise through the actions of this man. "So you believe in witches, do you, Uncle, like Captain Winship? The wrong person is in Slattery Asylum."

I'd rattled him. For a moment he looked confused. He glanced away, his hand with the knife now on the counter.

Keeping my eyes on him, I asked Patricia, "Is Anna all right?"

I'd been stupid, stupid, not to confess to breaking the frame. I should have known Uncle would blame Anna. When Patricia didn't answer me, I took my eyes off Uncle. Patricia was studying Anna's head wound, gently pulling back strands of her hair. "It's not deep."

Eli was trying to draw me away from Uncle. Uncle's eyes swerved to Eli, and he came back to life. "What are you about?"

I felt Eli's arm tighten around me as he pulled me to the side. He put his other hand out, palm toward Uncle. "It's all right, Frank. Why don't you go out and we'll tend to things in here?"

"Go out?" Uncle snorted. "I pay you. You're in my employ."

Confused, I turned to look at Eli. His eyes met mine, and he recovered quickly, but I'd seen the guilt on his face.

"What . . . does he mean?" I asked Eli, remembering now the fight he'd had with Uncle.

"I want to talk to you, Cecilia," he said, gesturing toward the door. "Come with me."

"Mr. Bauer is no university professor," Uncle said with a brittle laugh. "I brought him here." I felt his laughter in the pit of my stomach, as if it were burrowing itself there.

Eli said my name, but it was as if it were from a distance. My head began to pound, and my vision narrowed. I walked past Eli's outstretched hand through the door.

CHAPTER 46

"I haven't spoken to you much, I guess," I whispered. The cemetery was gloomy under an overcast day, so clouded over it felt like we were approaching night. I closed my eyes, listening to the quiet, trying to make the world stop spinning. "I wish you were here, though. I've often thought about you and what you thought of all of us. Did you feel alone too?"

"Cecilia."

With a gasp, for a moment thinking it was my father, I whipped around. "Eli."

Without waiting for a response, I turned back to my father's grave, lined up beside Tess and my grandmother. His stone simply read: JAMES CROSS, 1929. I would have had a lovely headstone made for him, one that mentioned he'd been an artist and a father too.

"You spend so much time out here," he said. "In the graveyard."

A hollow laugh escaped me. "This is where my family sleeps."

"Look at me," Eli said insistently. "Please."

"What are you doing here?" I asked, keeping my voice cold, my back to him still.

"Please turn around." I could sense a panic in him and wondered if he was afraid to see my face.

"Why are you here?" I asked again. "Are you friends with my uncle?"

"Absolutely not."

Then I did look at him. He stared at me hesitantly, as if there was something to say but he didn't know how to say it.

"What were you and my uncle arguing about?" I asked, clutching the journal to my chest.

"What?"

"I saw you out the window. He was yelling."

He nodded. "We were arguing about you."

"You did know him, then, before you came to Sanctuary," I said.

"I never met him before I came here," he said, tapping his fingers against his leg. "But I did talk to him on the phone."

"About the library?" I asked.

He paused. "Not only about the library."

"What else, then?"

He didn't look away. "I have to first explain—"

"Why are you here?" I asked, the fear growing within me.

He didn't approach, but he kept looking at me, as if he was pleading with his eyes. "I didn't expect to fall for you," he said very slowly.

My eyes stung and watered, so I looked away. "Are you going to tell me why you're here or not?"

When he stepped toward me, I thrust out my hand to stop him. "Just tell me," I said softly, almost unable to get the words out.

"Promise you'll listen to all I have to say before you react."

"Go on."

"A few weeks ago," he said, talking rapidly now, "when I was in my office in Bangor, I got a phone call asking if I would come to Sanctuary to . . . talk with someone here."

"To talk to Uncle?"

"You."

"Me?" I asked, confused. "Talk to me?"

"Yes."

"Uncle called you?"

"No," he said. "Dr. Brighton."

"Dr. Brighton?" I began to tremble.

"Cecilia," Eli said gently but insistently. "Listen to me, please."

"Go away," I said as I left him and walked deeper into the cemetery, crunching over the fallen dead leaves. I stopped under a maple, grasping the bark of its old wavy trunk, wanting its scratching against my skin.

"I didn't know you," he said, behind me. "I was doing my job."

I looked up at the branch above me. One bright red leaf in a sea of green dangled there. "Who are you, Eli? What do you do really?"

"I'm in private practice."

"A doctor?" I asked, turning toward him.

He gave a quick nod.

"A psychiatrist?" I asked, wrapping my arms around my stomach, pulling the journal farther into myself. Was it all I had?

"I didn't know you," he said again. "Not then."

"So you figure out if people are crazy?"

"I try to help people."

"Crazy people. Like me."

"You're not crazy. No one is going to hurt you. No one."

"I thought . . . I thought you cared for me," I whispered.

"I do," he said with a kind of ache in his voice. "So much, Cecilia. So much." His hands were shaking. "My professional hope is to help people with their own personal demons, not to hurt them." His words tumbled out. "My mother struggles with a sadness that seeps out of the core of her, and then she bursts out of it with this wild exuberance. She overwhelms my father, but he loves her. Others are not so fortunate. I want to help people who have no one else to help them."

"Like Dr. Brighton does, shocking them and injecting them with drugs?" I accused.

"No one is going to do that to you," he said.

"They do it to my mother!" I yelled.

"I know," he said urgently but calmly, putting a hand toward me but not touching me. "I know."

He looked off in the distance and then back at me. "I'm glad I came here. Otherwise, I'd never have met you. But I'm sorry I went along with your uncle's charade. I didn't know him then and what he's capable of. He's a fractured man, Cecilia. A man with demons that I can't begin to understand. And I believe he's trying to set you up."

"What do you mean?" I asked, confused.

"That he is doing things to make you believe you're losing your mind. He's already persuaded Dr. Brighton, telling him that you have the same mental instabilities as your mother."

Splitting of the mind.

I turned from him so he wouldn't see the truth on my face, especially at this moment when I was feeling vulnerable and exposed, and doubting of him, a person I'd grown to trust and care deeply for.

"So Dr. Brighton wants to have me committed?" I asked as steadily as I could.

I sensed Eli right beside me, within touching distance, but he still didn't reach for me.

"That's not going to happen," he said firmly.

Thoughts and longing for my lost family filled me up. I couldn't focus on his words any longer.

"Cecilia?" I heard Eli asking, but he seemed so far away. "Cecilia?"

"Are you sure?" I asked. "That it's not going to happen?"

His hand reached toward mine, but then it dropped back to his side. "I'm convinced your uncle is creating mysteries and ghosts just to prey on your mind."

"Did Patricia tell you about what happened here last evening?"

He paled. "She said you saw something that she didn't see."

I looked at him quite directly. "I see ghosts. And it's not Uncle's doing. I know Amoret is here, in this graveyard. I don't know why Patricia couldn't see her. She was right in front of her."

Condition within families.

"Is Amoret here now?" he asked.

"Yes, probably."

"Okay."

"You don't believe me, I can tell. You want me to believe you, but you don't believe me."

He looked tortured, exasperated, and very unsure of himself. He ran his hand through his hair. "I don't know what you want me to say."

I turned away.

"Wait," he said, his voice stopping me. He shook his head while I waited. "You want me to say I believe there is a ghost haunting Sanctuary? Is that what you want?"

"I don't want you to think I'm crazy."

"I don't think that."

"And I don't need you to take care of me, as your father does for your mother."

"It's not like that. That's not what I meant."

"What is it like, then?"

"I want us to be together. To take care of each other. That's what I want. Can't we be that for each other? The best kind of friend?" He turned beseeching eyes on me. "Don't you see? I need you."

"Even if I'm insane."

"You're not insane."

The fear inside of me snaked and twirled. "Was any of it real, Eli?" I asked in a frightened whisper. "Between us?" I doubted everything.

"All of it," he said with great passion. "All of it between us is real."

I saw them before Eli did. The fireflies drifted from the deep of the woods and began to circle us, these tiny lights. His brow furrowed in confusion as he watched them. I'd never seen them in the day before, but I had a feeling that Amoret had sent them.

228

"Ghost candles," I told him. "Do you see these?"

He nodded, speechless, as they settled into my hair and on my arms and shoulders, small lights of fire outlining my body. I remembered Tess's words—"our cousins"—and felt a kinship with these lights. *He sees them. He sees how they protect me.*

"I am not insane," I told him. "Please don't follow me." I walked off, the lights trailing me before most of them disappeared into the woods. But two stayed with me, alighting on my hand or my cheek and off again but never straying far away. I remembered how frightened I'd been of the fireflies and how comforting I found their presence now.

Quite deliberately, I went to my grandmother's cottage. Unlike the last time I visited, I strode right to the center of the ruins and sat down on the crumbling stairs.

I wished I could banish Uncle's babblings about Tess and my grandmother out of my head. He was just a modern version of his witch-hunting ancestor Captain Winship and was blinded by his own hatred. There was no truth in what he said. Tess wouldn't have burned down this cottage.

I also didn't want to think about Eli. Lovely moments from the last few days flooded unbidden into my head. I didn't know if any of the words he had said were real. Our whole time together seemed a lie. Mary, Anna, even Ben hiding the letter—everyone had been lying to me, Eli being the one that hurt the most, even though I'd known him such a short time.

Gusts of wind came off the bay. My grandmother had an excellent view. She'd wanted her cottage built farther from Sanctuary, on the north point, but Papa had said it wasn't practical. Did she want to look across the sea and imagine being back in Acadie? Then why come to Sanctuary to begin with?

Each step I took toward my family took me farther from them. Maybe I had been too young to really know them.

I took my aunt's letter out of my pocket, hearing her voice in my head as I read silently. The only truths I had were riddles of the past, dragging me to even more riddles, as if my family's past was indeed roots, a physical part of me, with the desire to pull and twist and strangle. I understood how I could feel bonded to my mother and Mamie, but the pull on my heart went even beyond my grandmother.

How could I be connected to a place I'd never been? Did our family curse begin in Acadie, or would it stretch back even further?

How far a reach does the past have on us? How long would I struggle with this—if I pulled too hard, followed too closely, would I meet the fate of my sister, my father, my mother, my grandmother?

The fireflies were still with me, both resting on my hand. They lifted up, so beautiful. They drifted toward the crumbling fireplace. I got up, compelled to follow them deeper into the ruins. They rested on the broken stone, slipping delicately inside an empty, dark space. They flew out and then back in. Again and again they did this. My heart beating wildly, I felt between the stones, my fingers finding a small object in the dirt.

A brass thimble. I looked at it closely, feeling Tess's touch upon it. *Aimée's*, someone whispered softly with love—not into my ear, but as if coming from my own heart.

I felt a painful yank inside of me. The sound of the sea was in my ears, as if it crashed all around me. My head throbbed from the noise. The sea spoke my name, calling. I was confused. Was it my name or another's name? I was drawn to the edge of the high cliff, but was afraid to look. There was something there that I needed to see. Finally, my eyes fell to the waves. There, a body floated, faceup.

I fell to my knees. But I wasn't myself. I was Amoret, and it was William's body. She didn't cry. The pain cut deep inside of us, slicing here and here and here. We didn't cry.

CHAPTER 47

I woke, my heart beating. Or was I still dreaming?

My hand held a knife. Amoret's rage burned inside of me.

I felt a presence. It was either Uncle or Winship or both. Weren't they the same? I swung open the door to emptiness. I turned on lights as I went, brightening up Sanctuary, not caring who came downstairs.

In the dining room, my hand went to the light, but I froze. On the table, hazy images showed candles already burning. Captain Winship was wearing the same coat he'd been wearing when I'd seen him in this room before. Amoret was in the same dress. She was waiting, just like before, almost like she'd been waiting for me.

The captain began to cough. I thought he might be choking. His hands went to his neck and his eyes widened like his throat was burning. But he couldn't yell or speak. He tried to reach for Amoret, but she stood and watched him, her face dead.

The captain fell to the floor, his eyes still open, but very still. Not breathing.

I watched, horrified, as Amoret stood there. She whispered, *I'm sorry, Papa*, speaking to a father not there.

Calmly, Amoret picked up the captain's silver fork and took a bite.

CHAPTER 48

I LEFT BEFORE THE SUN CAME UP, THE JOURNAL IN MY SUITCASE, THE suitcase in my hand. It was colder than I'd thought. When I got to the boat, I'd put on something warmer over my sweater, but not this minute.

I wanted to be away from the house, quickly. I was despondent about leaving and feeling guilty about abandoning Ben. I was breaking my promise. I had to leave before my spirit slipped away as Amoret's had almost two centuries ago.

But then Eli was on the pathway, in hat and coat. He put his bag on the ground. We stared at each other, under the yellowing trees in the low light of the morning.

"I'm so sorry I have hurt you," he said.

"You need to go back to Bangor," I said, my heart breaking.

"I won't," he said quietly. "I can't. I can't leave you."

"Then I'll leave you," I said, passing him by.

"If you leave me, I'm coming too," he said, picking up his bag and walking briskly alongside me.

"Don't," I said. And when he wouldn't stop, I repeated, but more vehemently, "Don't!"

Without looking at him, I kept walking. He wasn't following me now.

"Cecilia," he called out.

"What?" I asked, exasperated, wanting this to be over.

"Where are you going?" he asked. "At least tell me that."

I stepped toward him to see him better and realized he was crying. "Eli."

"I'll never . . . see you again"—his voice was breaking—"if you leave. I can't lose you."

Without thinking, I ran to him. He stepped back as he caught me, letting out a sound of surprise, and then, recovering, pulled me in closer, his gray hat falling to the leaf-covered path. I buried my face into his neck.

"Oh, Cecilia." I could feel the speeding up of his heart. We held each other for a long time, not saying anything else. He thought I wasn't going to leave. I didn't know how to tell him the truth. So I stayed pressed against him, wanting the moment to go on and on and never end.

He seemed to relax a little, taking a breath. "Aren't you cold in just your sweater?" he asked in my ear, trying to push me away to look at my face. But I just pressed in closer.

"Let me put my coat around you," he whispered, but I just shook my head silently, feeling comforted by the nearness of him, the smell of his skin.

He stopped speaking and said nothing else. We stayed like that, pressed against each other. His arms and chest were strong and warm, and I felt safe huddled against his heart.

A rustling in the bushes stirred me from my moment of bliss. I lifted my head. Eli smiled at me, his hands caressing my back.

But then he saw my face and understood.

I pulled out of his arms. "You're not the man I thought you were." His face fell. It pained me to see it.

He didn't follow me this time.

CHAPTER 49

LETTING GO OF THE THIMBLE ON A CHAIN AROUND MY NECK, I PULLED MY collar up against the wind as the ferry drew closer to the shore of marshy land rolling into hills. Bucolic idleness drifted over the water to us. A man in a blue cap and a tall boy on a long pier watched our boat coming in, the boy with folded arms and curious but cautious eyes. They moved slowly, coming toward our approaching ferry. No one was in any great rush.

My mother didn't fit in this sleepy place. But Amoret was easier to imagine in the fields of Acadie, now Nova Scotia.

A woman on the ferry had been bringing the past to life. She wasn't of French descent, but instead British, her ancestors the English planters brought in by the British after the Acadians were thrown out.

"You need to visit the church and the marker," she said, pointing. "But just stand on the land. You'll feel it."

"Feel what?" I asked.

"The sorrow of all those poor people taken from their homes and from one another. You don't have to be Acadian to feel it. That kind of tragedy—it lingers. It's in the air at Gettysburg, where all those soldiers, boys mostly, died."

"I am Acadian," I told her.

As we left the ferry, I tried to imagine what it must be like to be ripped from this place, everyone herded to the shore, a few belongings, what they could grab, what they could carry, forced to leave a life they loved—their homes, their animals, their fields, their church, their communities. Everything they'd been born to. The large ships in the harbor looming, the panic as neighbors or even daughters and sons were loaded onto different ships, many never to see each other again.

This wasn't Winship Island, my wild rocky island of cliffs and trees and few open spaces. Amoret hated my island. Sanctuary wasn't a home she'd been born to, raised on, anchored to. Instead, it was *this* land that held that special place in her heart. Strange how what was home to one was hell to another. Although Sanctuary had changed for me.

Something stirred deep inside of me, something primal and potent. I felt like I was coming home and that I was farther away than I'd ever been.

CHAPTER 50

THE CHILDREN WERE ON A WOODEN GATE, ALL LINED UP, SMALLEST TO largest. Beyond them was a two-story farmhouse with a garden and a flock of sheep.

The youngest, a boy with freckles and missing front teeth, pointed at me. "You're the lady in the red hat," he said with a slight lisp.

My hand instinctively went to my head. "It's gray."

His little finger moved to my suitcase. "What's in there?"

"My clothes," I said.

His face fell.

"And pirate ships?" I teased.

His older brother, maybe eight or nine years old, laughed, but the boy with freckles protested, "Don't be silly."

The oldest—a girl with solemn eyes—watched me. It was she I turned my attention to. "Does Blanche Bouchard live here?"

"She's our mother!" the youngest said. "Is she your friend? I don't have any friends." Before I could express my sympathy, he added, "Except for Evan and Martin!"

He jumped off the gate and unlatched it, but he couldn't budge it because his siblings stayed attached. "Move!"

His older brother actually did what he said, but the oldest continued to watch me suspiciously.

Just then, a woman ran out of the house. I backed up, thinking she didn't like me talking to the children. But she hardly glanced my way.

"Margrit, we must hurry. Get in the car, get in the car."

"Is it time?"

"It is, it is. Get in the car," the woman said, waving her hands. "Something's not going right."

"What's not right? Alice's crazy mother?" Margrit asked, concerned, taking her mother's bag from her.

"I want to come," the younger of the two girls said.

"No, no!" the woman told her. "Watch your brothers."

"I want to come with you, Mama. Margrit always—"

"Shush, Bridgit. You have to watch your brothers." It was only then that the woman glanced at me, and all of that excess energy fell away as she stared. Her face turned so white I reached for her, afraid she might faint.

"Who are you?" she asked.

"It's the lady in the red hat!" the youngest said excitedly.

Margrit tugged on her mother's hand. "Mama, we have to go." But her mother kept looking at me, finally giving me a weary smile. "Come, come," she said to me, "get in the car. We'll talk on the way."

CHAPTER 51

"You're Cecilia?" she asked as we sped off down the road, dirt flying.

I nodded at her. "You knew my mother?"

"The resemblance—"

"Yes," I murmured, interrupting, looking out the window.

"She told you about me?" she asked.

I shook my head, feeling uneasy with her scrutiny, especially considering we were flying down the road in an old car. She was quiet for a while, obviously trying to take it all in.

"How did you know where to find me?"

"A letter from my aunt, before she died."

She put a hand over her mouth, and her eyes swam. "I didn't know Laura had died."

"Yes," I said softly, "last month. I'm sorry to tell you in such a way."

Her eyes were back on the road when she spoke. "Is your mother . . . did Cora . . . ?" She stopped, not able to finish. Her lips were pressed together.

"She's not dead."

I couldn't see her reaction, really, if there was one. She just kept looking at the road. "Is she still in that place, the asylum?"

"Have you been there?" I asked quickly. "To see her?"

She stopped talking as we pulled up in front of another farmhouse. Margrit grabbed her mother's bag.

CHAPTER 52

BLANCHE BURST INTO THE HOUSE WITHOUT KNOCKING. TWO MIDDLE-AGED women were at the table, one with a rosary. "Blanche," one said with weary relief. "It's not going well."

A woman's screams pierced the air.

Blanche raced down a dark hallway, flying through the door at the end. Margrit and I were right behind her. A young woman, who looked barely my age, was on the bed, holding her very pregnant belly. She fell back against the pillows, her face exhausted. Another woman was in the room with her, so similar to the girl in features I knew she must be related.

Blanche was at the girl's side in a flash. "Why wasn't I called sooner, Irene?" she snapped.

"Bringing a baby into this world hurts," the woman said with a shrug. "Alice could never take pain well, even when she was a child." She wiped the girl's sweaty red face with a wet rag. "It'll be all right, my daughter."

Blanche waved Irene out of the way. "Now, Alice," Blanche said softly, "I need to see what's going on, so I can help you."

Alice's face was white. Blanche gently guided her, as I stood by her side, mesmerized. I could see the baby was trying to be born.

"Okay, I see why it hurts so much, Alice. Your baby is turned the wrong way. I need you to sit up."

The girl groaned.

"What?" Irene snapped. "She's not having her baby that way."

"Help me, Margrit," Blanche said quickly. "You too, Cecilia." She pointed to one side of the bed, then the other. "Leave, Irene. We'll be done soon."

"I'll say I'm not. Not while my daughter is having my grandchild."

My hand slipped on the girl's sweaty, hot skin when I took her arm, but she was so tired she let us maneuver her. We pulled her up so that she was on her knees. The girl's body buckled and she screamed again. Her weight pressed against us as Margrit talked gently to her.

"If you're to stay, Irene," Blanche said, "then take Margrit's place." Without further protest, Irene did as she was told. Margrit hurried out the door with the bag, and I heard her directing the women at the table.

Alice caught my eyes and held them, but I wasn't sure if she knew she was looking at someone. Her eyes were dark and miserable, until life flickered in them. "My baby," she whispered to me.

"Your baby is all right," I told her, as if I knew something.

The two women from the kitchen were in the room with us now, one of them with the rosary still draped over her hand. She hung it on the headboard.

Blanche ordered the women to get on either side of Alice. "Cecilia, climb up on the bed in front to help her and encourage her."

I scrambled up as Alice let out another piercing scream.

"Push, Alice," Blanche told her.

I cupped the girl's face in my hands, holding her head up when the screaming stopped and she drooped.

"This isn't the way it's done," Irene grumbled. "It's not the way I had my babies."

Blanche whipped her head over to Irene. "Out!"

The older woman stepped back at the ferocity of Blanche's order. Margrit bustled back in, carrying instruments in a cloth. Irene left in a huff, loudly shutting the door, as Margrit pulled a small table around to her mother and laid out everything carefully. "They're sterilized, Momma."

With Irene gone, the tension in the room eased. The woman who'd had the rosary was singing softly, a beautiful song in French. The light slanted in the window, suddenly shimmering.

Blanche talked quietly to Margrit. "The baby is coming out the wrong way. I need you to take Cecilia's place and help Alice."

With Margrit on the bed with Alice now, I stood by the door, trying to stay out of the way. Another spasm of pain hit Alice. Margrit wiped her face with a cool cloth, talking to her quietly, so quietly I couldn't hear what she was saying. The woman kept singing, the French words familiar to me, even though I didn't know what they meant.

"Push, Alice," Blanche directed.

I heard Alice murmur something. Her body hung limply. I wasn't sure how she'd find the strength to get her baby out. The singing seemed to comfort her. I saw her lips move as if she was saying the words too. Margrit talked quietly to her until Alice did push.

Blanche spoke softly, encouragingly. "You are doing so well, Alice. Your baby girl is almost here." Her brow was creased with worry, but still Blanche was calm and efficient. Her confidence steadied the mother—all of us, really.

Despite the seriousness, I felt a part of something amazing and beautiful. I began to feel disoriented and the room tilted. Before my eyes was another place, a familiar one. It was my mother's room at Sanctuary. A baby was being born. I was Amoret watching my own birth. *Aimée*, she whispered, her hands toward the baby. Whoosh, the vision shifted. It was the same room, but decorated differently. Amoret was now on the bed, an intense, focused look on her sweating face. Her body bent. A man and a girl were with her, helping her as her baby was being born.

Alice's scream shook me out of my trance, a contraction hitting her hard. Shaking, I pushed away my visions and focused on what was before me. Blanche comforted and reassured the mother. She reached forward as if she was just there to catch the baby more than to birth her. The baby's head fell out and forward, the little thing bending over at its waist.

"There, now," Blanche said happily.

Alice collapsed into Margrit while Blanche whisked the baby up. She wrapped her in a cloth quickly, cut the cord, and handed the child to me.

The unexpected warmth and crying gathered in my arms surprised me so much I felt tears rolling down my cheeks. I looked down into the new eyes in wonder.

I want one of these, I thought, and laughed at myself as the baby embraced her first breaths. She was so bright with life it was as if she'd come to us directly from another world, carrying over truths that needed to be heard. I stared more deeply into her blinking eyes, feeling she had something to tell me. But it was Mamie's haunting words that came to me, words I had forgotten: *Cecilia was the one born at Sanctuary, Cora. She is closest to it and to Amoret. You can't keep her from me forever.*

CHAPTER 53

THE ROAD WAS DARK, AND THE HEADLIGHTS MEAGER. MARGRIT WAS CURLED up in the backseat asleep, looking more like a child than a wise old soul. Blanche was exhausted and asked me to drive, and I had to explain that I didn't know how.

"You'll keep me awake by talking to me?" she asked. "It isn't far. But I'm exhausted. I want to lay my head down on this steering wheel."

"I can do that," I said, but I was so tired. I was feeling very unsettled by the visions, coming when they had. But I understood why. Seeing a life come into this world was a spiritual event, the air charged with meaning and bonding. That wonder could be seen on the face of each woman in the birthing room tonight. The wave of energy had even stirred Amoret inside of me, carrying me to my own birth and to Aimée's. It seemed a divine thing. I hadn't known I was born in the same room as Aimée.

Remembering—hearing?—Mamie's words had also shaken me. I recalled my mother's angry look when Mamie said it. As a child, I'd so wanted to please my mother. Any small attentions she gave me were momentous. Her beautiful face had distorted into ugliness when she'd snapped at Mamie. I'd thought Mother had wanted to push me away. She didn't want me to share in Amoret because she didn't want me close to her. Maybe that hadn't been it at all.

"Cecilia?" Blanche was asking.

"I guess I'm not talking."

"You must be tired. We don't have to talk."

"No, I have so much I want to ask you," I said. "How did you know my mother?"

"You know I live in her house now?"

"No . . . no," I stammered.

243

"The girls are in her old room upstairs. That's where I'll put you tonight. You'll have to sleep in their bed." She laughed. "You are staying, I assume?"

"If I may."

"Of course you're staying."

"How did you end up with my mother's house?" I asked, mystified.

"My husband, Earl, and I bought it from your grandmother when she left. We wanted to be close to my parents. I was here so much as a child, it felt like a second home anyway."

"My mother was raised in a farmhouse," I said in disbelief.

Blanche laughed again. This no-nonsense, industrious, happy woman had been my mother's friend. The people my mother attracted to her— Miss Owens, Blanche—were nothing like I'd thought they'd be. Was my mother drawn to them, or they to my mother?

"Cora never liked living on a farm," Blanche said. "She was desperate for life in New York City with dancing and poets and dreams."

"Was her childhood unhappy?"

Blanche shrugged. "Fine, I think. Your grandfather was a jovial man, filled with light and laughter. British descent, not Acadian. Mrs. Lancaster, your grandmother," she said with a nod at me, "was . . . well, you remember, more serious, a little crazy, perhaps, with all that obsessive talk."

Inwardly, I cringed at the description, but just nodded in the dark.

"Cora would roll her eyes when Mrs. Lancaster would go on about the Acadians, telling her that was forever ago and it didn't concern her, and your grandmother's eyes would flash, and she'd yell at Cora, and Cora would just flip the pages of whatever book she was reading and yawn and stretch like a cat."

We drove up to the front of the house. Looking back at Margrit, Blanche said, "Isn't she my angel?"

After she'd jostled Margrit awake, we went inside. I tried to think, This is my mother's house, where she was raised. But my thoughts were tired and jumbled.

I crawled into the bed with Margrit, her sister between us, in my mother's childhood room, listening to the breathing of the two sisters. I was reluctant to sleep, fearful of the dark dreams about Amoret that still haunted me at night. And alongside that fear was Eli tormenting me too with an endless, unceasing loneliness and ache. My feelings for him were beyond logic, springing from an unknowable depth within me. I didn't know how to exorcise him. Finally, I fell asleep.

CHAPTER 54

"You look just like her. Being in this kitchen, with you looking like Cora, it's shaking me up."

We were at the breakfast table, the kids wild and silly with their talking and their walking around the table, biscuits in their mouths. I thought of Eli's stories about his brothers and sisters and wondered if this was what his home was like. The thought of him hurt and pinched my heart. I turned my mind elsewhere.

Bridgit was helping her mother in the kitchen while Margrit still slept after our long night. Blanche explained her husband, Earl, was in New Brunswick to see his mother, who was ill.

"You were close to my mother?"

"Tight."

"I still can't believe she was raised in this house . . . on a farm," I added, lest she think I was criticizing.

She laughed. "She desperately wanted to leave it behind."

"She did leave it behind."

"Not her family, though. Your grandmother found her in New York. I'm ashamed to say my part in that. I gave her letters Cora had written me."

"Do you still have the letters?" I asked quickly, then blushed when I realized I was asking to read her private mail.

She shook her head.

I nodded, disappointed. "So my mother didn't want to be found?"

"Cora wanted another life, one that didn't have anything to do with family obligation. But your grandmother had raised her on family obligation, with every meal and prayer."

I fiddled with the tablecloth. "Why?"

"Your grandmother had plans for your mother. Cora often told me she thought your grandmother was crazy."

I shivered. There was that word again. "Do you know what Mamie's plans were?"

For a second, I caught her eyes gazing into some memory or thought, but she didn't share it with me. She looked uncomfortable.

I was about to ask something else, trying to nudge it out of her, when she said, "Come with me."

Behind her bed, lovingly placed on a high shelf, were six books. A small painting hung over the shelves, one of a woman with a bright red hat. One elegant hand with long fingers pulled down the wide brim of the hat, so only one of her eyes was visible, still conveying a coquettish gaze.

I put a hand out but didn't touch it. My hand dropped.

"She sent me that as an apology of sorts," Blanche said. "It didn't come with a note. Just the painting sent from Lady Cliffs. How like your mother to apologize by sending a picture of herself." She laughed again.

I went closer to study it.

"Probably why I knew you," Blanche said. "It looks so like you. I'm not sure who the artist was."

My father, I thought. "Why an apology?"

"She had a hard time forgiving me for those letters. She didn't want to be found."

"She looks contented."

"She loved your father," she said with a wistful smile. "So much. I think it made up for her having to fall into line with her mother."

"Blanche, you have to tell me. What was it that Mamie wanted my mother to do?"

Still, Blanche hesitated.

"You think it will make her sound mad. That's why you don't want to tell me."

Her eyes showed me I was right. Finally, she said with a sigh, "It's all about a young Acadian woman who lived a long time ago."

"You know about Amoret Winship?" I asked quickly.

Her eyes lit up in surprise. "When Cora and I were growing up, I paid more attention than she did to Mrs. Lancaster's long stories. So I heard how you're all descended from Amoret—"

"What?"

"Surely you knew that, Cecilia. You did know that."

"But . . . but Amoret . . . then . . . the baby . . ."

"Yes, the baby, who was your great-great-something-grandmother, little Aimée, taken from Winship Island and brought back to Acadie by a servant."

"Oh, no," I said, my stomach lurching.

"What is it?" Blanche asked, putting a comforting hand on my arm.

I was descended from Captain Winship too. But then something else occurred to me. Was I related to Uncle? I shuddered.

"What?" Blanche asked again.

"My uncle's ancestor is Winship. Is he descended from Aimée too?"

"Laura's husband? No, no. Most definitely not. Laura told me there was another child back in England. She inherited the estate and her descendants settled there."

Still, I thought. He is my distant cousin, as well as my aunt's.

And we were all of Winship's line. I shivered.

CHAPTER 55

With that news, I tried to put Amoret and Captain Winship and Sanctuary out of my mind. Uncle's vileness was wrapped up in all of it. I didn't want to think of it.

Blanche didn't ask how long I was staying. And so I just stayed.

The kids were always underfoot, following me when I walked across the meadows, or went to get water at the well, or helped their mother with the garden. They all had their chores, and school, which they walked to, but when they were home, they tailed me and riddled me with all sorts of questions I didn't know the answers to, about the sky, about other places and frogs, about me. It felt right here, as if I belonged. It was easy and light, unlike Sanctuary. But Sanctuary hadn't released its hold on me. A sharp longing pierced me with every breath.

The weather grew cold. Snow visited a few times. And still, I held Amoret inside of me, not wanting her out.

I took long walks, trying to re-create what my mother might have felt growing up here. How different her experience had been. She'd turned her back on her home and never returned and never wanted to. I wondered if she ever felt a pull back to it. I wondered if she resented Mamie and her fate so much that she disliked Acadie too.

The sea drew me to her. On cold windy walks along Minas Basin, I looked across the water and was comforted by the sight. I also thought of Eli and felt a heavy empty feeling at the loss of him. I wondered what he was doing and if he thought of me. I tried to shut him away, but he wouldn't disappear. There he stayed, in front of my eyes, and in the beats of my heart, intertwining my thoughts with his voice, his smile, his touch. Slowly, I was forgiving him. I loved him. It was very clear to me how much I loved him. But I didn't feel whole, and I couldn't be with him while I was in this state.

One night, after I'd been in Grand-Pré for almost a month, the kids were asleep and Blanche and I were on the swing outside. It was a quiet, cold night, and we were bundled in blankets.

"So when are you going to ask me, Cecilia?"

"Ask you what?"

She was silent, but she laughed so much, I could almost hear her laughing softly in the silence.

"About my mother," I said.

"About all of it."

"I'll be back," I told her, quietly sneaking upstairs and into the bedroom so as not to wake the girls, and retrieving the journal from where I'd put it in the dresser drawer given to me.

Blanche had moved inside and was in front of the fireplace. She stoked the fire and then settled in one of the chairs. "What's this?" she asked, taking the journal.

I curled up in the other chair. It was warm by the fire, but I still snuggled in a blanket. "It's a journal written by William Clemson, a doctor on one of the ships that stole away the Acadians."

"Really?" she asked, intrigued. Opening it, she began to read.

And there we sat in front of the fire, while she turned the pages. I stared into the flames, suddenly surprised that I was doing so. I hadn't been able to sit in front of a fire and relax and not think about Tess and Mamie before.

I must have dozed off, because I awoke with Blanche watching the fire, deep in thought.

"What is it?" I asked her.

She looked over at me, still someplace else in her mind. "It's sad."

"Amoret was strong, though."

She cocked her head. "I don't mean Amoret."

I was quiet for a moment. "You don't have sympathy for Amoret?"

"I do, of course. What happened to the Acadian people is a tragedy. But for most of us, life went on. But your family . . ." Her voice drifted off.

"Couldn't let it go," I said.

"Some of them couldn't. Some of them learned Amoret's story and it didn't affect them. But it touched deep inside of others. Your grandmother was one of those people."

"Why do you think? Why did it affect her in that way?"

"Isn't that the way of all of our beliefs? Their mystery. How they embed themselves in the souls of some, but not others."

"Not in my mother. Maybe in Aunt Laura?"

"Your aunt was very sweet and malleable. Marie—your grandmother—was a force of nature, a hurricane come to life. And I think she was surprised by Cora. She wasn't used to people standing up to her, much less her own daughter. People were afraid of your grandmother."

"I wasn't . . . well, maybe a little."

"Did you know your grandmother was born Marie Robicheaux? She used to say she married a Lancaster to show she'd forgiven the past." Blanche smiled wryly. "But every time she was angry with your grandfather, she'd throw up her hands and say, 'I expect no less from a man whose ancestors pushed out my people.'"

"Did she love him, you think?"

"She would never have married a Lancaster without love. She was a strong, strong woman."

"Like Amoret."

"She would have taken that as a great compliment. Your grandmother thought Amoret had magic in her. But what magic is as lethal as dark human emotion? Betrayal, rage, envy, hate, fear . . . they change people's lives."

"But why did Mamie even think that about Amoret? Was it lore passed down?"

"Yes, it was," she said, looking at me in the firelight. "Would you like to go on a midnight hike?"

My eyes lit up. "In the snow? Yes!"

CHAPTER 56

THE PURE WHITE SNOW CRUNCHED UNDERNEATH OUR FEET, UNDER A FULL moon. We didn't turn on our flashlights until we reached the dark of the woods. We were quiet as we moved through the brush and under the branches of the trees. I struggled holding the light with my thick fur-lined gloves. My free hand was buried deep in my wool pocket. The cold stung my face, but I welcomed it.

The trail ended at a sandy beach spilling into the bay. The moon was bright and hovering, its reflection upon the water a stunning path of light, beckoning us to follow it to the ends of the earth. A fierce cold wind whipped my hair into my eyes. I tucked the wild strands under my hat and pulled my scarf tighter around my neck.

Carefully we made our way over the slippery, snowy rocks until we came to a delicate icefall guarding an entrance to a cave. We ducked under the ice. Blanche kept walking into the cave, but I staggered forward, stunned by both a deep longing and a fierce hope that the longing was about to be fulfilled. The desire was strong and salty, encased in love for the sea. Recovering, I went into the cave, hiding my feelings from Blanche. I knew she wouldn't understand. I didn't really understand.

Blanche stopped in front of the cave wall, illuminating a figure that was carved out of the rock. I didn't have to see the face to know it was Amoret's likeness. I felt enchantment emanating from her. Blanche seemed immune. She studied the sculpture under the light, putting her hand upon one of the woman's outstretched palms. Amoret was covered in what looked to be offerings, seashells and rocks placed at her feet and ribbons of many colors dripping from her hair and arms—bloodred, sunflower yellow, white as bone, soot black, gray as rock, and orange as a sea sunrise.

Blanche looked back at me. "Are you all right?"

"Yes," I said, shaking. My eyes stung, and my cheeks hurt. No, I thought, I'm not all right. I'm both better and worse than all right.

Blanche stared at me for a beat longer, then turned away silently. Maybe she was frightened by my reaction, realizing I shared the family curse with Mamie. I believed in Amoret's spirit.

"This has been here a long time," Blanche explained. "The sculptor was very skilled. See the definition of the eyes and hands." She ran her fingers along Amoret's eyes. "And look at the strands of her hair." Blanche was enthralled by the artist's skill, but she didn't seem to be spiritually affected by the cave and the figure. Not like I was. She shone her light here and there over the statue. "Believers leave ribbons and buttons and things for Amoret."

"They worship her?" I asked.

"No, not exactly. She's not believed to be a deity. More of a gift."

"A gift?"

"From the sea. For many, she represents the feminine power of Acadie. They believe the sea was so pleased with the Acadians and the way they treasured the land and befriended the Mi'kmaq, she gave them a sea child, Amoret."

"And the sea child was stolen by the British."

"To some, she's like the Acadian Joan of Arc, in a way. Not a warrior who led armies. But a woman who should never have been taken from her home."

"There are still believers?"

"Oh, yes," Blanche said, looking around us. "They have ceremonies here in the spring, but you can see they visit her year-round. They have not forgotten her."

I walked to a fire pit in the middle of the cave, something wounded stirring inside of me. "What kind of ceremonies?"

She came to stand with me. "Their ritual involves fire, but it's very secret. You have to be part of the group to know what it is. They are very loyal to one another. They call themselves Amoret's Daughters, or the Daughters."

The walls of the cave shimmered, emitting female voices softly chanting. Blanche didn't hear them, it was clear, but she spoke almost reverently, as if we were in a holy place. "It is in their lore that two groups of Daughters disappeared. One sailed from Nova Scotia in the late eighteenth century, searching for Amoret. The second group in the nineteenth century. None were heard from again."

I shivered.

She glanced at me, giving me a small smile. "So they say."

"So you don't know what the Daughters are trying to do?"

"I know *what* they're trying to do. They want to call Amoret's spirit back to Acadie. They're secretive about how."

"I don't know why, since they've obviously failed." I felt Blanche's eyes searching out mine in the darkness, but if she thought my comment strange, she didn't say it. "Am I related to all these women?"

"No. Some aren't even Acadian."

"Do they live in the woods or something?"

She laughed. "They have normal lives, with children and meals and sewing. The ones who left Acadia in search of Amoret are said to be related to her, generations of her granddaughters."

"And Mamie was a part of the group?"

"Marie led them. Her mother—your great-grandmother—brought her into the circle." She hesitated. "Marie said the ceremonies were useless to Amoret, that they only comforted the Daughters. She was called, she said, to go to Winship Island, following the path of those before her."

I thought about that for a moment. "Why here? Why did they choose this place?"

"They say Amoret was found in the sand here, washed up from the sea during a storm, the waves crashing into the cave. This was the place Amoret was born. They believe the soul will always long to return to the place of its birth."

Blanche began to walk around the cave, as if she was giving me time with Amoret. I studied the figure under the light. I took off my gloves, stuffing them in my pockets. With shaking fingers, I touched her eyes, nose, and cheeks. The artist had captured her beauty and her strong spirit so well it seemed she might burst out of the stone.

I knelt down and took a handful of sand. I expected it to feel wet and cold, but it was warm and full of life, as if cooled embers from a fire. It pulsed as if it lived. Home, I thought with wild relief and abandon. I saw Amoret's face before mine, her reaching for me, as if she wanted to take it from me. Fireflies lifted from her palm. I opened my eyes, feeling ripped apart, as if I were home, finally home, and also not home. Both there and not there. I poured the sand into my pocket, breathing, breathing, breathing.

CHAPTER 57

THE ROASTED POTATOES AND SLICED HAM WERE ALMOST READY. THE TWO girls were setting the table while I finished the cooking. In my time here, I'd learned how to prepare a few things. Blanche was at the table, back to reading the journal. Peering over her shoulder, I realized what part she was reading.

"You read French?"

"Mm-hmm," she said.

"What does it say?" I asked her excitedly.

"Well, give me a minute," she said lightheartedly. Here this journal affected me so deeply and sorrowfully, and she—an Acadian—was able to read it safely from the distance of time and not feel the effects of it.

Blanche whispered some of the words in French as she read, and I thought of Mamie. I remembered her talking to us in French sometimes, and oh, oh, didn't . . . didn't Tess talk with her? And my mother too. Sometimes, my mother too. I wondered if she'd spoken French growing up.

"Blanche," I said.

She broke from her reading and looked at me.

"Who wrote those pages?" I'd assumed Amoret had written them. "The ones in French? Mamie?"

Blanche looked at me almost sadly. "No, Cecilia. It seems your sister did."

"Tess?" I whispered, wanting to reach out and touch the words she'd written but keeping my hands tucked tightly by my side. "What does she say?"

Blanche folded the book closed. "Let's talk after supper."

After we finished eating, I went out and sat in the swing. It was freezing, and I had bundled up well. Blanche joined me.

"So tell me."

"They all believed—your grandmother, your mother, your sister."

"Believed what, exactly?"

"That the spirit of Amoret was trapped in Sanctuary."

Blanche didn't believe it, I could tell. "How did her spirit get trapped?"

"Tess writes that Cora felt very close to Amoret's spirit," Blanche said, flicking her eyes to me.

I couldn't reveal that I felt closer to Amoret than even my mother.

"And that she tried," Blanche was saying, "to make your grandmother see that the deaths of the captain and Amoret didn't happen the way she'd always believed. Mrs. Lancaster was insistent the captain's murder of Amoret was the tragedy that anchored her to Sanctuary."

"That was why Mamie forced my mother and aunt to the island?"

"She thought your family would never have peace otherwise. She referred to it as *La Grande Fléau*. The Great Curse. And that it wouldn't be broken unless Amoret was released. It seems to me that Marie brought the curse to all of you." She shook her head. "What she did to your family."

"You think they're all mad, don't you?"

"I don't know what to think, Cecilia. I have wondered if your grandmother planted these seeds when everyone was so young that they had to believe. But . . ."

"But what?"

"Tess describes it like a compulsion. The words she uses—it reminds me of my feelings when I suddenly knew I wanted to be a mother. I knew in my soul I wanted a child. It seemed beyond my control, like a biological thing, my need to create. Which led me to midwifery. Your family's obsession reminds me of that, like it was a compulsion beyond their control."

It was odd they didn't pull me into their little mad circle, but I pushed those old feelings aside.

Blanche continued: "It seems almost wrong for me to reveal this, so I must've been a little affected by the mythology of Amoret and the secrets of the Daughters. But Tess writes that Amoret's followers had studied the ways of the Mi'kmaq and their sacred ceremonies. Sadly, they took one of their beautiful rituals and distorted it, creating some sort of exorcism ceremony. My interpretation, not Tess's, of course."

"This was the ritual," I said slowly, fear building. "What was the Mi'kmaq ceremony?"

"Have you ever seen sweetgrass before? It's a fragrant herb, even more so when burned. It is very sacred to the Mi'kmaq. They associate it with love. They would burn the sweetgrass and fan and breathe in the smoke, which cleansed out evil spirits and allowed them to be one with the Creator. They believed the ceremony would free Amoret from the evil spirit—the captain—who had trapped her."

"What did my grandmother do?" I asked slowly.

"Whatever it was, they hadn't done it by the last entry in the journal. What are you thinking?" Her eyes darted to mine. "No, you think . . ."

I looked away, with eyes stinging.

"Tess says they were trying to help Amoret's soul home," Blanche said. "You think they tried the ceremony in the cottage?"

"And instead they . . ." My voice drifted off, not able to finish my sentence. "They failed. Amoret is still on the island." I felt Blanche watching me. "Did Tess talk about seeing Amoret?"

"No," she said carefully. "She says they wanted to see her, tried to see her. Your grandmother felt her presence, though, as did Tess. But they never saw a physical form. Your mother apparently did."

The porch light went out, and for just a second, I felt a frightful stab in my heart. But then I heard one of the boys laughing. Blanche didn't yell at them, as she usually would, to tell them to go to bed. We just kept rocking in the swing in the dark, with a faint light streaming from inside the house.

"There is something else," Blanche began.

I turned to look at her, her face in shadows.

"They weren't only intending to free Amoret. According to Tess, there are many other spirits trapped on that island."

My heart felt dark and flat, not beating.

"Captain Winship's spirit is affecting your uncle. Tess thought your uncle was possessed by the captain. And then there are the others."

"What . . . others?"

"The women who left Nova Scotia to try to find Amoret, to free her. It sounds . . . well, I'll just say it . . . Mrs. Lancaster believed all these women were trapped on the island as little wisps of light."

"Fireflies," I whispered.

Blanche cocked her head. "She called them ghost candles."

Oh, no, I thought sadly. Tess. Mamie. My hands were cold and clammy. I waited, but Blanche said nothing else. "So how do I do it, Blanche? How do I release Tess, Amoret, and the others?"

"You don't believe this, Cecilia?"

I did believe it, but didn't want to see her doubt.

Blanche and I talked long into the night, about my family, about Amoret, about my cousin Marie Delacroix who left Acadie and never returned. Blanche believed that Tess was misguided, and that all her writings were the fanciful imaginings of my grandmother. She thought Mamie had poisoned young minds, and even my mother had fallen into her trap. But Blanche was kind, and listened to me, and reassured me, and I felt safe with her.

CHAPTER 58

THE DAY I WAS LEAVING NOVA SCOTIA, BLANCHE'S HUSBAND WAS RETURNING. Unfortunately, I wouldn't get to meet him because his train would arrive after mine departed. But at least Blanche only had to make one trip to the train station. I'd arrived by ferry to Wolfville, but had decided to take the train to Digby and cross on the ferry *Empress* to St. John's, a route Blanche had recommended.

As we drove away from the farmhouse—Blanche's home, my mother's home, my winter refuge—the children were hanging from the open gate in their places, youngest to oldest. I threw my arm out the window, fingers waving.

Blanche stopped the car in front of the church that had been built on the spot of the old church, the one that had housed all the Acadian "men" over the age of ten on the day they were told they would be removed from their country.

"Most were in disbelief," Blanche told me as we looked about the church, trying to imagine the scene. "The British had made threats before." She shrugged. "And besides, who believes such a thing would happen?"

We walked the grounds, the scene of the deportation.

"Your ancestors were deported too, then?" I asked.

"No," said Blanche, shaking her head. "My husband's were, but not mine."

"But you're Acadian."

"Oh, yes. But we never left."

"How could that be?" I asked.

"The Mi'kmaq took my ancestors in. They hid them for many years."

"You're not among the returned, then," I said, "not like my mother's family."

She didn't answer, just looked out over the meadow toward the bay. "There aren't many Acadians in this part of Nova Scotia, even after the returning." She sighed. "I can't take it in, what these people went through."

"Your people," I said.

"Yes," she agreed. "And your grandmother's. She never forgot it. She lived and breathed it. It defined her life." Blanche looked at me. "And her children's lives. She wouldn't let her daughters ever forget, even forcing Laura to marry Frank."

I hesitated. "I saw a picture of my aunt with Frank. I think she was in love with him."

Blanche's brow furrowed. "Was she? I'm sure that wasn't in your grandmother's plan. Mrs. Lancaster held that over Cora's head, that Laura had sacrificed while Cora had run off to New York. She had a great influence over Cora."

"Over my mother?" I asked, incredulous. "I didn't think anyone could influence my mother."

"Your grandmother was made of tough stuff, of the need for vengeance."

We stared up at the bronze statue of Evangeline, the heroine of a poem by Henry Wadsworth Longfellow. Her head was tilted back and her anguished eyes looked toward the cold blue sky.

"You think my mother is insane, don't you?" I asked softly. "That she should be in the asylum."

She paused. "I tried to find you, you know." I looked at her in surprise. "After your mother was put away, Laura wrote me in distress. I went to her—"

"At Sanctuary?"

"Yes. The only time I've left Nova Scotia, in fact," she said. "And I tried to find out where Laura had sent you, what boarding school, because I wanted to bring you here to live with me."

A warm feeling came over me as I contemplated that. How my mother had a childhood friend who loved her so dearly she'd tried to find her daughter and take her in. And I marveled at Blanche's kind, wide heart. What would my life had been like if I'd come here to live? Would I still have searched out Sanctuary, or would this have been enough?

"Laura wouldn't tell me," Blanche continued. "And assured me all was well, that this is what Cora had been planning to do for years. I met your uncle briefly and took a disliking to him right away."

I nodded at that. "So you don't think Sanctuary is haunted?"

She grew somber, looking around us.

"I know it's just a piece of earth," she said finally, "but when I stand here, on this spot, I can sense *something* in the air. Something that lingers here, that's sad and tragic. It does makes me wonder if the earth is alive and watching us. We die, and it goes on, but it takes a little of us with it before we go."

It was eerily similar to what the woman on the boat told me when I arrived. I believed it. I believed the earth and the sea had power. I had an idea about that and what it might represent to Amoret.

Blanche thought dark human emotion created this tragedy. Didn't it follow that the other end of the spectrum—love and kindness and selflessness—had equal influence?

We were quiet for a while, walking through the snow dusting the fields, finally making it down to the cross set up at the place of deportation. As we sat there watching the placid water of the Minas Basin, Blanche said, "She loved your father, you know. He brought her great happiness."

"It would seem."

"If you ever need a place to be, Cecilia," she said, "this is it."

I looked at her then, studying her kind eyes.

"You're always welcome," she said, "with me and mine."

CHAPTER 59

❧❧❧

HE LOOKED UP FROM HIS DESK WHEN I ENTERED HIS OFFICE. HIS FACE showed his shock. He didn't say anything, just stayed very still.

I sat across from him. He stared at me, his pen in hand, still poised to write.

"You look thin, Eli," I said quietly.

He blinked. He put his hand over his face and rubbed his eyes, then looked at me again. He set down his pen and said, "You look older."

I gave a hollow laugh. "It's the hat, I think."

"Would you like a cup of coffee?" he asked politely.

"That would be nice," I said, feeling uncomfortable and not knowing what to say and stalling until I could think of something.

With a nod, he left the office. The heat was barely on. I pulled my coat around me and looked out the second-floor window until he returned.

I sipped the hot coffee. "Good," I said, gesturing with the cup.

"*You* look good, well."

"I feel . . . rested."

"Where have you been?" His distance hurt my heart.

"Nova Scotia." Then more quietly, "Acadie."

He raised his eyebrows, clearly surprised. "I hadn't thought of that." I wondered if he'd been searching for me. "I thought you wouldn't want any . . ." His voice trailed off.

"Reminders."

He nodded.

"I had some things I needed to figure out."

"Did you figure them out?"

"Yes."

"Why are you back? Are you returning to Sanctuary?"

"I need to do something first," I said.

He nodded. I tried to tell him with my eyes how much I missed him, trying to see in his eyes if he missed me. But he wouldn't hold my gaze; he kept looking away.

"You could have written," he said finally.

"Yes."

"Just to let me know you were all right."

"I'm sorry."

"You haven't forgiven me, then?" he asked.

"I understand why you did what you did."

He studied me for a moment with unreadable eyes. Talk to me, I wanted to say. "Why are you here, Cecilia?" he asked.

I paused and looked at my hands. "I need your help."

"My help," he repeated.

"Is that such a surprise?"

"It is."

"You're angry with me?"

He looked so weary, I wanted to reach over the desk and put my hand on his cheek and tell him how much he meant to me and how sorry I was that I had left and that I did forgive him and that now I hoped he forgave me.

He took a long breath. "I'm relieved to see you're all right. Very. Relieved."

"So you'll help me?"

"With your uncle? I'd prefer you didn't go back. There's not anything for you there."

"Not with my uncle," I said. "But I do need to return."

"Why?" he asked, exasperated.

This was a new Eli. I had only seen him mostly calm. I realized it was because he *was* angry, and angry with me. I wasn't sure if he even knew it, but he was wrestling with it.

"I have something I need to do," I said quietly.

He stared at me for a long moment, then looked away, saying to the wall, "What do you need my help with?"

I paused long enough for him to look back at me. "I need your help with my mother."

"I've been visiting her."

My eyebrows shot up. "How is she?"

He hesitated. "I'm concerned about Dr. Brighton's medical treatment of her."

I pressed my lips together. "I want you to help me get her out."

He thought for a moment. "I'm a new psychiatrist just beginning my career," he said finally. "She won't be released because I say so."

"There must be something you can do."

"I've tried, believe me. Especially when I found out what Dr. Brighton . . . I'm sorry. I need to tell you."

"What?" I asked, in a panic.

"Cecilia," he said gently, "he wants to perform a neurosurgical procedure on your mother's brain."

"What kind of procedure?" When I saw him hesitate, I said anxiously, "Just tell me."

"The surgeon would remove parts of the cerebral cortex—"

"What? No!" I interrupted, sick to my stomach. I continued to stare at him as he looked at me sadly. "When is the operation?"

"Next week."

"You have to help me get her out of there! Help her escape."

He gave a long, slow blink. "Escape?"

"She can't stay there. You know they shouldn't do that to her. You're a moral person, an ethical person."

"Cecilia," he said slowly.

"We have to get her out."

"If I'm caught," he said, "I'll never practice as a psychiatrist again."

I looked out the window. "Yes," I said, realizing he was right. "I can't ask that of you. I'm not like Helen."

"What do you mean?"

"You said she, your fiancée—"

"She wasn't my fiancée."

"She asked you to give up your career. I can't ask you to do that. I know what it means to you." I stood. "Just don't tell anyone I'm doing it." I went to the door, my mind racing. I had things to figure out.

I told him where I was staying and left.

CHAPTER 60

I JUMPED AT THE KNOCK ON MY DOOR, THINKING IT MIGHT BE THE CRAZY man down the hall, who was still here. I'd hoped Mrs. Oliver, the landlady, had thrown him out by now, but it was a cruel thing for me to wish on someone suffering or deranged or both. I understood what it was to suffer.

"There's a man to see you," Mrs. Oliver said. "He's in the sitting room. There's no one else in there right now," she added, almost as an afterthought.

He was standing, playing with a clock on the mantel, his hat on a chair behind him.

"Hello, Eli," I said.

When he turned to me, I was hoping I'd be able to read his face. But I couldn't. He was even more reserved than when I'd first met him. I felt the loss of him and sat down in a chair.

He almost sat on his hat, but then moved it. The door opened without a knock preceding it. Mrs. Oliver came in balancing a tray of cups. "It's such a cold night," she said to me. "I thought you and your guest might want a cup of hot tea."

"That's very kind of you," I told her as Eli cleared off the coffee table so she could set down the tray.

"Thank you," Eli said politely, the edge gone from his voice, and I saw a little of the man I'd first met at Sanctuary. But when the landlady left, his distance returned. Politely, quietly, he made my tea the way I liked it and handed me a cup. He didn't take any for himself.

We sat together for a moment in the quiet with me drinking my tea. The crackling of the fire, the coziness of the room, the darkness of the night mirroring the window created an intimacy I hadn't experienced in Eli's office. But the sudden closeness meant I couldn't bring myself to look at his face. Instead I stared at his hand resting on the arm of the chair: a strong, capable hand that had caressed my eyelids . . .

"I've realized I did a terrible thing to you," he was saying. My eyes went to his and must have still held the soft look of memory because he stumbled trying to find his next words. "Betraying . . . your trust."

I nodded at him, not able to look away.

He cleared his throat, pressed on. "I thought I was doing a good thing, trying to help someone. I'd met your mother and consulted with Dr. Brighton and heard the case. Dr. Brighton believed—based on his interviews with your mother and what your uncle had told him—that you and your mother shared a mental illness."

I looked away.

"There was evidence to suggest this was true," he said quietly.

This was still a sore subject for me. I thought I had put my fears and my anger behind me. But I realized I still had some healing to do after all. Maybe it would be a journey I'd always be on. "You thought that after you'd met me?" I asked.

"I want to be honest. Yes, there were things you said and did that made me question your mental state. But I also felt you had a very rational mind and that you tried to reason things out. That trait in you conflicted with the other things happening and your reaction to them. But . . . I also realized I had . . . fallen for you," he said, faltering a little. *(Was that gone now, Eli?)* "And that might be affecting my perception of . . ."

"Of my sanity."

"Yes," he said reluctantly. "But when . . . when I saw the fireflies surround you that way, almost like they were protecting you, and I felt it too, not just saw it. Felt some strange energy there. And . . . now that I've had time to think about it, away from the island, I remembered sometimes feeling as if the house itself had some sort of presence trapped within it. I realized there were things that I didn't understand." He paused, leaned forward, put his elbows on his knees. "Part of me is intrigued by it. I was always drawn to the study of the mind. It's exquisitely incomprehensible. Perhaps there are other mysteries that I don't understand, that don't seem possible, but somehow . . . *are.*"

He looked up at me, and I nodded.

"So," he said, "I began to look more deeply into your mother's case. I interviewed her frequently. I realized Dr. Brighton was experimenting on her. He said it was to help. And I know he has a genuine interest in psychiatry, but it doesn't emerge from compassion. It's cold science to him. By being careful and observant, and with not a small amount of sleuthing, I've discovered he has several patients he's manipulating in the same way—patients who have no families or ties—how they react to certain medication, certain dosages, and other therapies."

"There must be something that can be done."

"I haven't figured out what it is yet. Dr. Brighton is a man of considerable power, wealth, and prestige in the local and in the psychiatric community. His family is old, and his money is old. He is well respected, well liked. He has well-placed friends and colleagues."

"But surely there is evidence."

"He is very careful."

"We must get my mother out."

"We must get your mother out."

My eyes went to his. He gave me a nod.

"Your career?" I asked.

"What good would I be to myself, to my future patients, if I look the other way? Would I be true to myself if I did that? I don't think so."

We were quiet for a moment. Finally, I said, "I'm sorry I said that all those weeks ago, about you not being the man I thought you were. I've regretted saying it. It's not true and it hurt you."

"I hurt you too. I'm sorry too."

I bit my lip, looking away. He still seemed so far from me. I wanted things to be like they used to be between us, but there was such a wall there, or a sea, a vast sea of betrayal and hurt.

"So," he said, still in that reserved tone he'd adopted with me. "So we'll get your mother out. And somehow in the future I'll figure out how to help the other patients, although I believe that will be a long, hard path. But we must get your mother out now, before the operation. We don't have much time."

CHAPTER 61

Eli and I were sitting on the bench in front of the asylum, watching as people entered the building for visitor's day. I felt agitation rising in my chest as I stared at the sanitarium, remembering my lifelong fear of the place and now my uncle's intent to have me committed.

I glanced down at my mother's watch. "She'll be here soon, I think."

He nodded.

Three days had passed since Eli had come to see me at the boarding house. In that time, he'd been visiting my mother every day, telling Dr. Brighton he wanted to observe the surgery and aftercare "to witness the improvement in the patient." The arrogant Dr. Brighton didn't even suspect an ulterior motive, so certain was he that everyone would find my mother's surgery as fascinating as he did.

"Do the nurses and orderlies know you well?" I asked Eli.

"Some of them very well."

I nodded.

He put his hand over mine. Startled, I stared down at our hands. I wanted to strip off our gloves and touch his skin. That need swept over me, immediate and primal. I missed him. Even as he was here right beside me, I missed him. He hadn't touched me in three days. I hadn't kissed him in ages. He was so far away, even though his hand was just there, resting on mine.

"Security isn't as tightly controlled as it should be," he said, removing his hand. "And they know me and trust me, especially these last few days, with all my visits."

"Thank you," I said very quietly, too quietly.

He leaned in. "What?"

"Thank you for helping me."

He smiled. "You're welcome."

I miss you, Eli, I thought, but didn't say. "And thank you for teaching me to drive these last few days. I know that's been trying," I said, attempting to inject lightness into my voice. But it only came out nervous and shaking.

He laughed a little and smiled at me. Then he looked at the sanitarium, his face suddenly sober again.

I almost didn't recognize Miss Owens as she was approaching. She wore a fur-trimmed coat and a stylish hat. Her face lit up in a bright smile. "Hello, Cecilia."

When she was closer, I saw that her coat was frayed on the bottom and some years old and one of her gloves had a penny-size hole at the wrist. But her face was radiant and eager. "You look very nice," I told her.

She cocked her head at Eli, and I introduced them. He was very serious, and I could tell he wanted to get on with things. She must have seen his worry because she patted his arm. "I have a friend on the inside." He nodded, but this information didn't make him feel more at ease, I could tell.

Miss Owens gave him a bag and we stood in front of the bench while he moved things to his briefcase and then gave the empty bag back to Miss Owens.

"Let's go," she said, taking my arm.

Eli with his long strides went ahead of us and had disappeared up the steps before we arrived at the receptionist's desk. My hands were shaking as Miss Owens signed us in with Miss Tilly, who didn't look up. She'd lose her job over this if she was found out.

Dr. Brighton smiled at us when we entered, putting his hands together. "Miss Cross, I'm delighted you're ready to talk about your mother's treatment. And who is this?" he asked, squinting at Miss Owens as if he knew her but couldn't place her.

"Miss Owens. She's a friend of my mother's."

"Ah, yes," he said, "welcome to you too. Please sit down."

As we settled into chairs in front of his desk, he eyed me as if I were a specimen for him to pick apart. My lips trembled as I remembered how Uncle wanted to have me committed. If we were caught, would Eli and Miss Owens go to jail and I be locked up with my mother?

I looked down at my folded hands in my lap for just a second, took a breath, and tried to rearrange my face from one of fear to one of pleasant interest, trust, and concern.

"So, yes, Dr. Brighton, you explained a little of the surgery to me on the telephone," I said. "I thank you for delaying it until I could get here to discuss it with you."

"Of course. I want you to be comfortable with the procedure." He cocked his head, and I imagined him thinking of all the things he could do to my brain if he had the chance. "You'll see your mother's demons will disappear after this is over. It will be a very good thing."

"Miss Owens," I said, "would like to hear about it. I didn't explain it very well. Do you mind?"

"Of course not. Miss Owens, the objective is to separate a person's emotions from her intelligence. Mrs. Cross's prefrontal lobe will be removed—"

"Will you do the surgery?" I interrupted. Miss Owens shifted in her chair. I was sorry for bursting out, but I couldn't stand hearing about it. My stomach had turned to ice.

"No, no. A neurosurgeon, Dr. Clark, will perform the surgery. I'll be there, of course. Your mother is my patient in my personal care."

I stared at him, imagining how my mother might do it, hoping to unsettle him. And I put my thoughts on Eli. Was he talking to the attendant at the locked door in his very calm and professional manner? I tried not to shiver as I remembered how horrible it had been to walk through that door when I'd visited my mother last fall and then to hear it clang shut behind me.

The attendant would come out with a set of keys and open the door for Eli. Without a backward glance, Eli would disappear into the hallway. I knew the routine because Eli had told me. It was the same thing he'd been doing for the last three days after he'd gone to Dr. Brighton and apologized for questioning his diagnosis and insisting he now wanted to observe the procedure.

But he asked to be allowed to talk to my mother and ask her questions that he would supposedly ask her again after the surgery. Dr. Brighton's eyes had lit up when Eli had told him it was for a paper that Eli would write on the procedure.

"Of course," I heard Miss Owens calmly say to Dr. Brighton.

"Yes," I agreed, though my heart was pounding.

Dr. Brighton put his arms on his desk and leaned forward. "We'll give your mother anesthesia so she won't feel anything. Dr. Clark will drive holes through the skull," he said, pointing to his own head, "and then, using a metal loop, will remove pieces of the white matter through the holes."

He discussed it like it was clipping my mother's fingernails, ridding her of something dead and useless, and then she'd be all pretty inside and out when it was done.

I composed my face, nodding. Behind my eyes stung fear.

My mind, however, was with Eli. At this moment, if all was going to the plan, Eli was walking my mother to the attendant, saying that he was going to assess my mother's intelligence through tests in Dr. Brighton's office. The attendant knew that Eli had been working with Dr. Brighton and that yesterday he had indeed brought my mother to the doctor's office for Eli's testing.

Yesterday, the attendant had called down to Dr. Brighton's office, and Miss Tilly had transferred the call to the doctor and he had given his permission. Today would not be so easy.

But if, *if*, Eli was able to get my mother past the attendant, when he was halfway down the stairs he would take the coat out of his briefcase and button my mother up in it and put shoes on her feet.

The peals of a bell filled the room, making me jump and my heart pound harder. Dr. Brighton turned to me politely, overly politely, evaluating my every move. "Are you all right? It's a lunch bell."

"No, no, I'm fine," I assured him.

But he looked at me a little suspiciously.

Calm yourself, Cecilia.

With a quick glance at me, Miss Owens leaned toward Dr. Brighton. "So how long before she's better?"

"Hmm?" asked the doctor, still looking at me. I met his gaze as calmly as I could.

"Will Cora go home then?" Miss Owens asked loudly, trying to pull his attention from me. Our original plan had called for me to come in alone, but we thought we'd more likely be able to distract him with two of us. Because of my current state, I knew we'd made the right decision.

"What? No, no," Dr. Brighton said. "We can't send her home."

"But isn't the idea for her to get better? To have the operation so she can come home?"

Dr. Brighton hesitated, choosing his words carefully. "Of course we want her to be able to go home. But she really is very ill."

He was never going to let her out. Never. He had some arrangement with my uncle and he would leave her in here and experiment on her until she died. I knew it. And he wanted me too. I could see it in his eyes. The greedy need to study both mother and daughter was tempting, especially since he had a willing, a more than willing, guardian.

There was a tap at the door. Again, I jumped, cursing myself silently as soon as I did. The doctor narrowed his eyes at me while he got up to answer the door.

"May I speak to you a moment?" we heard Miss Tilly's voice asking.

He snapped at her in a low voice but stepped out of his office, shutting the door.

Miss Owens reached toward me. "You're shaking. It's all right, Cecilia."

I took a calming breath, and then another. For some slightly unsettling reason, I thought of Amoret and how feisty she was in my dreams, the fire in her. I wasn't going to be trapped in here, and neither was my mother any longer.

"What do you think she's telling him?" I asked.

"Miss Tilly? She's making something up. He'll be angry with her for interrupting, but we need to keep his little mind occupied and distracted." She grabbed my wrist and looked at my watch. "Do you think your fella is done?"

"He's not my fella," I said quietly.

"Oh, baby doll, baby doll."

Dr. Brighton came back in, and Miss Owens stood, putting out her hand to shake his. I didn't know how she could bear to touch him. "Well, thank you."

"Are you going?" he asked, looking from her to me. "I apologize for my receptionist. It was a silly little matter—"

"I have to run an errand, but Cecilia has a few more questions. Is that all right?"

His eyes lit up, making me terribly uncomfortable. "Of course."

And then Miss Owens left me alone with the lunatic.

"I'm sorry for taking up so much of your time." I heard the receptionist's phone ring and tried not to freeze up. It might be the attendant from upstairs. "But I'd like to know how many times lobotomies have helped patients enough that they could have normal lives."

"This operation has not been done extensively in the United States, you understand. And currently, it's difficult—with the war—to get information out of Europe. Not as easy as before."

I nodded.

"Did you know that the first lobotomies performed in the US were on chimpanzees?" He laughed. "Their names were Betty and Lucy. After the surgeries, they were calmer, much calmer, and still able to do the tasks given to them. Maybe not as well, but sufficiently."

My hands tightened together so much they were white.

Through the window, I could see Eli walk down the front steps of the sanitarium with my mother in one of Miss Owen's coats. She stumbled down the steps, but I kept nodding at Dr. Brighton. Miss Owens drove up in the car. She helped Eli gently put my mother in the automobile. They drove away.

Dr. Brighton was watching me. I was still nodding.

"What?" I asked. "I'm so sorry. What?"

He turned around and looked out the window. "Why were you staring . . . ?" He squinted.

I stood, and he came around the desk. My hand was on the doorknob when I felt his hand grip my arm. I looked him directly in the eyes and said viciously, "Let go of me," jerking my arm away. He was shocked for just a moment, long enough for me to get the door open and almost fall into the outer office.

"What's going on?" he asked.

Stopping, he looked above him, as if he was trying to see into my mother's room.

"Is there anything I can help you with?" Miss Tilly asked innocently, coming back into the office.

"Where have you been?" he demanded.

"I just told you, Dr. Brighton. I had these papers to run to—"

He stepped toward her as I hurried through the half door into the hallway.

"Was no one watching the door?" He glanced at me again and disappeared on the stairs to the second floor.

"Thank you," I mouthed to Miss Tilly, and then was out the front door and down the steps, running, running. I got to the parking lot, started the car. I put it in gear and sputtered along. I saw Dr. Brighton at the entrance of the sanitarium looking out, but I was off to the side and I didn't think he saw me. I drove off, desperate to get away and see my mother.

Dr. Brighton was on the front steps, looking. He threw up his hands and ran back inside.

CHAPTER 62

THE MOTEL ROOM WAS SMALL AND FREEZING COLD. THE RADIATOR EMITTED very little heat. We wrapped my mother in blankets. She stared out at nothing, and then slept.

"Do they keep her so drugged up all the time?" I asked Eli, horrified.

"She was heavily medicated the times I saw her." He swallowed. "He's been giving her different drugs, using her as a test subject."

My eyes stung as I stared at her wan face on the pillow. "How many others is he doing it to?"

"Not any of my patients, I know that." Going to his coat, he pulled an envelope out of his pocket, which was addressed to a doctor I didn't know. "I've written a letter describing my concerns. I'm sending it to Dr. Smalling. He's a good man. He'll look into it, I hope."

"When will you mail it?"

"After," he said, going to tend to my mother when she groaned. He talked to her soothingly, so quietly I couldn't hear.

Someone knocked on the door. I was startled for just a moment, exchanging a look with Eli, but parted the curtain a fraction and saw Miss Owens's old fur-lined coat.

"It's so dark in here," she said. She looked at my mother tucked in one of the twin beds. "Ah, Cora." She grabbed my hand and squeezed. "You did the right thing, Cecilia."

"We did the right thing," I said. "All of us."

"Now we just have to not get caught." She lifted the suitcase, looking around. "Where should I put her clothes?"

We cleared off a place on the dresser. She opened it up, pulling out a pink nightgown with ruffles. "Cora is going to cast kittens when she sees what I've dressed her in," she said with a laugh. She laid it out on the extra twin and turned back to my mother. "She's out. Did you give her anything?"

"No," Eli told her. "She's sleeping off the drugs in her system. That's the best thing for her right now."

Miss Owens grew somber, and her eyes filled. "Do you think she'll be okay?" But before Eli could answer, she shook her head. "What am I saying? Of course she will." She looked at the two of us. "Why don't you go for something to eat? I can stay here with her."

"I don't know," I said slowly. "I shouldn't leave her."

"You two must be starving. Now there's a café right next door." She went to the window, pulled back the curtain, and pointed. "Right there, see. Just walk over, have something quick. I'll fly over if anything goes wrong."

Eli and I entered the small café. A bell on the door alerted everyone to our entrance, and a frazzled waitress in a stained green-and-beige uniform gave us a nod. A couple of the customers watched as we moved to a table. I appreciated that Eli procured us a place in the corner; it was slightly dark away from the windows, but more private.

We dined on identical $1.10 meals of minute steak and french-fried potatoes while music scratched out of a boxy brown radio on a table beside us.

"How long did you stay at Sanctuary after I left?" I asked.

"For a few days, hoping you'd come back. Then I couldn't take your uncle anymore and left."

I didn't like the thought of Mary having him all to herself. "You came back to Bangor?" I asked.

"No," he said, "I went home." He paused. "To my parents," he clarified. "It felt like where I needed to be."

"And to all your brothers and sisters."

He nodded, pushing his empty plate to the side. "They were as rambunctious as usual."

"You never told me their names."

"There are so many I forget," he said, smiling softly into my eyes. "Many sticks in my family."

I paused, returning his smile, his look. I couldn't think of anything to say that would make it better between us, so I just kept looking at him. I thought the waitress might have returned to clear the plates. I thought I might like to sit in this café with Eli for a while, and let the sun sink, and rise again, and here we'd still be.

Eli ordered dessert and coffee, which I declined. While he ate his pie, he told me about helping his father around the farm and how good it was to be working outdoors, saying it was exactly what he needed. He'd stayed for only a week, but it was enough time. Then he returned to Bangor and began looking into what was going on with my mother.

"I thought of looking for you," he said, "but I didn't know where to begin. I gave Anna my address and telephone number, just in case you returned to Sanctuary."

"I stayed with a family in Nova Scotia, a family friend. She had lots of wild children. They reminded me of you."

He laughed. "Well, thank you."

I smiled at his laughter. "I meant, of what it must be like to be you, to have such a family. So it seems we were on the same trip, just in different places."

"I would rather have been in the same place," he said gently.

I was quiet for a moment. "I needed the time. But now we're in the same place."

"When is your birthday?" he asked abruptly.

"In March," I said, scrunching my eyes at him.

"And you'll be eighteen," he said.

I nodded.

"Eighteen," he repeated.

He stirred more sugar in his cup. "Cecilia." He paused, grappling for words. "You don't have to go back to Sanctuary. Please don't."

Before I could answer, the waitress returned with the check. I left the diner and sat on a bench out front, waiting for Eli to pay the bill.

He sat beside me, quiet.

"I have to go back, Eli. I have to go back."

He didn't say anything, but I could read his face, filled with disappointment. "Don't worry," I said.

But he was worried.

CHAPTER 63

"I won't go there," my mother said, sitting up in bed but looking weak and drained. It was the seventh day.

"You don't have to," I told her. "I'll do what needs to be done."

"No," she said, plucking at the pink ruffles on her nightgown with a distasteful look on her face. "You're not going back either."

I pressed my lips together, not wanting to defy her when she wasn't well yet. Nevertheless, she saw it in my eyes.

"You have to listen," she said, glancing at Eli warily while she talked to me. "You don't understand what's to be lost."

"I do."

"Not this, you don't. You don't know what happened to your grandmother and to Tess."

I sat on the bed beside her, and she shifted a little. We weren't used to being so close to each other. "Do you know about the fire?"

She closed her eyes almost as if she were in pain and put one finger on her lip. "I want a cigarette."

"Did Aunt Laura tell you?" I asked gently.

She barked a laugh. "No, Frank made a special visit to tell me." She shook her head, her hair loose and wild. "He was different, worse. As much as I despised the man, I didn't think he was a murderer. But that day he came to the asylum, I knew he would do anything. He would have stabbed me straight through the heart if he'd had a knife." She looked at me, warning me with her eyes. "He hates everyone descended from Amoret. Because he . . . I think the fire . . . what Tess and your grandmother did . . . it released . . ."

"Released what?" I asked urgently.

She looked at me. "It seems like so long ago. Wasn't it a long time ago?"

"It's still going on, Mother."

She gave a weary sigh, as if preparing herself. "Mamie," she said finally, "had a plan, which—of course—had to include me. She pulled me from the bright city and brought me to that horrible island.

"All my life I'd heard about it over and over, how we have Mi'kmaq ancestry and it would be the thing that saved Amoret. But that it needed to be done on the island. The original ritual was peaceful, one of respect, but she changed it. She felt she could take the essence of it, capturing the power of the Mi'kmaq people that was in our blood, and combine it with her own personal touch." She paused. "It didn't work."

"I'm surprised Mamie thought that kind of thing would work on Amoret."

She looked at me, her eyes suspicious. "What do you mean? How would you know what would work on Amoret?"

"I'm just guessing," I said quickly. "What happened that night?"

"Some of Mamie's hocus-pocus," she said, waving her hand in the air. "I think they released Amoret's spirit from the house, but it only made things worse."

"But Amoret is still there. I've seen her. She's . . ." *Inside me.*

She looked at me, putting a hand out as if she would touch me. But then it dropped to her lap. "Laura saw her too."

I looked over at Eli, who was leaning against the wall, listening quietly.

"But, Mother," I said, "Patricia couldn't see her."

"Patricia?"

"Anna's niece. She and her sister are on the island too."

"Not anymore," Eli said. "Anna made them leave. She didn't give a reason, but we all saw that Frank is a danger. He's getting worse, Cecilia."

I nodded, turning back to my mother. "So why couldn't Patricia see her? And Ben, he hasn't seen her, I don't think."

"I think . . . I came to believe that Sanctuary is filled with spirits, showing themselves in different ways to different people, depending on who"—she gave me a quick, worried look—"they feel a connection to."

I knew she meant me in particular. "Sanctuary seems alive to me, like it holds souls within its walls, even sometimes just a brief feeling from its past."

"Cecilia," she said after a quick glance in Eli's direction, "we shouldn't speak of these things." She looked frightened.

I only nodded. I was trying to figure out how to tell her about Tess and Mamie. I wasn't sure she knew. I wasn't sure anyone had known but Laura.

"Mother," I said gently, "I went to see Blanche."

She looked at me cautiously, her eyes narrowed.

"Aunt Laura mentioned her in a letter to me," I said. "When I was still at Sanctuary, I found Dr. Clemson's journal, you see. Tess had made entries in French in the back."

She nodded slowly. "Mamie taught her French."

"Blanche read Tess's section to me. And Tess had written about the ghost candles."

"So you know about Tess and Mamie?"

"Do you know?" I asked, surprised.

"I've guessed." She leaned back against the headboard. "I was trying to protect you, you know."

"You mean from Uncle?"

"I could handle Frank." She let out a gasp, which turned into an empty laugh. "At least, so I thought." She pressed her temple as if it hurt. "No, I meant from my mother. If I gave my mother Tess, I thought she'd leave you alone. And she did for the most part. You were safe. I'd kept you safe."

I tried to digest this, so different from the way I thought of things. "You didn't want to protect Tess?"

"Tess and I were close. Very close. I was good to Tess," she said. "It turned out she was the one to take on Winship. And I did have to protect you from him as well. To protect you from my mother was really to protect you from Amoret and Winship and their hold on us. Quite selfish hold. I wouldn't let her pull you into that like she did me."

Eli wore a perplexed, intense look, as if he was trying to sort it all out.

I had to press on, though. "So you think Winship is still on the island?"

"Of course he is," she retorted. "I'm sure Frank has seen to that, by putting me away and having you sent away."

"Aunt Laura sent me away."

"Even so, he was most glad to see you go," she said. "You were a threat."

"A threat?"

"To Winship. The old captain doesn't want to let Amoret go, even in death."

I thought she was wrong about that, but I couldn't tell her Amoret stirred inside of me, in my dreams, my heart. That the strength I felt welling up inside of me at times seemed to come from her.

"Evidently he's in the house," my mother was saying. "She's on the grounds, in the graveyard. At least, that's what Frank told me. Gleefully he told me that Tess and Mamie were dead, killed in the fire meant to set Amoret free. So they failed. And now they're trapped too."

"Then we need to release them," I said.

Eli looked at me steadily, and I returned his gaze.

"Mother, let me show you something." I unwrapped the pipe and the thimble from Mamie's handkerchief. I held the treasures out to her, but she wouldn't take them.

"Where did you get the thimble?" she asked me, her voice shaking.

I sighed. "I found it at the cottage." With Eli looking on, I couldn't bring myself to tell her about the fireflies showing me the way to it. "Why was it at the cottage, Mother?"

She closed her eyes, clearly disturbed by it. "It was Aimée's. Amoret's sister's, passed down through the generations. Your grandmother said that it would be the difference, that it would make the ritual . . ." Her voice drifted off. "I don't want to talk anymore." Her hands started to shake, but she said with steel in her voice, "We've lost too much. We should just run, Cecilia."

Looking at Eli's face, I could see he agreed with her.

"I'll never have peace if we don't finish this," I said.

"There's no one left. If we fail, you'll know what it really means not to have peace." She leaned forward then, her eyes frantic. "And there'll be no one left who could save us."

I drew back from her, catching her fear. She was right. We would be trapped on the island forever, surrounded by Winship's vileness. A dark fate.

She became very agitated and we had to work with her to get her settled down. Finally, she was soundly sleeping.

Eli put on his coat and left.

I followed him. He was leaning against a car, perfectly still, just staring into nothingness.

I leaned on the car next to him. "You don't believe her?"

He shook his head a little. "Cecilia."

"I thought you were open to figuring this out."

"I'm trying."

"So if you don't believe her, that there's an Amoret Winship still at Sanctuary . . . but you saw the fireflies—"

"Cecilia," he said, looking at me now. "I'm here. I've given up everything for you. Does it really matter if I can accept"—he struggled for the words—"a ghost wandering the grounds of Sanctuary?"

"For me?" I asked, hope fluttering. "You said it was because it was the right thing to do."

His look had so much love my heart stumbled. He looked away then, into the night. "It's what I told myself. And it was a part of it. If it wasn't for you, would I have done it? I wish I knew that answer, but I don't."

Inside I was soaring. "I don't care."

His eyes quickly swiveled to mine. "About what?" he asked carefully.

"About the why of it," I said, returning the look he'd given me.

He didn't reach for me. We just stayed in the moment, staring at each other.

"Thank you," I said, not thinking about the words.

"You're welcome," he said, probably not thinking about them either.

I looked down at his hand and took it in mine. Our hands were freezing. He squeezed mine then, and I looked up at him.

Our eyes locked. *Finally, finally.* He put his hand behind my neck and gently pulled me to him. *Finally, finally.* He kissed me gently, or was it urgently? The air so cold, our faces cold, our lips so warm. I missed you, I said. I love you, he said. We kissed again. I love you too, I said. He pulled my forehead to his, his eyes looking deep into mine. Don't leave again, he said. Never, I said. We sealed the whispered promises with another kiss, long, tender, passionate. I lost myself.

I rested my forehead on his chest. My eyes burned with happy tears that I didn't want him to see. He kissed my head. We stayed that way for a long time.

"We should go in," I said finally. "My mother."

"Yes," he said. "But I want you to myself one day."

"I want you to myself. All to myself."

"And you shall have me. When this is over."

"When this is over."

Our arms were wrapped around each other's waists as we walked, not wanting to be parted. Each step was taking us back to Sanctuary's troubles. I hoped we could withstand what was to happen next.

"Do you remember what we learned about the woman who drowned?" I asked.

"Of course."

"I found out some things when I was in Nova Scotia."

"Tell me."

CHAPTER 64

MISS OWENS WAS AT THE DOOR WITH BAKED CHICKEN SHE'D MADE. WHEN I let her into the room, I was surprised to see my mother's eyes filled with pain. She turned from Miss Owens and looked at the wall. "Cecilia said you were here, Stella. I can't believe you did this for me."

"Cora," Miss Owens said, sitting beside her on the bed and wrapping my mother in her arms. Mother patted Miss Owen's hair awkwardly.

She visited with my mother, getting her to laugh. Mother seemed to finally let go of the fear that made her stiff and reserved. As I watched them, I thought of her with Tess, how she relaxed with her in a way she didn't or couldn't with me. Was she telling me the truth, really? I thought she might say whatever she wanted me to believe. I still loved her, though, despite all of it.

"You're a good daughter," Miss Owens said as I walked her out to her car, wrapped in my coat.

"I'm trying to be, Miss Owens."

She grabbed my cold hands with her gloved ones, looking right into my eyes. "Call me Stella. You're all grown up now, Cecilia." She leaned in and whispered, "I'm no longer your governess." And then she laughed and opened the door to her car.

"As I said before," she told me, "your mother has always been good to me. Very good. Better than you know." She looked at me as if she wanted to say something, but was holding back.

"What?" I asked.

She shook her head.

"What did my mother do for you?" I asked her, a slow dread coming over me.

"I told you. She took me in when I needed someone. My husband had abandoned me. I was poor and a mess." She laughed, trying to make light of it. Kissing me on the cheek, she said, "It's not her fault the way things turned out. I don't hold it against her."

With that, she got in the car and left.

Slowly, I walked back into the motel room. My mother was eating the chicken, talking to Eli. I could do nothing but stare at her.

"What is it, my darling?" she asked me. She tilted her head, her long hair spilling to the side, looking at me so earnestly and innocently, in a flash the mother I remembered.

She pulled a thin cigarette out of a silver case, which was engraved with the initial *C*. She saw me looking at it. "Stella brought it. She has one just like it, with an *S*, of course."

"I wish you wouldn't smoke."

"Oh, but I like it."

I sat down in the chair at the desk, watching her. She picked up an ashtray on the bedside table and flicked some ashes into it, then put it in her lap. "Don't look at me like that, Cecilia. Surely I deserve a smoke after being locked up for five years?"

"What did you do for Miss Owens?"

She gave a little shrug and shook her head, about to say nothing, I could tell from the expression on her face. Then her eyes grew sad and she closed them.

"Tell me," I said, the truth dancing madly around the edges of my brain. "Tell me about Tess."

"Oh, I wish you wouldn't keep going on about things." When she opened her eyes, they were filled with tears. "I did care for her."

"You sacrificed her."

"I didn't know it would be like that," she said testily. "I just wanted to protect you." Her voice dropped almost to a whisper. "I couldn't let Mamie have you."

"Is Tess my sister?"

"I never saw two sisters closer than the two of you. Laura and I were never like that."

My heart thudded slowly in my chest. I remembered Tess's face, so different from my own: the roundness, her light blue eyes, the way her nose twitched when she thought deeply.

I put on my coat and went to the café next door, ordering a hot cup of coffee. I couldn't drink it, just let the steam rise up into my face. I thought of a friend of mine at school, Daisy, who found out her mother was actually her grandmother and her sister was her mother. "I think I always knew," she'd told me.

I'd never even guessed. The feelings I had for Tess were complicated, but they were sibling feelings, when you came down to it. Blanche's kids had shown me that—despite our particular odd circumstances—the essence of Tess's and my relationship was all part of growing up, and birth order, and a struggle over who does my mommy really love most.

So much time wasted on struggling with that issue. But I recognized it wasn't really wasted. The struggle had led me to this point. And as precarious as it all still was, it felt like the place I was supposed to be.

But . . . *Tess.*

It was so unfair to her. She'd been a child manipulated by the adults around her. And now she was trapped in a living hell.

The coffee had long grown cold by the time I left the café. Both Eli and Mother looked up when I came in. I sat on the edge of the second bed while Mother straightened up, looking at me, waiting to hear what I was going to say. Still cold, I kept my coat on and put my hands in my pockets.

"Did she know?"

"Of course not. Stella and I thought it best for everyone to think she was my daughter. James and I brought her with us to Sanctuary as a baby, saying she was ours."

"So Mamie thought . . ."

"Yes, Mamie thought Tess was her granddaughter. Mamie was very selfish, Cecilia. She didn't care about any of us. I accused her once of having children just to create an army of Daughters for Amoret. She didn't deny it."

I thought of the blueberry pies she used to make for us, the card games she used to play with us as we sat before the fireplace in her little cottage. But Mother had made up her mind long ago about Mamie. "And so she brought Tess up as one of Amoret's Daughters," I said.

"She took to Tess right away." Her eyes grew sad. "I enjoyed putting one over on her at the time." She picked at some invisible thing on her blanket. "She taught Tess everything she'd wanted to teach me. Mamie wasn't very kind about Laura either, you know. She always said Laura wasn't very smart. So it had to be me, you see."

"That's a cruel thing to say about Aunt Laura."

"Laura had always been the obedient one, eager to please, listening to our mother's stories about Amoret, agreeing to do whatever was expected. Tess wasn't like that. She didn't want to please anyone. She was fascinated by all of it. Mamie saw that in her, that Tess wasn't doing it for anyone else but herself. Tess could be more clinical about it. Less emotionally wrought. She didn't carry the family curse in her blood."

"You put her life in danger."

"I didn't think of it that way. I honestly didn't. And I tried to make it up to Tess, the bringing her into all of this. I tried to be good to her. I was very grateful to her, actually."

"Grateful," I repeated.

"For keeping you out of it."

"She was just a child."

"It wasn't why I took her. Stella was in a terrible way, and James and I wanted to help. We were in love, newlyweds. It was the perfect solution."

"Except for Tess."

"Tess had a good life."

"Mother."

"Who expected the crash, the money gone?" she exclaimed. "And your father's . . ." Her voice drifted off. She was still not able to talk about his death after all these years. "It changed everything."

"That had nothing to do with Tess's fate."

"If your father had been there, I would have handled Frank better. And if I'd still been at Sanctuary, there wouldn't have been a cottage fire."

I looked down at my hands. "I think you should stay here, Mother. Miss Owens could take care of you while I'm gone."

"You should stay here too."

I shook my head. "I'll be back—"

"If you're going back, then I am too."

I looked from her to Eli and knew both of them didn't like my plan. But I couldn't leave Tess and Mamie, and all the others. And I couldn't live with this heaviness on my heart where Amoret waited. This had to be done, so we could all go on with our lives. I didn't know how Mother could even contemplate leaving her own mother and leaving Tess—my sister, no matter what she said—trapped at Sanctuary.

I wanted to be able to excuse Mother, as I remembered what her life must have been like the last few years, being imprisoned and experimented on. But some part of me wanted Tess to be my real sister and someone else to be my real mother.

"What are you going to do?" Mother asked. "Mamie and Tess already tried that inane Daughter ritual."

"Rituals have their purposes."

"Do they? These failed."

"Maybe the ritual was for the Daughters," I said. "Anyway, they had the wrong idea."

She narrowed her eyes. "Cecilia, what could you know that they didn't?"

I know Amoret, I thought. But I said, "It's something Blanche told me, about how powerful human emotion is."

"And?"

"I have a plan."

She looked at me askance. "Oh, my darling, I hope so."

CHAPTER 65

On the Lady Cliffs dock, Eli was counting cash into the hand of a stocky man with wary eyes. We were taking a boat over to Sanctuary. The island hid in the mist across the water.

Two people caught my attention: the Scotts from the library. They didn't approach us, but waved when they saw me looking. They were staring at my mother, dressed in Stella's clothes.

My mother was tall and aloof, even after being in a sanitarium for years. She was smoking a cigarette, looking at the Scotts. Her eyes appeared dead almost, just a spark of something there, like she was choosing to show very little of herself to the onlookers.

I was sure there were others in Lady Cliffs noting her return. The deranged woman from Sanctuary.

Mother had been healing for two weeks. We didn't want to wait any longer.

The sun was low in the sky when we pulled into Sanctuary's harbor.

"When does she appear?" Mother asked.

"Between dusk and dawn."

She nodded and pulled into herself. She had been very quiet on the journey home.

"The two of you should wait here," I said.

Mother screwed up her mouth in an *absolutely not* expression as Eli said simply, "No."

"Just until dusk, until it's time. I have to find Ben."

"You're not going into the house?" Eli asked quickly.

"I'm not leaving without Ben." Even though I'd done it twice already, I wouldn't do it a third time. He was coming with us.

"Well, come on, then," my mother said as she tried to get out of the boat.

297

I didn't see anyone as we climbed the hill, which was dusted with light snow. Mother walked between Eli and me, each of us with a hand on one of her arms. She hesitated when Sanctuary came fully into view, but then we continued on. As we got closer, she kept looking over toward the graveyard.

Eli opened the door for us, and the walls spoke: *Witch. Witch!* I felt the captain's corrosive venom oozing out of my dear Sanctuary's walls and quickly led us into the library. Winship's dark presence had grown strong in my absence. Mother was white. I knew she'd heard his voice too, but we didn't speak of it.

She moved to the love seat. "Cecilia," she said, taking out another cigarette. "Do sit here with me."

I did as she asked, wanting to rest for a moment while I gathered my courage to go deeper into the house to look for Ben. We were safe in the library, but the thought of hearing that unnatural voice again made me sick to my stomach.

Eli sat at my desk. I wondered where everyone was, if they were in the house, if they would find us before I found Ben. Amoret's spirit pushed and prodded inside of me, a frenetic energy of need and will.

The door flew open. Eli and I stood as Uncle barged into the room, followed by Anna and Ben, with Jasper trailing behind. Uncle stared at my mother. He stepped back toward the doorway, either from shock or because of his general fear of the library. This was a place of love and goodness. It didn't welcome Uncle or Winship's evil.

Mother's lips turned into an amused smile. I was close enough that I could see how her hand trembled as she put the cigarette to her lips. "Why, Frank," she said. "You look so much older."

He said nothing.

"Ruling over Sanctuary hasn't brought you happiness, I guess."

His mouth was set in an angry, trembling line. Eli came to stand beside me. Uncle's eyes flickered to him, and then back to my mother, who continued to look at him as if he were a fascinating specimen to study. I wondered if she'd learned that look from Dr. Brighton.

"You haven't destroyed me after all. I heard about the little operation you and Brighton had planned. You probably should have just killed me instead of letting the deranged doctor play around in my brain," she said, her fingers turning circles beside her head. "Was it the deal you made?"

Uncle's eyes were like slits, narrowed and venomous, and he said the strangest thing: "I'm not afraid of you."

Mother tilted her head, gestured at me. "It's my daughter you should fear. She's really quite amazing. Resourceful, smart," she said, then paused. "Determined, actually. Determined to see it all through."

His head swiveled from one of us to the other. He was obviously not at all sure what to do next. But in his eyes, I could see him beginning to make plans, scheming.

Mother looked out the window, taking a draw on the cigarette and blowing the smoke out slowly. "The lawn looks nice, Frank."

He finally exploded. "How did you get out?"

Eli put his hand on my shoulder.

"Is this your doing?" he roared at Eli.

But it was Mother who answered. "I see Anna back there." She gave her a little wave. "Or should I say, the new Mrs. Wallace?"

Anna wrung her hands, and I gave Mother a sharp look. I felt protective of Anna and wished she'd leave her alone. Mother kept staring at her with a calculating look, but in that aloof way she did so well. Anna paled and averted her eyes.

Uncle pointed at Mother. "You, witch, out of my house."

She rolled her eyes. "Witch? Come on, Frank. That's Winship talking, not you." She peered closely at him, moving her head to and fro as she looked. "Or is there any of you still left in there?"

He trembled visibly then. I saw the conflicted madness in his eyes, the tightness of his fists, as his deranged mind jumped from thought to thought, trying to find a way to save Captain Winship from Amoret and her kind. "Get out of my house, off my island."

"We're staying until this is done," I said, glancing out the window, noting the beginning of night.

He pointed at Eli. "I'll have him arrested. I'll have all of you arrested," he said, his arm sweeping toward all of us. "And you," he said, pointing at me, "you'll go into the asylum with your mother."

"What about the murder of my cousin?"

He paled then, sputtered a little. "I don't know what you're talking about."

"I have proof that Marie Delacroix left Nova Scotia to come to Sanctuary," I said, beginning my lies. "She wrote a letter to her mother, describing a visit with you, in which you threatened her if she ever returned to Sanctuary. Also, I have a photograph of my aunt wearing the pin that was found on Marie. I have a witness," I said, hoping Ben would stay quiet just now, "who saw you disposing of the body. Two friends of ours know about all this and will go to the police if something happens to us."

Everyone in the room was staring at me, all except for Eli, who I'd already confided in while we were at the motel. Ben was shaking his head, his eyes afraid. I couldn't read Anna's expression, as I hadn't been able to read her all my life.

"What do you want?" Uncle asked me viciously.

"You have to let her go," I told him.

He looked at my mother, confused.

"Amoret," I clarified. "You have to let Amoret go. That's what we're going to do. We're all going out to the graveyard, and we're going to free her. And in freeing her, we free everyone: Tess, Mamie, all the granddaughters of Amoret who've tried to release her, as well as Captain Winship." And me too, I thought. "And it'll be over. All of it will be over."

He left the room. We could hear him running up the stairs.

"He's going to get his gun," Mother said, flicking me a look.

I helped her off the love seat and brought her outside, with Eli following us. We walked the path and went through the gate. Jasper's little head was shaking, as if he thought this was a bad idea.

We went to Amoret's grave. Everything was hushed in a dark, worrisome way. It didn't feel natural. Something felt wrong.

Then my mother gasped. I looked up and there was Amoret, standing in the trees. Even though I was afraid of her, of her strong will that had created all of this tragedy and what she could still do to us, I walked toward her. Eli looked confused, and I knew he couldn't see her.

"It's time," I said into the shadows. Then her features became clear and standing before me was Amoret, with her long flowing hair and deep fiery eyes. She wasn't demure or sad. She was fierce and desperate.

"I know what you did," I said.

Her face distorted.

"It's all right," I said again, stepping toward her, feeling my mother's sudden grip on my wrist. "We're your granddaughters, my mother and me. And we'll go back to Acadie to live. To Grand-Pré, where you're from. Of all the places in the world, that's where I choose to live."

She continued to stare at me.

"I know you killed the captain. You poisoned him with the foxglove from your garden after he killed William and beat you. And then you poisoned yourself. My grandmother had it all wrong, and that made things worse."

Slowly, I took the chain off my neck, dangling the brass thimble in front of her. "It is Aimée's," I whispered, knowing she could hear me. "I know you know it."

I felt the pounding of her heart, the sharp hurt of it.

"Your guilt keeps us here. Others expected you to move the sea itself, and you think you ended helping no one. But you saved me. You showed me the path I needed to take and gave me the strength to take it. Because we're alike. We both wanted our families back. Just the way they were. But we have to accept it won't be like that again. I've found my way because of you. It's time for you to find your way. You need to go home."

I pulled a bag out of my pocket. Reaching inside, I brought out the sand and held it up. I walked toward her, my hand out, letting Acadie's earth slip through my fingers, hoping earth did remember. "This is home, Amoret. This sand is where you were found, where you were born. I've learned that childbirth is a sacred thing. I was born here at Sanctuary, connecting me more strongly to you than any others since Aimée. I'm not Aimée, Amoret. And I'm not you. I have my own life to live. You need to let us all go."

Something changed in her eyes, and I saw the yearning in them. I felt the yearning in them, like she was inside of me.

She came toward me, reaching, wanting what was in my hands, the sand from Acadie, her sister's thimble.

She was almost to me when we heard the shout.

Uncle's voice and footsteps were coming toward us.

"No, Papa!" I heard Ben shout.

Eli gave me an anxious look as he turned toward the entrance, putting his body in front of us.

Anxious, I quickly turned back to Amoret, but she wasn't looking toward Uncle. Her eyes were fixated on my hands. She continued to come forward, and when she was close enough, I put the thimble in her hand.

Aimée. I heard Amoret's voice inside my own head.

"Yes, your sister," I told her. "Your daughter's name too. Your daughter who is a part of me too."

I poured the sand into her hand. She stared at it, sifted it through her fingers, and looked up at me, tears in her eyes.

Her lips moved. *Home.*

Uncle appeared as she disappeared. Tiny lights exploded out of where she'd stood. Uncle raised his gun at Eli, but hesitated. At that moment, Ben grappled him from behind. A shot rang out.

I tried to see, but the lights swirled around me and my mother. One grazed my cheek tenderly, and I could feel Tess's heart inside my heart. The emotion was so strong, holding me so tightly, I gasped from the love I felt from her. And I saw a look of contentment on my mother's face as another light grazed her cheek, and I knew it was Mamie's spirit being released. Something shifted deep within me. I felt a sensation of lightness as Amoret lifted away from inside me.

I struggled through the emotions to see Uncle and Eli on the ground. I shouted out as the lights disappeared and ran to Eli. Ben was holding the gun, backing away. Uncle shot up and started reaching for the gun, screaming at Ben to give it to him.

Eli was on his back, struggling to get up. I was kneeling beside him. "Are you hurt?"

"No," he assured me, standing up, looking toward Uncle.

Eli ran to Ben, who let him have the gun.

Uncle's eyes were dark and blank when he stared at me. "What have you done?"

"Don't move, Frank," Eli said, the gun in his hand, but pointed at the ground. But his eyes made clear that he'd do anything to stop Uncle.

"I've made it all go away," I said. "It's done."

He backed up from all of us, uncertainty in his face. "It's not. He's still here," he said, hitting his own chest hard. "And there," he said, waving his arm toward the house.

Somehow I knew that he was right, that Winship remained in Sanctuary, tainting the very essence of the house.

Uncle ran from us.

"Let's go," Eli said.

I scooped up Jasper, feeling his warm body against my chest. As we hurried through the graveyard, I said good-bye to them all, knowing they were at peace, and would continue to be at peace finally. We strode through the light snow on the ground, past the front door, seeing Anna standing under the portico.

"Come on," I told her, but she shook her head at me.

The four of us made our way to the harbor. Eli threw the gun in the sea, and I was glad to see it sink, although Mother looked a little forlorn. I got in the boat first, but realized Ben was standing down the pier a few feet away. I could see his intention.

I jumped out of the boat and grabbed his hand. Jasper barked.

"I can't leave," Ben said, refusing to look at me.

"You can," I said urgently. "You must."

His eyes were teary. "He's my father."

"No," I said, my eyes tearing up too. "Don't you see? He's in a pit. A deep dark pit."

"I need to pull him out, then."

"He doesn't want to be out! He wants you to be in the pit with him!"

He looked back at Sanctuary, his eyes showing his struggle.

I was about to speak again, when Eli spoke. "Ben," he said calmly. "We're your family now."

Ben looked to Eli, then to me. He was about to say something, but stopped.

"We must go," Mother said in her best bored tone, but her tight mouth showed her worry. She would leave Ben, her sister's child, I knew. I hated that about her. But I loved her too. So I understood Ben's struggle.

"You don't need me," Ben said to Eli. "Cecilia has the two of you now."

I could feel my mother's hand on my arm, pulling at me, pulling me away from my cousin. I put Jasper into her arms, and her mouth contorted distastefully.

"Ben," Eli said, "I love Cecilia"—my heart soared at this—"and she won't be happy unless you're with us. Please come with us."

My eyes stung. "Please."

"I can't," Ben said, sounding like a child.

"I won't survive without you," I said.

"You always do."

"I won't go without you."

Still, he wouldn't come. Mother got in the boat with Jasper, holding him off from her body, and stared toward Lady Cliffs. Eli began untying the boat.

"It's too much loss, Ben. Don't you see? We've all been in Uncle's pit." I took both his hands and squeezed them. "Come with me. Help me out of it."

He looked back toward the house and then gave me one slow nod. Relief flooded me.

Once we were all in the boat, he said to me, "Anna."

"I know."

CHAPTER 66

WHEN WE WERE OUT IN THE BAY, I LOOKED BACK AT THE ISLAND, suddenly pierced by the sight of Sanctuary in the distance. Then I saw the flames. I stood in the boat, almost falling over. "No."

My mother reached out, steadying me. I heard her say, "What has that idiot done now?"

My library, my books, my memories were burning. Ben and I gave each other a long, slow look that stretched back across years. "Sanctuary," he whispered, as if it were a holy word, or one of magic and meaning. He was silently crying, tears on his cheeks.

We all watched Sanctuary burn, all except Eli, who kept his eyes toward the shore. As much as it pained me to see it, I knew it was the right thing, the only way to finally be rid of Winship. I hoped they renamed the island or deserted it and let the sea have it to heal it.

Places would always have a hold on us, like Acadie did with Amoret, like Sanctuary did with me, but what I'd been seeking all along was the people I belonged with, who may or may not be family.

Home moves with your heart, and right now this boat—with Eli, my mother, Ben—was my home. I could live with any one of them, but I was fortunate to have all three. Home moves and grows with the heart.

I wanted desperately to look back at Sanctuary, knowing I always would, but fixed my eyes on the lights of the mainland.

In the end, I did look back. But I didn't see Sanctuary burning. I saw three wild children running the island, pulling one another along, throwing rocks into the sea, calling out at birds, laughing at silly things, and holding hands watching the tides of life flow in and out.

ACKNOWLEDGMENTS

Much respect and gratitude to the three women who helped shape *Sanctuary* into what it was supposed to be: my editor, Lisa; my agent, Trish; and my daughter, Christine.

JENNIFER MCKISSACK is the author of *Sanctuary*.
She lives in Texas, not too far from the sea.